# GONE WEST

# GONE WEST

*Novellas*

*Typesetting and interior design: Ivica Jandrijevic*
*Proofreader: Max Rhinehart*
*Cover design: Agnesa Mahalla-Meha*
*Front cover photo: Frank Tozier*
*Back cover photo: QT Luong*

ISBN:

978-1-7345396-0-8   Paperback
978-1-7345396-2-2   Ebook

DISCLAIMER
*This is a work of fiction. All the characters and
events of the story are a result of the imagination.*

# GONE WEST

## Novellas

KEN JANJIGIAN

*For my mother and father*

# ACKNOWLEDGMENTS

*Gone West* was originally published by Pocol Press in 2005 as *Trapped Doors*. This is a new edition with the originally intended title.

Greil Marcus' book, *Lipstick Traces*, was a key source for the art history used in the novel.

# CONTENTS

*"Go west, young man."*

HORACE GREELEY

*"i will wade out
till my thighs are steeped in burning flowers"*

E.E. CUMMINGS

# BOISE REDUX

*Henry Fields*

I was on the bus on my way to my first day as a cabbie. The bus chortled down Haight Street. Two healthy looking twenty-somethings were panhandling on the corner of Clayton Street. Cloud Nine had a line out the door for breakfast. Seamus O'Brien was unlocking the door to his bar, The Gold Cane. A guy in white overalls was slopping soapy water on the windows of The Gap. A squeegee rested nearby. A man twice my age, head slouched low, sat next to me sucking on a brown-bagged bottle.

I picked up a dog-eared newspaper from an empty seat. It was already open to the comics, horoscope, and crossword page. My horoscope read, "You may be a little erratic today. Question the events that have recently taken place." I already do that every day. I looked at this day in history: "In 1933, the 20th amendment to the Constitution, the so-called 'lame-duck' amendment, was declared in effect." Finally, the Reflection for the day: "Love is what you've been through with someone." – James Thurber.

We passed the Ashbury sign. My old bookstore, Great Expectations, was on the left, its doors locked. I had worked there for four years and quit two weeks ago. My wife was happy that I quit, but she wasn't happy about

my next step, becoming a cabbie. I was thinking back to
an indelible conversation we'd recently had. The catalytic
conversation that got the wheels turning to this recent
change in my life.

Nancy was sitting on the couch drinking coffee and
holding one of our cats, Billie, the sociable one. I could
see introverted Bear in his usual spot under the couch.
I was at the kitchen table, sitting in front of my typewriter. I was about to start typing, or writing I should say,
though lately it felt more like the former. I was working
on a collection of sonnets about Rimbaud and Verlaine,
focusing on their sordid, tragic relationship.

Nancy said, "Henry, can we talk before you begin?"

"Sure. You sound serious."

"I am. It is."

I got up and sat on a rocking chair, diagonal to Nancy.
Bear popped out from under the couch and surprisingly
jumped on my lap, settling in comfortably.

"Henry, we've been in San Francisco six years and
I'm tired. Really tired. It's not working out the way we
planned," Nancy said, some blend of frustration and
despondence lacing her tone.

"Life is what happens when you're busy making other
plans." I responded, quoting John Lennon.

"I'm so tired of you using that quote. It's bunk."

"It's truth." I countered.

"No, it's an excuse for missteps."

"Plans never go the way we want them. We aim and
hope to come close to the target."

"We don't even have a target anymore, Henry."

"What's not working?" I asked, knowing it was a ridiculous question.

"Everything."

"That's a lot."

"Are you going to continue this sarcastic avoidance? The playfulness is not charming anymore."

"Wow, you seem really tense."

"I am."

"No one said it would be perfect, Nancy."

"No one said it would be this imperfect, Henry."

"Have you made a decision that I should know about?" I asked.

"Yes. Yes, I have. Listen, Henry, youth is over. It's time to quit before it gets even more embarrassing. I can't live this life anymore."

"What life? Us?"

Nancy explained, "This life. Your life of poems in minor journals and half-finished novels. Your life of screenplay ideas developed into nothing more than napkin notes. The whole art escape. It's got to change."

"Well, Nancy, I've been—"

"Let me finish. I've got to change, too. My life tolerating your endless youth has to change. We're sadly, pathetically co-dependent in our malaise. I go to work. You kind of go to work. This isn't a life. It's a treadmill. It's time for a real job, Henry Fields. It's time to make some money. I want to have children and time is running out."

"Ugh, time and money. Such annoying concepts."

Nancy rolled her eyes. "Henry, I need to tell you something."

I looked at her and forced my smile into serious expression. "Yes," I said earnestly.

"This is real. We need a change. I want children, but not with you this way."

The thought of children was paralyzing except for the act of conception. At least we'd have sex. I didn't invoke our celibacy at this moment because I had enough to handle with my lack of a career. My lack of money. My napkin novels. Of course, our asexuality could have been the cause of all the causes. What causes the cause that caused the previous cause? What was the first domino?

"Henry, this conversation is real."

"I know."

I didn't.

We'd had this conversation a few years back, but it was the genesis of many more like it. One of those moments in marriage that starts you on a permanent detour, gradually tarnishing the original bliss. I bought some time by letting Nancy allow me to go to grad school. I had told her I'd become a teacher by getting an MFA in creative writing, which I did all the while working at the bookstore. My last semester Nancy and I worked hard putting together resumes and cover letters for teaching jobs. Nancy was so excited. She even thought our sex life would resume once I got a real job. We talked about moving back to Boise where I could teach at Boise State. I had an old writer friend from my glorious wayward twenties in the Land of Trees who could get me into the English Department. He was sleeping with the Dean...

"We'll have children and time with both our families that we've lost in this San Francisco experiment. I'm so excited to change our lives."

And what did I do? I took all those resumes and letters and dropped the possibility of change right in the trash on Haight Street.

A few weeks after I graduated and with obviously no response from the un-mailed resumes, I unveiled my plan.

"Honey, here's what I'm going to do. I'm going to take one more shot at it. I've been talking to Mike upstairs and he's got me convinced the cab could be my answer, my ticket."

"Henry, everything's an answer for you. Answers. Always answers. Henry, kids look for goddamn answers. Adults realize there aren't any. Three and a half years getting a master's and now you're going to drive a goddamn cab! What the fuck!"

"I don't buy it. I mean, I get you, but I'm not looking for *the* answer. I'm just looking for my own little solution. I just feel I haven't let it all hang out. I want one grand shot at some art world success. Not this little underground niche I've been hiding in, wallowing in. Mainstream success. If it fails, I'll get a professor job and we'll make decent money and buy a little house out in Santa Rosa or go back to Boise and garden together and have kids and live the years out peacefully."

Nancy was shaking her head slowly, the gesture speaking volumes.

"Look, the MA is the firewall. If I fall flat on my face this time, it's there to staunch the bleeding. Teaching is such a white flag. Let me fully fail first."

"I don't know, Henry. I'm tired."

"I am too. I just need one more avenue to explore. Then, I'll be at peace with it and we'll slide gracefully into the life you want."

"I want?"

"We want," I quickly corrected.

"And what's the cab got to do with it anyway? How is that an answer?"

"Mike says the cab is full of characters and plot, which is what I need. I can put the blood flow in and flesh on, but it's the skeleton I lack. I've even started taking notes on Mike's experiences. Wait until I have my own," I said enthusiastically.

"Maybe you mean just the backbone."

"What's that supposed to mean?"

"You have to ask?"

"Taking shots at me isn't going to help."

"I know, but I'm at our limit. We've got nothing after all these years."

"It all depends on the method of measurement."

"Henry, I don't want to get into any philosophical discussions. We've got nothing and you know it, so cut the bullshit detours."

Nancy was very adept at cutting me off at the digressive pass. She had years of practice.

"This time, it really feels right. It's not a detour. I've been a fool in my own word folly. I know. I can handle anonymity, but it's un-attempted effort that eats me up. It's not big time success or a major publisher. That's the veneer. The truth is it's a physical, almost biological need to accomplish a vision that I've had teasing and tormenting me since freshman year at Boise State. If I don't materialize the vision, it will materialize itself into the bitter later years. I don't want the bitterness. I want peace with you. I want you to be proud of me."

"I am sweetheart, but I don't want bitterness in my early thirties. There is shame at teaching at a university. And you've already tried. Your Idaho novel got no takers.

You put the vision down and you even had connections from the bookstore."

"My Idaho novel was visionless, all self-absorbed and flawed. It was shit. The cab will get me into the lives of others. I'll just be this Cooper-like tenderfoot driver caught in the maelstrom of others running here and there. Everybody going and I'm in the same place."

"Hasn't it been done before?"

"Everybody going and I'm in the same place."

"It has been done before."

"Everybody going and I'm in the same place."

"Henry, Christ. Kill the mantra."

"I like the repetition of that. That's why I like simple, piercing poetry. A few more lines to that repeated verse and it'd tell what the novel would need three hundred pages to tell."

"It actually fits us well."

"Screw the Joneses. You never cared about accumulation when we met."

"When we met, I was 22. A decade has changed me, Henry. It should have changed you. You're almost forty!"

"Thirty-seven!"

"Like I said."

"One year's all I want. Six months to ride and take notes. Six months to churn the notes into a chiseled piece. Chiseled spontaneity. Let me be a footnote to history, but let me do it with a fight. I'm alive just thinking about it."

"Jesus, Henry another year. I don't think I can take it," Nancy sighed.

"You don't get it. We both win. I take a last stab at art and we'll be getting more money than ever. Mike says I can take in $500 a week clean, which is double what I'm pulling in at the damn bookstore setting up podiums and microphones for the overrated local literati. We'll put some money into some funds or CDs or whatever it is people do with money, so we'll be ready to get a house when I'm all done. We both win, Nancy."

"It doesn't feel like victory. It feels like more like another lap around the same track, but fine, Mr. Fields, you've got it. One year, Henry. Then you start applying for teaching jobs while you try and publish. You're not expecting a best seller. You can teach and write like everyone else."

"It's a deal."

"I hope you appreciate this. No other sane wife would put up with this. There must be something wrong with me."

"I wouldn't have married you had you been sane," I said.

"Likewise," Nancy responded with a hint of a smile.

"You'll see, honey. It's all going to work out. Spiritual and material peace will be in our grasp. The real truth will emerge, not some disguised lie."

Truth. Yellow Cab became my truth.

As the bus crossed Market Street, I tried to recollect what Mike had told me about the system. Mike was as regular as they came. He'd been cabbing for twelve years. He made great money because he loved driving and he was American. Plenty of customers gave him big tips saying, "It's nice to ride with one of our own. One who speaks the same damn language." He lived upstairs from me and had two kids. His connection to the mind warp of San Francisco was his first wife. She was of the crystal, herb, and numerology mold. When she began dabbling in Haitian voodoo and consequently constructed dolls of her parents, Mike had had enough. Mike belonged in the suburbs amidst sports bars and strip malls, but he said that Haight Street and San Francisco had hooked him. "There's something about these fuck-ups that I like. Having them around is good schadenfreude scenery. Kind of keeps me balanced and content with the insignificance of my life. Everywhere else I'd be dull, but here my life seems exceptional in its dullness."

So Mike told me to tip the dispatcher, Delmore, to get my medallion, which I'd hand to the mechanic to get my cab for the day. A two-dollar bribe would get a decent cab and five a "mint job." He said Delmore weighed about 400 pounds and was one fine asshole. If you didn't tip, or just a buck, you'd be breaking down twice a week, which is a cabbie's Achilles heel. "Screws the whole week up." A good bribe would give some precious airport runs as well, which is a "cabbie's bread and butter."

As I walked from the bus stop to Yellow, I remember having these strange, tragic epiphanies swaying my thoughts from gleeful to bleak extremes. It was suddenly crashing my senses that Mike had just offered my wishful thoughts another exit into self-absorption, a romance of the self. The cab would give my failing thirties the path to revisit my innocent twenties and the eventual crash would be so much harder than those of a decade ago. Back then it just seemed like necessary tragedy that I'd mold into a great and potent creation of salvation. A new way of hitting the winning shot in the state championship. This time, though, the stakes had changed. I'd lose my wife. The parachute would be off and the fall would be achingly lonely and harsh. Too real. Simultaneously, I felt so aware of my flaws and past and self. The worry seemed so ridiculous. I could control the ripcord this time. I'd know when to pull it before Nancy would leave. This was the last chapter and its completion would lead into a new book. The old one would be forever closed. As I wavered from spiritual nothingness and mockery to the waves of wide-awake, I kept saying nothing mattered because Nancy would be there. Can't lose Nancy. Can't lose solid ground. Can't lose Nancy. I knew she'd be there. I knew one truth to be true. Nancy and I would ebb and flow, flounder and stumble, but we'd always end together.

Can't lose Nancy.

"New driver, eh?" snorted a grossly rotund man in a cage elevated above the floor of cabbies and mechanics. He had greasy black hair, thinning on top, and dark half-moons hanging under his eyes. Plumes of smoke rose from the cigarette in the ashtray to his left. Welcome to Delmore.

"Yeah, first day."

"You ever cabbed before?"

"No, but Mike Shore has given me some prep on what to expect. I slid two dollars through narrow slot in the cage. I had planned on five on day one, but in the moment, I didn't want to kiss his ass. I was feeling like a new kid in sixth grade paying a bully with my milk money. In every job I've ever had, there's always been one asshole to make it unpleasant. I knew Delmore would play that role.

"Mike's one of the best," he shouted, spit splaying in various directions.

"Yeah, so I hear."

"You do half as well as ole Mike and you'll be pullin' in some decent change."

I nodded, looking forward to the aloneness of my cab. Kind of my own boss for the first time in material existence.

"You seem too white for a cabbie."

"Didn't know there was a color requirement."

"Too educated, too."

I rolled my eyes and raised my shoulders not sure what I was trying to express. Delmore stared unblinkingly into my eyes. "What is this, some sociological research for some half-ass college, some college professor looking for recognition by researching the salt of the earth?"

"Not at all." I said, laughing awkwardly and realizing this guy was starting to turn me transparent.

"Or maybe you're some artist. What are you, professor or artist?"

"Does it matter?"

"You want a cab?"

He'd taken my two dollars, but my medallion was resting in his fat, sweaty palm beneath his curled fire-hydrant fingers. I immediately wanted to lie, which I was never good at. Horrible, in fact. Truth always comes out of me, which has made writing fiction no easy task. I wanted a lie, a good one, something I could pull off. Just once I wanted to undermine the ever-present tormentor in my life. Out-do the prick before he got the upper hand on me.

"I sculpt," I mumbled. Not quite what I was looking for.

"Huh?" Delmore asked, face skewed in surprise.

"I said I sculpt." This time louder and with some semblance of conviction.

"Really? You don't seem like a sculptor. Let me see your hands."

"What the hell is this? How 'bout a cab?" I asked, my voice rising trying to sell my new artistic lie.

"Hands first."

Shaking my head, I put my hands up to the opening at the base of the cage and he aggressively grabbed them, squeezing and examining them. "You ain't no sculptor."

"How would you know? Who made you an expert?"

"I know two things, immigrants and artists, 'cause that's all we got here. I know third-world accents from south of the border and I know who's the musician, or the writer, or the painter. These ain't sculpting hands."

"They were."

"Why *were*?"

"I've stopped. Kind of ahh, sculptor's block, so to speak. I'm hoping the cab frees me and puts a little money in my pockets."

"We got 'em all here. Every failure in art finds their way here. The immigrants, I respect. Artists, no. They're too fuckin' good to drive a cab. They're driving because their so-called *muse* done got up and left 'em or the masses don't appreciate them. Muse, my ass. You should hear the shit that flies in here from the fuckin' writers. They're ahead of their time, post-mortem fame bullshit, Buddhist bullshit to get them through this lifetime. I've heard all their crap. You'd think artists would sling some good shit too, since their whole thing is based on twisting so-called reality. I'll take the Dominicans and Brazilians any day. The immigrants work for their family, but you artists lower yourself to work."

"Yeah, we artists are a terrible breed, but I'm a cab driver now, or at least I want to be if you'd give me my damn cab." I loathed Delmore, but begrudgingly respected his analytical candor, despite it eviscerating me.

"You seem like a writer to me. I know a writer when I see 'em."

"I like clay and sometimes bronze, not words."

"What's your name?"

"Henry."

"Henry, I'm Delmore. Remember one thing, writer boy, don't write about me. I'm telling you straight now because I've seen you writers come in here and use us lifers for your little hobby. Found some bastard's notebook in his cab and had pages and pages on a character based on me and full of dumb imaginations of my past and crappy fuckin' metaphors about me in the cage."

"I don't write. Maybe, I'll sculpt your cage, but no metaphors," I said, grinning. This guy was all over me.

"Remember my warning. You better not use me for your pathetic efforts at art. I'll write my own novel, if I want. I ain't gonna be a part of someone else's. Take your medallion. Cab number 2874, see Hal, he'll take care of you."

"Thanks." I walked away, finally free. If every morning's like this, I'll quit by Friday. Delmore was the goliath of all previous assholes. He turned all the others Lilliputian.

"The funny thing though, is even if you do write about me, it will never see the light of day, because all you so called artists first, drivers second are here because it's the opposite. You're all failures. Fucking losers. You're cab drivers, don't you get it? Nothing more, nothing less." He laughed big and loud and cigarette stained. "Too good to be a cabbie, huh? Let's see how you fare. There's a pun for you writer boy. Farewell, cabbie. Just another cabbie. Mike, I respect, you candy ass artists…"

And on and on he droned as I walked away. Mike never told me to expect this much. Sad thing is, I agreed with just about everything he said. He knew me in less than thirty seconds. I spend thirty-seven years trying to figure myself out and he's got me in less than a fucking minute.

While I was walking toward this Hal guy, Delmore's effrontery had spun some memories to my mind's forefront: My old man whipping my ass with his belt for the last time in good-old-fashioned, raise-the-kids, big-sky-Boise style; his big farmer hands grabbing the back end of my neck and spinning me around at age ten when I finally fought the power and glared at him, clenched fist cocked and aimed, blood blasting my face and my old man startled, and losing the stare down; he put his belt back on through the loops, met my eyes one final time, slightly nodding in approval (or acceptance) and then calmly walking out. He'd never hit me again. Carrying a paint brush in one hand, a book in the other, painting the old halls of Boise State to pay my tuition. Delmore types, who were lifers painting the school over and over, given to their fate and I was envious and condescending toward them all at the same time. Those Delmore types were always asking what I was reading and what I wrote about when I would stop to jot in my little dime store notebook I carried in the thigh pocket of my painter pants…all the while I was writing about them and their words and lives and complaints and quotidian feats…selling Christmas trees…meeting Nancy…sportswriter for the Boise Press…thirty years old…married…San Francisco…stuck…in San Francisco…bookstore…fighting with Nancy…little poems in little places…un-channeled visions and half-way ideas…last chance in Yellow Cab.

"Hey, are you Henry?"

"Huh?"

"Are you Henry? The new guy. Cab 2874?" I looked at my medallion.

"Yeah, 2874, that's right. Are you Hal?"

"Yes, sir. Are you ok? You look, ahh, a little frazzled."

"Yeah, yeah, I'm fine. First day, I guess I was trying to remember a few things my friend Mike Shore told me."

"Mike said you'd be in today. I was looking for you. Wasn't hard to find you."

"It's that obvious?"

"Well, when Delmore reads someone the riot act and tries to get under their skin, I know it's a new guy. You should hear what he says about the immigrants. He just turns the story upside down, elevating the artists and putting down foreigners."

Regardless, the speech still rattled my core. "Yeah, no big deal. He's a caricature," I said, thinking maybe I was describing myself. "So, what now, Hal?"

"You know how it works right? You went to the big Yellow seminar upstairs where the guys in ties tell the Yellow philosophy."

I nodded. "Sure did."

"Well, now all you got to do is drive. You know your zone?"

"Yeah, Haight and the panhandle."

"Lucky you, hippies and punks with no money, but plenty of needles. Never take them unless they show you green first."

"I know, thanks."

"Mike set you straight, right?"

I nodded.

"Well, you got a good cab. Purrs down the road. Here are the keys. You got any problems, call me or let me know when you return. You got the day shift, so it's really a piece of cake. Might get some speed queens finishing the nightshift and besides the Haight-Ashbury refugees, you'll get lots of businessmen going to the airport. The Haight's more yuppie than revolutionary now."

"Times have changed."

"I'm glad. I'll take the Gap over some burnt-out phony protesters and angry youth above work."

"Thanks Hal."

"Don't sweat it."

Hal was a good guy, but I felt like a young kid being sent out into the trenches for the first time. I was thirty-seven and he couldn't have been more than twenty-eight. Goddamn Delmore hit those real spots inside that go untouched for so long, getting covered and masked and walled in like an old, medieval Italian city. I'd felt individualized, using the cab as a vehicle to right my life until he strung me together on a fragile thread with so many others in this ashbin for artists taxi universe. As I wallowed indulgently, I reminded myself to just drive. Silence the damn internal voice and drive. I talked too damn much to myself when all I had to do now is let others talk to me. Hell, what better start could Delmore have been, considering my purpose? It's a constant struggle trying to right the ship of my mind.

So I started up my yellow angel and went up the grimy, tire-stained ramp leaving Hal, Delmore and the bleak taxi underworld behind and into a clear San Francisco blue sky day. My mind ceased digging within and everything suddenly seemed so open. I felt young. I felt like something might happen that would lead all the detours and exits into their manifest destination.

What does a cabbie do between fares? You either park at a hot spot like the airport or you ride around an assigned area. My area was basically my neighborhood, Cole Valley, a couple blocks south of Haight Street. It was a little more civilized than the Haight or lower Haight, which was still full of anxious youth and 20-something seekers. Cole Valley was a little older and jaded, but of the same seeker soul, just worn down over time into a role. There were quite a few academics and artists, literary revue owners, and some schoolteachers. I put myself somewhere between Cole Valley and the Haight, some netherworld not quite locatable.

I had quite a few friends, but I didn't truly like many of them. Mostly I was just passing time in conversations and looking forward to goodbye. One friend I actually liked was Samuel Connells. He worked at a café in my neighborhood. I figured I'd get a cup of coffee with an old friend I'd made during my bookstore days. Hit some level, familiar ground after Delmore's invasive assault. Sam was a regular at Great Expectations, always buying either biographies of tortured artists, from Judy Garland to F. Scott Fitzgerald, or the latest leftist economic theories. Samuel was a true scion of the legendary Diggers of Haight-Ashbury back in its late 60s glory days.

On the way several hands were waving to get a lift, but I just ignored them. Their faces writhed with frustration upon seeing an empty cab whiz by them. I enjoyed the little semblance of control I had. Hell, this was my cab, and I was the boss. My own little private, mobile office. I could do whatever the hell I pleased.

"Henry, how are you, amigo mio?" Samuel asked from behind the counter of the Paris Commune, which was worker owned as its name implied. A Marxist café alive and well in San Francisco. Where else? "What can I get you?"

"What's today's coffee of the day?"

"Kenyan dark roast. Enough caffeine in it to make you think you did a line."

"I'll take it."

"This will get your blood flowing. Are you pounding the keyboard or just thinking about it? It's always one or the other."

"Samuel, today's my first day behind the wheel."

"Oh, shit, I forgot, and you were all nervous for a week and here I damn forgot. So what's the word of your new world?"

"Well, I haven't picked anyone up, but there's my little yellow angel out front."

"That thing's gonna give you some cash and poems of everyday existence."

"That's what I told Nancy, kind of."

"She give you hell?"

"Little bit. We're at a crossroads right now. Kind of beyond it, maybe, more like Lombard Street rather than crossroads. I don't know, we'll figure it out. Something's happening or happened, I just don't know what. Anyway, if I were her, I would have left me long ago."

"Life is more crooked than Lombard. Can't expect it otherwise. Just put it in verse and you'll figure it out. Get it out and the truth will stare right back at you with big relieved eyes."

"I told you I'm done with poems. They're dead."

Samuel recoiled, tugging his black apron. "Dead, how dare thee. Poetry is eternal, everything else a fling."

"Well, I'm having a fling with prose. Good, solid capitalist writing. Make it up for money."

"Fields, you're a Robert Lowell guy and you know it. Lyrical confession is your only truth."

"Who's me, you or me?" I asked with a grin.

"Great question. Some days, I might be more you than yourself."

I took a deep breath. "Good luck with that identity. Can we change the subject?"

"To you or me?" Samuel said, grinning wryly.

I looked around the Commune. The ten or so tables were empty save for one where a young hippie-type woman was sketching in a big pad. "How's business?"

"Seeking a grounded, real dialogue Fields? Can't swing the philosophical swerve today, huh? Well, we're not killing each other here, getting an equal cut, and decent time off. Operational Marxism better than the real Paris Commune."

"You're off next week, right? What's your plan?" I asked.

"Reading, jotting down truths. Confessions to myself."

"Why don't you travel for a change? Get the hell out of here."

"Don't have the bourgeois wallet. Besides, traveling's bullshit. I travel through books. Real travel, not some roll of film bullshit. Don't need to take one step and I can travel thousands of miles and centuries of time. I got a ticket for the library and it's free, baby."

"I think I'd take a beach for a week."

"Henry, you buying into that? Absolutely not you. Stupid humans lying on the sand trying to turn my color. All crowded together, drying out in the sun, thinking they're having a good time. I don't subscribe. I'm gonna continue with my truth trend. I'm in a healthy, self-destructive groove. Baudeliere, Rimbaud, Artaud, Modigliani, Plath, and now I'm into this white bread 50s cat, Ross Lockridge."

"What did he write? Ahh, that film with Liz Taylor, *Big*, right?"

"Close. Same era and actress. *Raintree Country*. This Indiana guy writes a goddamn great American novel and kills himself the day before it hits the best seller list. They made him edit it for years after he'd taken years to get it out and then after it's sculpted and ready, he says that's it and buys the farm hours before fame. Had a wife and kids, the whole great big picture of tragedy. Some giant subconscious eruption moments before the world would have saluted him. Fame is toxic, my friend. Thank your anonymity and the peace it provides. And I'm also getting into this Japanese madman Mishima. He—"

"Don't you get depressed in this suicide groove?"

"No, strangely exhilarated."

Samuel was about 6 foot 5 and weighed 250 pounds and he was a naturally honed mass of muscle and the kindest man I'd ever met, giving money to anyone he deemed in real need. His hair was in 70s style afro. He was the manager of this socialist experiment that began in the 70s with him and a few friends. He's the only founder left and has no intentions of leaving. All the worker-owners share all the profits and everyone makes enough to live. He was proud of that and had no reason or want for more money. He's never had a car nor taken a vacation and he's lived in the same modest one bedroom above the café for twenty-five years.

"Coffee's great," I said.

"You feeling tortured."

"Huh?"

"Oh, you know subterranean artist life in a cab."

"You, too. Christ, everyone's an analyst today."

"I'm impressed by it."

"I'm not. Maybe, I just want a goddamn job."

"Fields, my soulful San Francisco kinsman, the bullshit won't work with me. We're of the same spirit. Remember their hands."

"Whose hands?"

"Your future characters. Get their words but remember their hands. The eyes lie. Everybody thinks the eyes are the window, but it's the hands that signal the soul. Like Homer in West's *Day of the Locust*. Whole novels exist in how one moves and rests their hands. Look at yours."

I looked down at my right hand holding my left tightly and let go.

"Fields, look at that tension. Christ, you need to talk it out," Samuel said.

"I gotta drive, not talk."

"I want some taxi epiphanies."

"I just want some fares."

"Epiphanies are why we are, Henry. Let 'em come. The hands, Henry. Neurosis has nowhere to extend after the hands. It's the last stop. It's all there. Trapped doors, Henry. We're all knocking on trapped doors."

I've got to get out of this damn city and all the prophets hazing the periphery. The dull materialism of the rest of America is looking pretty profitable right now.

"Let the roiling internal tornado blow itself into poesy," Samuel hollered as I was halfway out the door.

"Bye Samuel. Thanks for the coffee, not sure about tornadoes," I said as Samuel was still rambling on about some epic poems beyond color and into existence and something about Thomas Chatterton and arsenic and water cocktails.

I hope my first fare's a plain old suit and tie insurance man, wife and kids, mortgage, retirement plan, and two weeks' vacation.


"Hey, 2874. That's you, Fields," bellowed Delmore's gravelly baritone voice on the radio.

"I know my number."

"How you doing out there?"

"Driving."

"Got an airport for you. Pick up at 1487 Fell between Clayton and Ashbury. Can you handle it, soft hands?"

It's a damn conspiracy and I'm the marionette. "I'm on it."

"You know where SFO is?" Delmore said amidst a loud laugh that slipped quickly into a thick and liquidy cough that he must have aimed completely into his microphone.

"Been there once or twice."

"Go get 'em professor and remember this isn't your little pottery wheel. It's a real job in a real world where real people go to real places. Don't get lost."

"Thanks, Delmore, You're ahhh, ahhh, a real pal."

"The professor seems a bit…"

I muted the radio before the next aspersion sliced into me. There's got to be a reason this guy's all over me. Some purpose, some response to his whole vaudeville act that will help me pass into the next level of Buddhist enlightenment. Or everything has no reason and he's just an out of orbit, free flowing asshole.

Probably the latter.

I took a right onto Ashbury, down to the panhandle and circled around it via Oak and Masonic and then onto Fell where a pick-up basketball game was going on. I glimpsed at the players, almost equally black and white. I ought to go play, I told myself, but I seemed hell bent on recollecting events rather than living them. This cab could be considered a new turn at life or just another disguise trying to resurrect something that could only be recollected, likely trying to fix the failings of twenties, rather than recognize that time had won. Little did I know that my lost twenties would soon enter the back seat of my cab.

I noticed a small playground with some kids and mothers. There was a bearded man nearby in black martial arts attire doing Tai Chi or something similar; a young man playing Frisbee with his dog; a big circle of Hare Krishna types, flaky flower children dancing in a crooked circle and assorted hippies surrounding the retro be-in.

A group of well-dressed men and a few women were watching the flashback spectacle with some big video cameras and one guy, who had a clipboard, was looking at the group and occasionally writing on his board. It all looked artificial, maybe producers casting a movie. San Francisco, real and re-imagined, was happening and I was making my first pick up.

I pulled up to a three-story, semi-Victorian and leaned on the horn a couple of times. As I was waiting, I noticed a black woman on the second floor of the building next door, a drab, dirty, sky-blue, boxy post-Victorian with a tan fire escape front. She was sitting crossed-legged by the large bay window overlooking the busy four lanes of Fell Street. I tried to figure out what she was doing but had no idea. Her eyes were lazily looking downward and her hands slowly moving about. The sunlight shone on her dark face, large eyes, thin puckered mouth and small, narrow chin. She was terribly homely and upon my recognition of this, she looked up at the park and her eyes took in the gently wayward Golden Gate Park scene. She had no visible facial emotion other than the seemingly pained sadness permanently etched around and within her eyes.

My voyeuristic moments were suddenly interrupted by a door closing loudly. I turned and saw a woman descending concrete stairs. I looked back at the sad window woman when a big, black gate crashed shut and my fare approached the cab. She had red hair, long and shiny partly flowing down her back and the rest split evenly down the front of her shoulders. My mind oddly darted to memories of Nancy, of our early, magnificent days when we kissed. Real kissing. Passionate, meaningful kissing undamming youth's bursting sexual energy. Not the kind of kisses that we had now, those reserved for aunts at holidays.

"Hi. I'm going to SFO, but you probably already know that," she said, sitting down in the back and snapping my thoughts back to now.

"Yup, I'm on it," I said.

"My flight isn't until 11:30. We've got plenty of time, so don't kill yourself."

"Ok. We'll go nice and steady," I assured her, wondering why she said we, when I was just her cabbie and not traveling with her. Perhaps it meant something. After five years of virtual abstinence, I was foolishly willing to hang my eunuch hat on anything resembling a hint of flirtation.

As I pulled from the curb during a break in the rushing Fell Street traffic, I took a last look at window woman and saw her holding up a piece of something in the sunlight and staring at it. I focused and it came clear—a jigsaw puzzle piece.

*Perfect*, I thought.

After some silence, I tried to think of a conversation starter and came up with something confessional. "Actually, I'm glad we don't have to rush because it's my first day and, to be honest, I'm a little jittery."

"First day, really? Actually you hide your nerves well."

I smiled into the rear view mirror. She was wearing a spaghetti strap yellow silk shirt that glided alluringly across her breasts. She had ivory white skin that made her blue eyes more luminous and the straight red hair was sexy in its simplicity. She smiled back and we caught reflected eyes for more than a moment before we both giggled in what I perceived to be mutually recognized attraction, something so foreign for so many years. It was like relearning a language that one had forgotten, but it comes back quickly.

But her beauty and the attention had an strange effect on me. It catapulted my libido into absurd intensity. Pathetically, I began sweating with desire. The so-called hidden nerves were exposed. I remembered contempt for Nancy and our marriage and how it had reduced me to this teenage state. I blamed her, me, it. Perhaps many men would be the same way, happily married or not. However, this had gone too far, into surreal Modigliani-like elongations. Suddenly, her image seemed to be receding in my mirror, drifting away in my now rubbery mirage of a cab. I felt beads of sweat seeking rivulets along my temples and down my nose. Each time I looked back at her, avoiding eye contact, I saw her further and further away, my cab now a stretch limousine. I took deep breaths, hoping I could breathe this trippy panic attack back to normal, but oxygen didn't help. Looking away from her and focusing my vision on the road ahead was worse as the road turned into melting tar.

Christ, all this without even any LSD!

Thoughts of adultery had drugged my neurons. Why had she ceased talking? How long had it been? What was she doing during my own personal drama. Thirty-seven years old and I'm hopelessly pubescent. I engaged reality enough to stop at a red light. I decided to meet this head on and stared at her in my rear view mirror. She was preoccupied with something in her purse, not noticing my madness which was clearly all just dreamily in my head. I wiped my forehead with the back of my hand, confirming the physical reaction was real.

Her breasts, shoulders, chin, all of her being, was so beautiful. Her collarbones were slightly visible. Her face was tender with a few freckles on her small, rounded nose.

She had no accent of cheekbone, just the soft skin of a round face, all so unlike my wife's angular, sharp edges. The more I looked at her face, and not her body, the more it soothed, rather than seduced.

"Phew," she exclaimed pulling a ticket from her purse. "I thought I forgot my ticket."

I wiped my still sweaty brow with a tissue from a box that Nancy had given me.

We caught eyes again in the mirror. "Are you ok?" she asked.

"Yeah, yes, I'm fine. I had the heat on too high," I said, somewhat honestly.

"It's fine back here."

"So, where you headed?"

"LA bound."

I nodded and recognized my cab had returned to normal size. Got to keep a conversation going and just look at her face.

"So, why'd you decide to drive a cab? You don't seem like a cabbie if I can say that."

"I've heard that before."

"So what gives? It's a means for something else?"

"Isn't every job?" I asked.

"Yeah, but careers and jobs are different, right?"

"Well said. Yeah, I'm an artist. A sculptor." Might as well stick to the script. All the world's a stage…

"So this is the day job?"

"Yeah, kind of. I've been stuck creatively and haven't sold anything for a while. Figured I should make some money and maybe find a muse along the way." I was starting to like this sculptor stance. It wasn't a complete lie so it was finding its legs.

"Really?" she said without much surprise. San Francisco didn't produce the same effect as Boise. I missed ole, slowed down, banal Boise. I missed a reaction of surprise toward my life; missed the attention and feeling different.

"So what do you sculpt? Heads?" She asked raising her brow as if it might be silly question.

I was unprepared for any follow up. Delmore had immediately seen through my lie and leapt past it into derision, denying the lie any depth. Then my conversation with Samuel popped into my head. "Ahhh, well, I sculpt hands actually. I have this thing for hands. I know, it's odd."

"No, it's not. All's fair in love and art and it's different. Well, being a sculptor is interesting. Don't meet many of you. Don't think I ever have. At least you're not a writer using the cab for material. That would be so trite."

I nodded. "Right, yeah, done to death, but, I guess it depends on the writer. There are always new angles." Clearly some higher powers were conspiring to mock my life.

There was a lull in the talk. I desperately wanted to redirect to her life, not mine. I was so sick of me. "So, how 'bout you. What's in LA?"

"Phonies, sunshine, wannabes, and so on," she said grinning.

"I take it you prefer northern California."

"Actually, I think the LA world is phony but in a real sense, while here, people think they're hip to some truth or being, but it's all bullshit. In LA they're phony and aware of it without shame. They own it better than up here."

"We're all full of shit, I guess. North, south, whatever."

"Hard to argue that. So for me, in LA, there's business. I'm in real estate."

"Sales or rentals or—"

"Whatever they want I'll do, but mostly sales. That's where the money is."

She was dressed well with nice jewelry and makeup put on with class. Most of the women I'd been with were earthy, artsy or cheap, none of which fit this lady.

"May I see some of your work?"

"Right now this is my work."

"You know what I mean."

"Well, let's talk about something else. My work is a sore spot right now."

"I only ask because, well, to be quite honest, I'd like to go deeper and further than just small talk."

"Huh?" I asked, wide eyed. Had she really said that?

"I'd like to know you better. There's something about you. How's that for cutting to the chase?" She giggled a bit, but not shyly. She was confident and sexy. "Am I being too candid too quickly for you?"

"No, no. You just surprised me. Doesn't happen every day."

"We don't have a lot of time and I trust the energy I feel when I meet someone. I like our energy."

Was this yang paying back for the yin of Delmore? Universal whiplash. Was some balance suddenly entering my tilted, teetering life?

I smiled into the rear view mirror. She was smiling back.

"We're almost there," I said.

Candlestick was on my left. I realized I hadn't seen a single Giants game during my San Francisco years, but I'd read poetry in a dimly lit lesbian club on the periphery of North

Beach. I needed balance. I needed this woman. I wanted to say something bold with minutes to go before we parted. She had open the door and I just had to follow her lead.

"What airline are you?" was all I came up with.

"US Air shuttle."

She was fidgeting in her bag again and leaning lower than before. I used every bit of my ocular muscles not to stray there.

"Listen," she began, "I never got your name. I'm Eve."

"Henry, Henry Fields."

"Well, Henry Fields, I'd like to see your work when you're not feeling so down about it. Maybe I could lift your spirits. It would be a nice change from my phony real estate world."

"I'd like to show you my work, but, ahh, I'd rather just get to know you better. I'm really not successful."

"Success is overrated. Maybe you're hypercritical of yourself."

"I've had help from others."

"Well, that could be why you can't get the momentum going. Maybe I can help you with your momentum, artistically and otherwise."

"I have a feeling you could."

"I feel you could help me, too."

"I wish I'd started driving a cab ten years ago. That is, if I'd known my first customer would have been you."

"You're a very sweet man, Henry. I can tell you've never cheated on your wife, but my sixth sense tells me that's just what you need to do to get out of an unhappy marriage if I may be so presumptuous."

I looked at my wedding band resting on my hand clutching the steering wheel. The ring looked big and heavy. "Well, ahhh, you certainly have a knack for jumping ahead, but really, I'm not that unhappy.

"Not happy and not unhappy."

"I don't like the word happy anyway. Peaceful is better."

"Peace can be dull. Artists need chaos, no? Peace isn't prone to creation."

I nodded. "Can't argue that." She knew just how to prod. "You're killing me, Eve."

"I'm trying to do the opposite."

"You know, I don't blame my wife."

"There's not always blame to be given," she said as I pulled into an open spot at terminal B. She reached into her bag while I got out of the cab and opened her door.

As we stood on the curb she gave me a $100 bill for a $22 fare. "I don't have change, Eve."

"I don't want change."

"Please, this is too generous," I said.

"It's just good luck for your first day."

"No, really, I—"

"How 'bout you keep the money for dinner tonight with me. I'll need a ride at nine o'clock and then we can have a late dinner."

"I finish at six," I said foolishly.

"I don't want you as a cab driver."

"Of course."

"Tell your wife something creative. You're a creative man, Henry."

"I'm not thinking straight. I'm a bit jittery. Been out of the game for a while."

"It makes you more attractive. See you at nine." Then she kissed me softly on the lips while gently gliding her hand across my cheek. It had been so long since I'd been with a woman besides Nancy and so long since I'd been with even her. She moved her hand behind my head and pulled me tighter into her mouth, moving her tongue slowly, and all so erotically. Then she stopped, whispering "our first kiss," before disappearing through a revolving glass door. I stood there, watching the door spin round and round, for what must have been one hundred revolutions before a cop's shrill whistle snapped me out of my mesmerized state.

Perhaps, this whole cab affair…my desire to take this job…move into the apartment below a cabbie and thus be inspired to leave my dead-end, bookstore job surrounded by the poems and adventures and of others…lives being lived…to quit sports writing…to have met Nancy while working three menial, tough-skinned, salt-of-the-earth jobs—painter, Christmas tree salesmen in the windy, dry, cold Boise Decembers, and sidewalk scrubber—while keeping Verlaine in one hand and Rimbaud in the other… to have taken ten years to finish college…set ablaze all the journals, poems, lyrics, stories, confessional novellas, every form in which we've caged the written word…an ego sacrifice near the ending of the great writer ego in Ketchum…A big blaze in the Spring twilight, watching the smoke twirl *nightward* as if new openings would be burrowed free by torching failed past releases and the misalliances of inspirations, incinerating youth, and all its misdirection…If I hadn't ended my relationship with Arlene Murdoch…hadn't gotten hung up in 70s hedonism, anti-ideology, the middle-class bourgeois life is the bane of modern life with friends like Elgyn Simmons penning metaphorical sci-fi stories only to end up an L.A. bell hop hated by Nancy for his feckless ways…

past symmetry knotting and confounding the present… It all rests on Nancy, got to get us back, sexual, together, coming, touching, or is Nancy all false and the desire all real?…and this woman, this new, strange tantalizing woman named Eve.

More fares and maybe more temptations. More stories and more Delmore accosting my existence in its transparent armor. Penetrating my shaky, spiritual core. Maybe all these things going further were the catalyst to something I wasn't wholly aware of. Thirty-seven years haven't taught me much, but I constantly remind myself that the present is never really what it seems to be. The moment is quicksand. There's so much more going on. The subconscious reigns the palace infinite. But, just maybe, this time I was onto something. Further awareness. Deeper knowledge that would penetrate the veneer of the comic kingdom I've so painstakingly been creating. I had a notebook and pen for time between fares. I jotted some things down after L.A. Woman left, recording some dialogue untrusting of my memory to recollect it right. I was off to a novel start. I was beginning to realize the cab was going to concretely confront my papier-mâché present. Perhaps the novel would never be, but my life might.

The rest of the day was normal, just regular workaday folks going here and there while my mind pinballed varied scenarios and notions. I told Nancy over dinner that I had a rescheduled therapy session and then was going to meet some local poet friends for drinks and a reading at a bookstore on Polk Street. I offered that she could join me knowing there was no chance she'd have any interest.

When I arrived back at SFO, Eve was waiting for me right where I left her.

I jumped out to open her door.

"Such a gentleman, Henry. It's refreshing."

We made some small talk about her flight and work in L.A. today. She asked about my day and then she initiated real talk.

"You seem tense. You ok?"

"Eve, this isn't easy for me."

"Because of your marriage?" she asked, seemingly not rhetorically.

"Of course. Otherwise, there'd be nothing stopping me from kissing you immediately."

"Is a bad marriage worthy of fidelity?" she asked as we merged onto 101 in my shitty '84 Ford Escort.

"Yes and no."

"Not everything has to be vague."

"Maybe."

Laughing at my response, Eve asked, "Are you in love with her or just respecting the vows?"

"I don't think I'll know unless it ends and I can see it from the outside. I need a new perspective."

"Henry, we've known each other for less than an hour, but I feel comfortable asking you anything. Do you mind?"

"Not at all. I like it. Actually, I love it."

"How's the sex?"

"There isn't," I said.

"None?"

"No, not for years."

Eve, this stranger, took my right hand with both of hers as she leaned towards me. She slowly caressed my fingers and then pressed my hand between her palms as if to warm it before leading it along her breast, moving it slowly over its firm slope, up and down several times along the thin silk covering. Then down her leg and up her skirt. This game continued for most of the ride. There was no conversation, just the sounds of heavy, on the verge, breathing. Thankfully I didn't have another surreal experience, but staying focused on the road was a herculean task.

When we arrived at her house, she said "Come up, Henry. I want to change and then we can go to dinner."

I tried to think with my brain. "We'll never make it to dinner."

"We will eventually," she said, smiling coquettishly.

"Ahhh, I don't know, Eve."

"Your resistance makes me want you more. You actually respect your sexless marriage enough to hesitate."

"Strange, huh?" I said, adrenalin outflanking my resistance.

"Sweet and noble, so out of male character, especially for an artist in this lost city."

"How 'bout tomorrow?"

"For?"

"To see each other. Let me sleep and think and do the right thing."

"You're a good boy, Henry Fields."

"I wouldn't go that far. It's not as if I've stopped this snowball from rolling down the inevitable hill."

"It is inevitable. I feel it, too. Henry, don't think I do this often. I haven't felt an instant ease and attraction to a man in ages like I feel with you. My instincts are directing this play. It feels so good and free."

"What time tomorrow?" I asked.

"Four o'clock. The Delta gate. Off to Santa Barbara early in the morning."

"Ok. Four o'clock it is, Eve."

We kissed passionately before she pulled away. "I won't take no for an answer tomorrow," she said as she left the car. I watched her head up the stoop, hearing the big black gate crash shut. At the door, she looked back and blew me a kiss, which I immediately returned. She laughed before disappearing into her building.

I sat in my Escort, grinning ear to ear for a while like a high schooler who just hooked up with someone out of his league, before guilt and indecision ruined the moment. I pulled onto Fell Street, glancing up to see if jigsaw woman was there. Indeed she was, but this time she was looking straight out the window. I think we caught eyes in the dark of night, but I wasn't sure.

On my way home I tried to channel my sexual energies resurrected by Eve into desire for Nancy. I considered relieving myself of the libidinous tempest at a construction site port-o-potty, but decided to dam the flow for Nancy. Besides, I'm too Boise, and not enough Bukowski.

"So how was your first day? Give me some details," Nancy asked as I settled myself on the couch while she fed our cats a few treats. After they ate, Billie relaxed at my side, pressed comfortably against my thigh. Bear went under the chair wear Nancy was sitting, lying down directly below her and staring at me as if I had done something wrong.

"Ahh, not so bad. Of course, there's the requisite asshole, but that's no surprise. He's the guy Mike had warned me about, but he seemed particularly up my ass."

"That seems to happen at all your jobs."

"Yeah, you know, my father's ghost follows me around."

Nancy shrugged, never really buying into my paternal complaints, or just tired of them. She redirected, "So potential novel material?"

"Only day one, but there was a nugget or two."

"Do tell."

"No, no. Verbalizing kills it. It's *muse-icide.*"

Nancy shrugged again. Apparently it was a shoulder-shrug kind of night. "Well, I did make some good money. That I can share."

"How much?"

"Well, after the $50 for the cab's use I took in about $150."

"You're kidding?"

"No, ma'am. Like I told you, more money and my last shot as a writer in one mobile package."

"Jesus, Henry, that might be $600 take-home, $750 if you worked the same five-day week as everyone else."

"Nancy, sticking to the plan, one day for writing, four for money. That'll leave us with some weekend time together. I'm not a five-day-a-week guy."

"That I know."

I could see this going beyond shrugs. We had enough skeletons to fill the closets of Versailles, but she let it go. "Anyway, that's more than double your bookstore salary. Maybe, we can actually take a vacation this year, besides driving to Boise to see family. Done that to death," Nancy said with hope in her voice.

"I like it. Maybe a nice week-long drive down Route 1, all the way to San Diego. We've never done that."

"Yes, or maybe even something grander, more exotic that gets us out of this state." We rarely dreamed, even little dreams. "How 'bout an island in the Pacific, like

Fiji or Bali, and just sitting on the beach? Why can't we be middle class for just a week?"

"Well, if we could just get the credit cards down," I said stupidly raining on the conversational parade. I was great at self-sabotage.

"That fifth day would take care of it. Do you realize you're losing $600 a month by working four days a week? Hell, we'd have a vacation and zero balance in less than a year."

"Nancy, let it rest. Let me write the damn book and then I'll work six days a week and we'll take two vacations and do all the other crap that the bourgeois life buys."

Whenever we had these conversations, I remembered how Nancy fell in love with me as the young poet trying to sidestep society. The notion of seeking internal sanctuaries, rather than external trappings. She didn't see through my pose, nor had I. We ran on that for several years. Now she'd gone from idyllic romantic affection to South Pacific beach vacations and I'd seen so far through myself that I was trying to prose my way out of it for redemption. Still, despite my transparency, I couldn't look at myself in the mirror and see a cab driver, just like Delmore had said. Seven hundred fifty dollars a week wasn't enough. Zero balances weren't enough. Island sunshine meant nothing. Delmore was spot on. One day in the cab and I was indulging in epiphanies and peeling away poses. I just had to get it right with Nancy. The rest would follow. I did love her.

Can't lose Nancy.

"You know, honey, driving gives me a lot of time to think, and today I realized it's not about credit cards or vacations or Boise trips or any of those accessories. It's about renewal."

"Of what?"

"Us."

"Is this about change? About you leaving me?"

"No, it's just the opposite. It's about entering you, and I don't mean that crassly at all."

Nancy squinted at me in recognition of what I meant.

"Jesus Christ, Nancy," I said followed by a deep breath and exhaling sigh, "I want to make love to you. No, I want to screw like we'd screwed before. Angry, passionate, as if it were the only worthwhile thing in life. It's the only goddamn chance to get out of this sorry world, if only momentarily. We can't go on without it. How did five fucking years go by?"

"I'm flattered, I think, but no, Henry, you're wrong. It is about material comfort and peace. We had passionate sex back in our early days. Where did it get us? Marriage changes sex. I think it does for everyone. No one says it, but very few are doing it. And those that do are just going through the motions. I don't want us deceiving each other. Fake orgasms, lying pleasure."

"Why the hell does it have to be fake and lies! If I don't turn you on, say it directly. It's bullshit. We're deceiving ourselves if we think a sexless marriage can endure."

"Why, all of the sudden, are you so horny?"

"Five fucking years Nancy!"

"What happened at the therapy session tonight or was it in the cab today?"

"It's got nothing to do with tonight's therapy. This has been building for a half of a decade and maybe the time in the cab today just crystallized it. You don't think our dead sex life is an issue? You don't think about it?"

"No, I've accepted it. I think maybe it'll return when your life is together. When we have a house, a normal life, some kids, stability."

"How the hell can we have kids? Immaculate conception?"

Nancy rolled her eyes at my sarcasm. "When we're finally settled. When you get your art fix saturated and accept its course as secondary and our life and future as primary. I think about it, but within reality. Henry, I'm convinced our sexual troubles are related to your juvenile writing need."

"Juvenile! What the fuck are you talking about?"

"Your vulgarity is obnoxious. Keep it on paper."

"It used to turn you on."

"On paper and I was twenty-three years old, Henry. You see, you can't get over twenty-three. It's like this giant hurdle and you just trip every time. No, you don't even jump, you go around and around, without ever going ahead. The cab's another fantasy."

"Nancy, you're the one going around with periphery bullshit. Vacations and good-on-the-outside jobs so you can tell your family and friends that your husband's not a cab driver, bookstore clerk, failed poet, but at least a teacher, or better yet a professor. That's acceptable failure to you and others. To me, it's surrender. We agreed to one last year. But with us, damn it, I want to rip your clothes off and give you pleasure. That's not going around and avoiding. That's looking straight ahead at the hurdle. You on the other—"

"I don't feel it, Henry. I can't just manufacture passion—"

"No, but if we try, maybe it'll happen."

"It's bullshit. Our problems are larger than sex."

"Nancy, I think are problems begin with sex."

"As usual we see things perfectly diametrically. Henry, wake up! It's a result, a symptom of the big picture. I want you to change and evolve from juvenile art whims into adult practicality. I'm tired and sex won't relieve the fatigue."

"What will?"

"Have you not heard a word I've said?"

"I've heard too much."

There was a long silence. This argument, although more heated than others in recent memory, would drift away as usual with no climactic end, no resolution. It would be superficially forgotten, but kept within, interred, but lurking. We always ended with dignity, but I felt we needed depth, finality, danger. Dignity was getting us nowhere.

Nancy broke the silence in our typical way. "So, what about dinner? What should we do?"

"We should finish our fight and not do our British policy of avoidance."

"What else is there to say other than time will tell?"

"Why can't you make love to me?"

"Let it go, Henry."

"Nancy, make love to me. Let me make love to you."

"Honey, I'm touched by your desire, but I can't force it. We decided to let it return naturally. I just don't have the energy for it. It's not there for me and maybe you're just kidding yourself. It will return beautifully one day in the future. I believe that."

"Nature's taking too damn long, Nancy."

"Concentrate on the cab and your book. Get it done for me, so we can move on, wherever that leads. I don't give a shit about friends and family perceptions.

I wouldn't have married you had I cared. I want to be proud of you. We need to bury our twenties with forty so close."

"Well, hate on the twenties, but they felt wide open and free. Now I feel caged."

Nancy was shaking her head and then took a deep breath before scooping up Bear, who only allowed her to do that. She put a lot of her affection into those two felines. Looking sweetly maternal with Bear peacefully resting his head on her shoulder, she said, "Henry you're chasing a sentiment that requires a time machine. The cage is not so bad if you accept it."

More silence before I pushed the envelope, "You know, if I were an outsider listening to us, I'd swear you're trying to change me and using the possibility of sex as bait."

"You're not an outsider. You're right here."

"Am I right?"

"You're paranoid, but if it would finally snap you forward, then bait it is."

I walked over to Nancy, took Bear out of her arms, who hissed at me before scurrying under the chair, and held both of Nancy's hands, looking into her eyes.

"What," she said, almost embarrassed at this minimal level of intimacy. I remained undeterred. I kissed her softly, touched her shoulders, arms, and breasts. I wasn't deluded, becoming aroused immediately. I led her to the bedroom and she willingly followed.

"I'm sorry, Henry."

I heard her, but continued as if I hadn't.

"Henry, stop, please. It's not going to work. It hurts. I tried because I do still love you. My mind's not ready so my body isn't either."

I had tried fingers, tongue, penis, sweet nothings, everything.

And nothing.

"So, it's hopeless?"

"I prefer suspended."

"Do you really believe that? That it'll all just come back when I mold myself into what you want?"

"I'm not trying to mold you. Or maybe I am, but I believe it's for the better. It's not some Orwellian mind trap where I'm the puppeteer, like you're implying. I just want a normal life. Is that so bad, so wrong? Oh, Henry, I don't know anymore. Maybe I'm wrong. Maybe we're wrong."

She began to cry and I took her in my arms, her head nestled into my shoulder and neck much like Bear's was to her. I caught a partial glimpse of our entwined naked bodies, her back heaving from the sobs, and just felt pure sadness.

"No, no, you're right honey. It's time for me to grow up." I kept holding her until she stopped crying and we both slipped into sleep. It was as if the attempt at sex was enough to knock us out.

I woke up at two in the morning, fixed something to eat, and sat at our small kitchen table next to the window open to a brilliant, starry black night. It was September, summer in San Francisco. Halfway through my sandwich, visions of a better scenario with Nancy interrupted my appetite for food. I tried, but I couldn't even imagine it. Our sex life had reached such a nadir that onanism couldn't even conjure consummation. However, the dead end detoured into Eve and me on our date. Effortlessly I indulged.

After finishing, I scribbled a quick note for Nancy in case she woke up, ate the rest of my sandwich on the fly and jumped in the Escort heading into the San Francisco night for Coit Tower, my favorite spot in the city. Nancy and I used to park at the base of Telegraph Hill, make the football field-length walk up to the top where Coit stands tall and proud. Sometimes we'd even get lucky and see the famed wild parrots on the way up. We'd usually end the little hike with lunch or dinner in North Beach or Chinatown, but after a while Nancy grew bored with the excursion. The repetition dulled it for her (or was it another kind of repetition?), but it never did for me. So I started going alone, which gave me freedom to sit, think, and write poetry perched by the tower overlooking the city of my escape. The poetry usually flowed better there and it often rescued me from those dreaded creative dams and dry spells. Coit provided tonic days of youth, alive with possibilities and poetic moments hitting high notes in between all the toxic arrows of self-doubt.

I liked to think there was a certain magic in the tower from its namesake, Lillie Hitchcock Coit, a free-wheeling, firefighting, 19th century feminist with a penchant for gambling, cigars, and wearing pants long before Coco Chanel did. Or maybe it was the great New Deal public art along the walls inside, especially Victor Arnautoff's *City Life.*

Then there was the magnificent 360-degree view of San Francisco. Sure I'd take it all in at times, but I always wrote facing the Bay Bridge, the unheralded, but much larger and more imposing bridge compared to the famed Golden Gate. So many flock to the Golden Gate and its undeniably majestic qualities, the royal, red carpet exit to the end of the west. Yet, it was the Bay Bridge, buried in the shadow of golden royalty, that is all power, testosterone, all simple blue-collar strength extending much longer across the great expanse of America's last bay. It's a mighty iron behemoth piercing Treasure Island halfway across like a medieval sword before emerging again connecting east and west. It was all awe and wonder to me while the Golden Gate was more imposter. I knew if my father ever came here, he'd agree. We could have connected on that.

But he never came.

"So you're back for day two, Mr. Sculptor, writer, artist or whatever it is you THINK you are," Delmore said to me as I gave him my bribe.

"Did you have doubts?"

"No, I figure you're some month or two cabbie. Once you realize you ain't getting' no kick here and nothing comes from it except the money, you'll move on or back to wherever you were last. You guys are all looking to go backward anyway."

I laughed uncomfortably. "How 'bout the medallion?"

"You don't like talking to me, Mr. Sculptor?"

"No, no, Delmore, I just regret we didn't begin these delightful morning talks long ago."

He let out a loud, hearty, cigarette-hacking laugh. "Hey, Fields, I got you a special fare today. Old lady McCabe. Every Tuesday morning, she's a 9:30 pick up, 712 Steiner. She goes to Safeway, then the Chinese Tea garden in the Park, then down to Ocean Beach and back. Meter's running all the time. It's an easy C-Note."

"Japanese Tea Garden," I said, pushing my luck.

"Big fuckin' difference, Mr. Poet. You want it?"

"Sure."

"It's the goddamn Korean Tea Garden for all I care. You frauds are all alike."

For a moment I actually liked Delmore in some strange, veracious way. He provided boundaries, recognizable lines that are too often blurred by those we know.

"I'm a caged bird and you're a cabbie. You ain't nothing more."

I nodded semi-affirmatively. "We could do worse."

"Not much. Cab 3762. Step on it. Old Lady McCabe hates tardy artists."

I got to Old Lady McCabe's at 9:29. She was waiting on her porch, standing with the aid of a tripod metal cane, and wearing an old zipper back, polyester dress. I wondered how she got the zipper up because I assumed she was alone. She lived on the first floor of a beautiful pristine Victorian, one of the famed "Painted Ladies" on Steiner Street. Heading down Hayes Street, the city skyline was picturesquely in view behind the ladies. Postcard scenery, though, did little to distract me from thoughts of Eve and the momentum of adultery. I had tried so hard with Nancy last night, and the failure felt worse than not trying, but it also seemed like a Rubicon of sorts for us. Maybe that explains our policy of avoidance. We didn't want confirmation. Floating is easier than sinking.

As I pulled up in front, she nodded at me and begin her slow approach to my cab as I got out to help her. She was all sagging, withered skin on crooked, bony arms and hands covered with large, purple green veins rising and falling like the hills of Alameda County.

"Ma'am, let me help you," I offered.

She didn't look at me, but she did say, "You're a new one, young man."

"Yes, ma'am, I'm a newbie."

"Did Mr. Oliver tell you the route I go?" Delmore, I thought, as I held her feathery arm. Damn, he didn't fit the image of a Mr. Oliver.

"Yes, I've got it. We're all set."

We made a quick stop at Safeway to start the trip. I had coffee near the checkout area while Miss McCabe shopped. As soon as she paid, I carried the couple bags out, put them in the backseat next to her and we made our way north to the Richmond. At that point Old Lady McCabe wasted little time diving into segments of her eighty-plus years on the planet. She was monologist.

She was from a tiny town in Iowa and grew up on a farm during the Depression, dust bowl years. She reminisced about hiding from chores between great stalks of corn and reading Jack London novels and western adventures until her father got suspicious and yelled at her for slacking off. She'd put the book in a plastic bag and bury it underground otherwise her father would've burned it. She'd resume harvesting or planting between paternal screams and dreaming of the sea and mysterious lands. She had to quit school after the 8th grade because that's what girls did in Bucaine, Iowa back in those days. "The Roaring Twenties never hit Bucaine." The oral autobiography spun along as I drove north on Great Highway along Ocean Beach, where Nancy and I often walked during our early dreamy San Francisco days gone by.

We drove by the coarse, brown sand and solemn brown water energized by scattered surfers, artists, and teens smoking. They sat along the three-foot cement beach wall randomly adorned with skilled and unskilled graffiti. This was my windshield vision, while my internal sights were woven with the movie of Eve and me undressing tonight and the sexual end of Nancy and me last night. We'd become siblings. Another love had grown, but not the one of forever. Meanwhile, a diametric love, wanton and sensual, seemed inevitable tonight. I tried to escape what some hyped-up therapist may call the virgin-whore syndrome and instead turned my thoughts to the history pouring out of my back seat. I was here to escape myself and absorb the tales of others, wasn't I?

"I got hitched, as we said back then, at twenty-one, like a tiller to an ox. It was awful, life that is. I was damned to a dead, servant life under the rule of a man I didn't love. The only difference between me and the farm animals was that I slept inside. I remember those years, all my years with frightening clarity. My hair and skin have been beaten by time, but my memory is always in a state of spring, if I may be poetic."

"You most certainly may," I said.

"We stayed married for ten years. Ten long, sad years. Oh, he never beat me or physically injured me, but he also never pleased me. I wanted more out of life. My friends thought I was crazy and selfish when I dreamt aloud of running away to the West, but I couldn't get it out of my daily thoughts. Those soil stained, London novels had permanently disheveled my soul. You see, the way I thought then, was my whole town had resigned itself to waiting for the tombstone, while the world outside of Bucaine was brimming with life and adventure. It was a different time. Mystery existed. So you know what I did? I laughed at the tombstone and put on the coat of the black sheep, the prodigal daughter in the 1940s, twenty-five years before the foolish hippies. One friend and I plotted our escape. A run into the night on a train into the great western escape."

I was thinking only in a San Francisco cab could one hear a female forerunner of Jack Kerouac speaking poetically of possibility. Only here could a seemingly crabby, old lonely woman bury the secret treasure of escape in her heart. Or perhaps, it was only here that one would let it out.

Her tale so outdid my newly married pedestrian flight from Boise at the edge of thirty. I should have paid my dues covering varsity softball games for the East Boise Press, so that today I'd have a decent, respectable journalist career. Nancy was right. Instead, I took the exit in hopes of finding secret treasures, which I'd assumed would reveal themselves on the fringes. These alleged treasures that I'd staked a life on, stayed buried. It was all some sad, Halloween costume, worn all year, whispering a lingering mockery of adolescence.

Tell me more Old Lady McCabe. Take me out of me.

I tried to listen purely as we cut a swerving swath through the seven miles of Golden Gate Park. Colorful flowers, powerful trees, green grass, and blue and yellow above. I knew why she wanted to drive along the vast Pacific and into the Park's verdant path. I tried to unhinge myself of me and see, truly see the natural panorama unfolding in front of me and hear, truly hear, the oral history unraveling behind me.

Her friend convinced her to hop a freight going west during WWII, at a time when newspapers were discussing the potential of a German Europe. America hadn't even entered yet. It was around late 1940, but there were jobs aplenty for women, as men began to train for the inevitable. The two soon-to-be Rosie the Riveters stashed a little money away for a couple of months. Then the night they were going to leave her friend got cold feet.

"You should've gotten cold feet on your wedding day, not today," I told her, but she didn't listen to me. So what did I do? I went anyway, all alone on an evening train for $11 one-way and I haven't been back since. I left a note for my husband and I'm sure he just replaced me. It wouldn't have been difficult, like hiring a maid."

She had some glory years alive and free along the elevated ebb of youth before the flow settled and dissipated into the mundane. She worked in a factory and danced with sailors during the war. She romanced more than one of them as she put it. Peace brought the end of work and short-term romances.

"I was a single woman in my late thirties in the postwar euphoria and I couldn't have been sadder. My whole family and life was a half a country away. Yet, I refused to return. Those glorious moments of life during war kept me from surrendering back to an Iowa life. I put my personal sadness aside as San Francisco and the rest of the country began to rise up after the victory and, young man, anything seemed possible then, unlike now."

She had more romances, all with sailors, but soon they lost interest in her. She took a job at AT&T as an operator in 1947 and stayed there until 1985. Several times she almost went back to Bucaine. Her parents' deaths were the closest, but she never returned. She'd divorced Iowa and never saw another person from her past. She married a Filipino man, who was involved in real estate, but his true passion was alcohol.

They had a daughter in November of 1963, just before Kennedy was assassinated. Old lady McCabe's voice flattened to a grave monotone. She spoke but a few minutes about her divorce and daughter, who had a child whose father disappeared during pregnancy. The three of them shared the apartment where I picked her up.

Generational mimicry is virtually inevitable. Apples never rolling far from their trees especially ones resembling cantankerous Oz trees.

Then silence.

My wife, Eve, and my life began filling the spaces. What was I repeating from the past? What was my mimicry driving this cab? Or was I unconsciously trying to redirect the flow of my earthly time? Those questions were too big. I had a decision about Eve ominously dangling ahead. It was my own little Genesis in a cab. What I really needed was a clean and precise suspension of my obsessive self-analysis in order to let instincts take over.

"What does your daughter do, Miss McCabe?"

"She's a nurse at Kaiser."

"That's a good job. She's done all right for herself."

"She's made mistakes, but so have I. Her boy needs a father. We're not enough. It's sad how things happen again and again. No matter how far from Iowa I am, Iowa never leaves. Maybe, it's God's way to say my way was wrong. Running's never the answer."

"Maybe not, but it's irresistible at times. I ran and I might run again."

"Young man, I suggest the opposite. Look your problems square in the face and go at 'em head on. It took me too many decades to realize it, but I see my mistake every time I look in my daughter's eyes. Too much ruin. Do you have kids?"

"No."

"Well, running is still wrong, but at least you bear your own cross."

"Yes," I said, while I thought, keeping your orbit small may be the answer.

"Young man, can you pull over at the Japanese Tea Garden?"

"Certainly."

"I'll be back in ten minutes."

"Take your time."

"That's good for you," she said looking at the meter.

"No, no. I'll turn it off." I pulled the red arm down and the little purr of money and time clicked off.

"You don't have to," she said, exiting the car. I helped her out, but she waived me off and headed on her own to a bench on the top of a small hill overlooking the manicured garden. I sat in the cab and momentarily pondered what she could be thinking—I concocted images of Bucaine, her ex-family, her marriage, divorce, daughter, grandson, Navy men days. I thought of the ephemeral, cosmic rush of her Jack London escape years and the sad, earthly eternity of her AT&T bondage, but all roads led back to Eve, of course, and the coming reality that my marriage, or the growing falsehood that it was becoming, would end tonight.

There was no question that McCabe, Delmore, the Cab, were all face-slapping signs of life change. It wouldn't take some metaphysical, warped San Francisco twirp to point out that our life is dotted with a clear path. We've just got to open our eyes and water down the misfired energy. We pursue or we stand still. Every epiphany this week led to pursuit. Morality and fidelity to a lost cause were static. I even convinced myself that it would be better for Nancy if I chose Eve. A kinetic choice would circulate so much energy in both our lives that had simply grounded to a scarily numb halt.

Beyond this, my life as a poet had been a sham. I'd belittled my passions and been deaf to internal voices for far too long. It was as if my very existence has been to debunk my very existence. I've been like the designated rabbit runner setting the pace early on and then drifting to last, a pawn for the others get ahead. I got struck hard by Whitman's youthful cries and then drifted passively in the very face of their call. This weekend I'd pen some fruitless poem about an old lady and her past, have it picked up by some local journal, feel a moment of redemption, and slither onward until Nancy finally left me. But this time, there'd be no poem. There'd be life with another woman in a new world real and unimagined.

McCabe was still bench-bound and my watch read 3:30. I was supposed to pick up Eve at the airport soon. The giant contradiction of myself rolled onward. I played picaresque poet-manque, except I drank only two beers a night, never cheated on my wife, had no sex at all, no pain, and no boils burned off my adolescent body like Bukowski by some insane, Christian witch doctor aunt. I was Exley without the nut house and the booze. Lukewarm and all watered down. I was jealous of pain. I had no right to pose as a poet, but I had a right to cataclysm. I had to see Eve, so I could look back on all the ennui and feel it for the pain that it really was. Visions of sex and explosive creativity became my sunrise horizon.

"Ok, young man, I'm ready."

"Do you need a hand?"

"No, no," she said, getting in the cab.

My Bartleby like, I-prefer-not-to-tonight wife had snowballed me into a delirium of Eve. I could think of nothing else. I was dazed and delusional yet simultaneously crystal clear.

"Young man, slow down," McCabe said nervously. Unbeknownst to me, I was going sixty in the twenty mph park drive.

"Sorry, I got a little carried away."

"What's the rush all of the sudden?"

"No rush, I'm just trying to get you home. Are you tired?"

"Do you need to be somewhere?"

"Actually, I have an appointment."

"Mr. Oliver said you have the dayshift?"

"Yes, well, I promised an old friend I'd meet her at the airport pretty soon. I don't want to be late." I couldn't even lie about the gender.

"Who's your old friend, if an old, bored lady may be so intrusive?"

"Just an old friend from Idaho, which is where I am from."

We didn't talk for a while. I zipped out of the park, down Fillmore and towards the Painted Ladies. I pulled over at her house, trying to disguise my haste for efficiency. I got her groceries out of the trunk, put them at her front door, and then I went back to help her.

"Young man, I'm all set. My daughter's home and she can help me with the groceries."

"Are you sure? I don't mind."

"I don't want you to be late for your appointment."

"I won't be."

"Please. I'm all set," she said, slightly irritably.

"Ok, Miss McCabe, you have a good day and it was quite nice meeting you and talking." I turned heading down the stairs.

"Do you want some money?"

"Oh, I completely forgot. Let me check the meter."

"Here, don't bother." She handed me a crisp $100 bill just like Eve.

I was about to politely refuse, but she cut me off.

"You're not special. Every driver gets this and I'm sure they told you as much. Now get to the airport and do whatever it is you have to do." She looked deeply into my eyes with a mysterious half smile and an inscrutable glare. "Thank you, young man."

"You're very welcome. By the way Miss McCabe, I'm not so young."

"Sure you are," she said, unlocking her door.

"Money and material," Delmore's voice bellowed from the radio as I headed east on Steiner en route SFO and Eve.

"Huh?" I asked, not wanting to deal with him at all.

"Good money and old lady's life to, ahhh, sculpt so you claim," he said with hacking laughter punctuating his mockery.

"So what did you try, stories from behind the cage?" I snapped back.

"What?" Delmore asked, intoning surprise at my parry.

"You're a failed writer, right?"

"Fields, I just watch failures. I wouldn't make things worse by thinking I'm more than I am, like you types."

"Did you get anywhere? What was your title? Behind the Cage?"

"Going on the offensive, professor. Look at you. Finding your mojo behind the wheel?"

"I'm just trying to get a little more out of you to add some depth to my sculpture when the block ends. I think your mockery might ironically be my muse."

"You're a bad liar, Fields. Try being a cabbie, and get off your high broken-down horse."

"Delmore, you ought to be a therapist, except you've got the touch of a hungry grizzly bear."

"How's old lady McCabe? She take care of you?"

"Sure did."

"You're welcome," and he clicked off before I could say thanks.

Just maybe, I had gotten the best of the Delmore in my life for a change. Maybe the wall between me and my life was cracking.

In my haste to get to Eve, I actually arrived early. I parked near all the other cabs waiting for their bread and butter runs. Delmore was howling out for pick-ups, but not up my ass. I turned the volume down so I could kill the time peacefully in the driver's seat before the big night began. The only true anxiety I felt was lust seeking conclusion. I was the dealer of my own tarot cards for once.

Except somebody decided to throw a new card into the deck.

A woman approached my cab looking right at me with a slight, nervous smile. It wasn't Eve. The lie I had just told Old Lady McCabe had turned true. An old friend from Idaho was entering my cab. Nothing had really happened to me in five years and, now in a few days, my past, present and future were colliding in a time-warp cauldron. The future was offering sexual salvation. The past confronting me with the one that got away. My present crystallizing its lost cause truth. Where to go?

I rolled down the passenger window.

"Hi, Henry."

"Arlene. Wow."

"It's been a while."

"Indeed."

"Are you busy?" my past asked.

"I've got a few minutes before my pickup gets here."

We sat on a bench near the possessed cab with the sounds of cars, planes and people on the move all around us, but all my attention focused on Arlene. Her dark hair was cut shorter and her eyes reflected the decade gone by, but not much else had changed. She still had that simple, natural Idaho beauty that I didn't see here in San Francisco.

I'd devastated Arlene in our mid-twenties between my University of Idaho and Boise State years. I was too full of arrogant confusion, convinced that the potential poetry brewing and boiling within would create great American verse. I left her, but returned capriciously off and on for five years. She took me back every time. I always knew she'd be there for me and I recklessly took advantage of that power when I was at my most lonely and powerless. I caused her so much pain. She loved me and I loved her, but I loved her all wrong. I couldn't let myself completely be with her because I was too committed to the mirage of artistic salvation.

She was the one ex that I thought about as Nancy and I eased into our catatonic marital state, but was too afraid to reach out.

"So you're a cabbie," Arlene said.

"Yes, ma'am," I said with feigned pride.

"And your poetry? Still at it?"

"Well, actually, playing with an idea for a novel."

Arlene nodded. "Good for you, Henry. Still fighting the good fight."

"Maybe more the foolish fight ala Don Quixote. I should probably quit, but I guess I need one more windmill."

"You were always stubbornly persistent."

"But not very good at seeing what's right in front of me."

"So how long you been driving?"

"Less than a week."

"Really?"

I nodded, embarrassed.

"You seem nervous, Henry. Relax, I don't hate you anymore. Really I don't. I hate what you did, but that was a long time ago, and I'm over it now. Therapy and time help. There's forgiveness."

"Thanks, Arlene. That's very kind of you. I'm in therapy, too. Many years now."

"Glad to hear that. Has it helped?" Arlene asked.

"Sure, a little, I think, but I probably wouldn't be in this cab if it truly had."

"And what if the novel doesn't work out. What's next?"

I sighed, "Oh, I don't know, teaching, maybe at Boise State. Professor Gettings thinks she can hook me up with a faculty position. I just got my MA, so who knows, maybe I'll go home again."

"So the future is wide open."

I shrugged. "And you?"

Arlene had always worked in her family business. Her father owned a successful commercial farm north of Boise and she did the bookkeeping. She quit Boise State, where we had met, when the business was going through a tough stretch. She hated numbers, but was good at it and her father needed someone he could trust. I remembered lying in bed listening to her complain about being a "dead end numbers cruncher" while we took turns reading aloud passages of her favorite writer, Colette, or mine, Hart Crane. She'd say our reading to each other was her therapy from spending eight hours punching a calculator and hearing the receipt endlessly churning.

But that all changed. She went back to Boise State, got her BA and then grad school for psychology. She was a therapist now and in town for a conference.

"That's great, Arlene. I'm proud of you and I bet you're great at what you do."

"Thanks. I like what I do," she said with a smile. She looked at her watch. "Hey, don't you have to pick someone up?"

I pretended to look at my watch. "Still got a few minutes. Don't worry."

Arlene took a deep breath. "This is quite a shock. I wasn't sure we'd ever see each other again."

"I had a feeling we would," I said.

"Really?"

"Yeah, I mean not here, of course, but Boise's small. Thought we'd run into each other there during a visit home. I was hoping to so I could say I'm sorry about how things ended."

Arlene ran her fingers through her hair pushing her bangs back as they often fell into her eyes. She looked at me and then looked away.

"It took a long time, Henry. A long time to get over you. To get over us."

"Me, too."

"Bullshit. I don't believe you."

"Well, it did. It just hit me later when the mistake sank in. I really regretted it and the regret lingers."

Arlene nodded. "I really hated you at the end, but I also hated myself for letting you come and go. That was on me as well."

"I really hate me, too."

"You ought to do something about it."

"You free for an appointment later? We can work on it."

Arlene laughed. "That would be a kick." The heavy air took on some much needed levity. Arlene then shared that she was getting married in a few months. He was a therapist, too. They had met in grad school and she was happy.

"Wow, two therapists. Jesus, constant analyses," I poked

"Actually, we barely speak about it. We try to keep it separate otherwise it would go on and on," she said grinning.

After I shared a bit about how Nancy and I were on the rocks, there was a pause. We had mostly been looking straight ahead as we sat side-by-side until I turned to her and nudged her leg to look directly at me. "Arlene," I said as we locked eyes, "so...ahh...you know, I meant what I said about regret. To be perfectly candid I think I married the wrong woman."

Arlene shook her head slowly. "Don't be ridiculous. You're getting caught up in this moment, Henry."

"Right, I know. True, but I have to ask you something since we're laying it all out there."

"I think I'm afraid of this question. And maybe we've laid enough out there."

"What if I said give me one more chance? Give us one more chance."

"What!" she shrieked and pulled away from me nearly following of the edge of the bench. "Stop. Stop this now. We don't get do-overs after a decade. And you already used up your share."

"I know, it's crazy. It's out there, but talking to you now, looking at you, listening to you, I see my whole flawed road was from the end of us. With you, I finished school, got some minor fame in Boise poetry circles. Without you, it's been nothing but false starts. You made me better."

"You didn't make me better."

"I know. I wish I could make it all up to you."

"Henry, you're desperate and going backwards for a miracle. And what about Nancy? You are still together."

"No, together, but the relationship is dead. That much I know. I just truly realized it."

"Just now?"

"Actually, yes. I'm having epiphanic moments, Arlene. I mean, why did I get this cab job? First, the crazy obnoxious dispatcher woke me up that my whole poet existence is a mask, then the artifices began falling like dominos. My marriage was next. Now you. I don't believe in God, but I believe in some mad kinetic energy connecting all of us. This isn't a coincidence."

"You're not going to throw the destiny card at me, are you?

"You'll never guess why I'm here."

Arlene was shaking her head. "For a fare," she mumbled.

That really got me. I laughed hard and cathartically.

"What? What's so funny?"

"I'm here for an affair."

"Huh?"

I told Arlene all about Eve and the plan to meet her right now.

"Henry, you are all over the place. You need help."

"I know, I know. It's just that, seeing you has, ahem, well, it's hitting me hard. Brought up so many things that have been begging for release for years."

Arlene was shaking her head and breathing heavily.

I continued, "sorry, I know it's too much, but it's been ten years and it feels like yesterday. Look how deep we've gone so quickly as if we last saw each other yesterday rather than a decade ago."

She took a deep breath. "Well our conversations were never superficial. We were good at that. Maybe too good."

"I miss that. Never came close to our depth since we broke up."

Arlene nodded. Unable to control myself, I pushed it further, an impetuous fool. I told Arlene that we should just jump in the cab and go away together. Drive down the coast, find a romantic spot, San Luis Obispo, or somewhere such, and see if what he had could flourish again. Maybe the timing was just wrong then. It wasn't our fault. We were meant to be together later. We were an anachronistic casualty.

Arlene laughed at my idea. But I plundered forward in my blind vision.

"I'm serious. Skip the conference, we'll spend the time together and your fiancé will never know. You'll catch the same flight back."

"So when I tell you this is too much, your response is to up the crazy ante! Henry, this isn't happening. I'm not taking it seriously and I won't hold it against you in the future."

"We'll stare out into the Pacific and rescue the memory."

"Still the romantic poet. Maybe, you ought to find that other woman. No memories to rescue with her. Work with a clean adulterous slate."

"Arlene, you said maybe. I think there is still something there for me."

"Fuck, Henry, you push so much! Of course, there is. You were the love of my life. Always will be, which pisses me off. Look, I'm going to the conference and not on some crazy runaway trip befitting a 21-year old. How about this compromise? You drive me to Marin for the conference. Be my cabbie, Henry. Forget the affair and end your marriage the proper way. I'm flattered by the insanity and would have done it years ago, but not now. We can keep in touch as friends and who knows the future?"

"Meaning?"

"Meaning, I don't know. Never mind. Just leave it alone, ok?"

We got in the cab and drove by the Delta gate where I saw Eve. We caught eyes as I drove past her. She looked disappointed and I tried to emote *sorry*. She probably thought I got cold feet and chose my marriage. I wanted to thank her for helping me choose divorce.

The inevitable end of Nancy and me didn't quite go as planned, of course. While I had been taking a few days after meeting Arlene to muster up the nerve to tell Nancy it was over, she beat me to it.

I had been gone all day driving and then went to dinner with a poet-friend of mine in North Beach where I talked incessantly about Arlene. It was late when I got home and I arrived to an empty apartment. Almost all the furniture was gone save for the kitchen table with my typewriter on it and one chair. I checked the bedroom and all her clothes were gone. There was a note on the kitchen counter under the keys to the Escort.

> *Dear Henry, sorry for leaving this way, but I couldn't bring myself to do it in person. I've been trying for months. It just makes me so sad and I know you would convince me to stay. Our conversations always buy you time. To be perfectly honest, I met someone else and didn't have the courage to say this in person either. I'm sorry. I wish you the best. You're a good man. The car is yours. Let's make this simple – Nancy*

I dropped the note and watched it fall to the floor, landing word-side down. Nancy saved me the trouble and us the drama, but instead of feeling liberated, I slumped to the floor and wept away our ten years and failure at forever, surprised at the flood of tears that rushed uncontrollably out of me.

The next night I drove to the Corda Madera Hilton, where I dropped Arlene off a few nights ago. I knew it was her last night at the conference and hoped she wasn't out with colleagues for farewell festivities. The front desk woman kindly gave me the room number. I knocked on room 914 moments later at nearly ten o'clock.

"Who is it?" Arlene asked.

"Henry."

There was a long silent pause before she opened the door. "Why are you here?" she finally said.

"She left me," I said.

Arlene didn't say anything. Instead, she opened her arms and gave me a long, loving hug, one that felt like a place I hadn't been to in a long time.

Home.

We sat down at a small table in the corner of her room. She had been drinking a glass of red wine and she poured me one. We talked for hours about Nancy and me, the *whys* and *hows*, and then shifted to her excitement and fear for her upcoming marriage. The intimate conversation became an aphrodisiac that overtook us, naturally and beautifully.

The next morning she insisted I take time to process and heal. "You have more trauma than you give yourself credit for. There's a reason you're a poet, Henry Fields. I knew your father."

"You know me so well. Better than I know me."

"I don't believe that."

"So when's the wedding?" I asked.

She smiled, gently shoved my chest and said, "Never mind that."

We kissed and hugged a passionate goodbye.

"It was a wonderful night, Henry. Take time to heal," she said before closing the door.

I stood there for a while, not wanting to leave, before I finally did.

A few months later I was still driving the cab, had a roommate, and spent my evenings after work sitting outside Coit Tower on my favorite bench with its stunning view of the great bridge. I sat there bundled up in a hat and scarf, writing in those old-style, black and white speckled composition notebooks. I even bought an old miner's light that I would wear on my head so I could write after sunset, probably looking crazy to the tourists passing by, but for the North Beach locals I fit right in. A miner's light struck me as perfectly appropriate for the task at hand. I feverishly wrote down what had happened during that first week as a cabbie. Mike had promised plot, but little did we know that I would have all the plot I needed in just a few days. I intertwined past and present, Boise and San Francisco, the inimitable Delmore, Nancy, the temptress Eve, everyone and everything. And I had the perfect ending with Nancy leaving me and then the night with Arlene. The writing came so easily, unfettered visions flowing uninterrupted to the page. I could almost feel the words coming through me to the pen and page.

I was 950 pages in, almost five full notebooks and three months of writing, aching hand and back from the uncomfortable bench (but an ache I cherished) when I came to the farewell with Arlene at her hotel.

Except that didn't feel like the end of the story. That final scene still had to be lived before written.

I stared out into the bay beyond the bridge. I could only see a few scattered ship lights and the soft glow of the deep night city. I didn't know how long I had sat there, but it must have been hours; a peaceful nothingness that came with a task completed and a truth to pursue.

The next day, I packed up the Escort with a satchel of the notebooks and a small suitcase with all the possessions I cared to bring with me to Boise. You can go home again. I would prove that and let the escape of San Francisco slip into my wake.

Fields Wake.

# IMAGINE INCARNATE

*Dixson Naturian*

I packed up my Chevy Chevette with my art supplies, some clothes, a few books, and two thousand dollars. As any youth on the run from the tired east would do, I went west.

To San Francisco. Of course.

I was blazing a trail where countless trails had been blazed. The roads were well-trodden…San Francisco had been played to death by youth, but that didn't matter to me. It still had subterranean renaissance in its imagery. It seemed the only city worth a damn in America. The end of America. The edge of the new world aging.

It wasn't really my idea. I wasn't original or daring enough. It was Xeno Waterfield's idea. Xeno was an eccentric college friend of mine. He'd been in a few of my art classes, but he wasn't much of a painter. He liked all forms of art. Writing, film, photography, sculpture, paint, whatever. He'd throw his hat into any ring of creativity. He was also a big fan of found art. He would scour the streets the night before garbage pick-up and find things to use for artistic endeavors. His whole existence was about creation. "Start with nothing and end with something," Xeno would say. "It's that bloody simple."

Xeno headed west with a plan. He wanted to start a literary journal that celebrated all forms of his religion.

Creativity.

He had a title, *Imagine Incarnate*, a desktop publishing program, and all the mad cerebral energy circulating under his fiery red hair. He convinced me to join him out west to get the flighty journal off the ground.

But he had bigger ideas than the journal. *Imagine Incarnate* was just the starting point of his fantasy. At the University of Rochester he had been part of what he called an "art house." A bunch of student artists and writers lived together communally and sold their art through local auctions. Occasionally, a local businessman would make a sizable bid on a young artist's future success. All the money was shared. Xeno called it artistic socialism.

"Socialism went astray with politics," Xeno would say.

Xeno hoped the journal would create a group of artists committed to a new order, a path beyond resumé and capital building.

"Beyond money lay something far more enchanting. A real Oz, my friends. Let's open the doors."

These artists would start up a new, mature art house. An Art House West.

I thought the whole thing was delusion. Bunk. Xenology. At least, the post-journal fantasy. I had no interest in living with a group of artists. I would prefer to live with a group of auto mechanics. It'd be more real, but Xeno was cut from a different cloth. He was born in Berkeley and moved east as an infant, but Berkeley circa 1966 never left his blood. He was certified Bezerkley. At the time, I refused to fully realize I was a kindred spirit to this aspect of Xeno.

Xeno wanted my sketches and paintings to illustrate the first issue. I figured I had nothing to lose. It'd give me a little taste of micro-fame. Maybe I'd meet some strange, perverse women who dug my paintings. I had a whole regular life in front of me. Why not detour a bit? Leap into the now.

I'd go west, let youth holler for a while, and return home and become an art teacher in my hometown. I'd teach the kids who hated spelling tests, just like I did. Yes, life would get simple and logical down the road, but for now, I was drawn to complexity and disorder. I'd look back from the rocking chair and say, "Yeah, I had my reckless days. Sowed my spiritual, artistic, and sexual oats." I would regret action rather than non-action. I'd heed Greeley's "Go west, young man."

I'd say I was gone west. Really gone.


I drove out to California alone, as did Xeno. We figured we'd use the loneliness for a muse and arrive in San Francisco with materials for a first issue ready for publication. I didn't paint or sketch a lick the whole trip until I hit the California coast. It was an uneventful, lonely drive. I stopped only for gas, food, or cheap motels. I didn't meet any women, nor take in any sites. I just drove, ate, smoked cigarettes every 25 miles, and slept. It would have made a good, avant-garde minimalist film. True minimalism. Nothing happened.

Once I hit San Diego though, the switch turned on. Nothingness crept up on my being. The energy of nada can be potent. On the way up to San Francisco via the Pacific Coast Highway, the notorious route 1, I stopped along the wild, rugged coast. I sat on the edge of cliffs overlooking the mighty Pacific and painted small abstracts. I didn't paint landscapes or any Ansel Adams or John Muir fit for the office waiting room scenes. But the landscape motivated the abstracts into new directions for me. I had done all my painting in the coffin-like basement of my parents' home, university art studios, or dorm rooms. Since I didn't paint nature, I never thought of unleashing the subconscious with nature all around. I lost myself on the edge of the Pacific. I found moments of intense serenity, moments of feral energy that seized me and put me into that trance where creation takes over. An internal slingshot had been pulled back all along the 3,000 mile drive and once I hit the end of the road, the end of America, the slingshot sprang forward with savage velocity. I was prolifically producing paintings and sketches, stopping two or three times a day and painting for hours. Most importantly, I liked the output days later rather than having that awful desire to slash and tear the work to shreds. I thought, just maybe, the painter that most influenced me, Arshile Gorky, would have been impressed. Yes, one of these would be my *Liver is the Cock's Comb*.

The trip from San Diego to San Francisco took longer than the trip across the country. It took me a week to reach the Pacific. It took me three weeks to go from Coronado Island to the Golden Gate. I stopped immediately after crossing the bridge, parked at a vista point where tourists were everywhere. Herds of Japanese were photographing every nuance of vacations they weren't actually taking. I walked down to the base of the majestic entrance to escape the clicking cameras and packs of humans and painted my final coastal abstract right there before entering the great city of escape.

I found Xeno's apartment on Divisadero Street and entered with more than a dozen creations. He was ecstatic. Red headed, burly, mad cap excitement, bouncing up and down with giddy fury as I laid the work out on his studio floor.

"Dixson, my crazy friend, with my words and your abstracts, issue number one is going to be a home run!"

In the meantime, Xeno and I were in different situations. He had already been in San Francisco for a few months, had a job and a girlfriend. He'd met Hannah at a café. He was taking an acting class next door to this café and went in after every class for a coffee. They went from trading smiles, to small talk, and a first date after three cups. Before long, she was spending every night at Xeno's small studio in the Western Addition district. There were three of us there. Three of us in a very small place. Tight and compact. A lot of energy and little space.

Xeno would go off to work every morning as a delivery driver for the March of Dimes. He worked way out in the East Bay so his days were long with a traffic-filled commute each way. I'd kind of look for work and half-heartedly search for an apartment for part of the day. I didn't want to be alone. The loneliness of the 3,000-mile drive lingered. The muse left upon arrival, leaving behind anxious energy devoid of outlet.

The other part of the day Hannah and I would work on the journal. We'd do rough drafts, and jot down ideas. Get something ready for Xeno to see after work. Most of the time, though, we just talked about our lives. The excitement and the unease.

I knew I was in deep and on the edge of no return when I saw her reading Anaïs Nin. She had just seen the film,

*Henry and June*, and got turned on to Nin's diaries. One day we snuck out for a matinee for me to see it and her again.

She had already been keeping diaries for years, but the film and Nin turned her into a pious diarist. Xeno wanted to publish sections of the diaries, but she wasn't sure. They were honest, raw, and revealing as any diary should be. Xeno thought a pseudonym would take care of that. Hannah didn't think so.

"The words enter the universe regardless of the name," she told me.

"Well, that's probably what you secretly want anyway."

"Maybe so, but I want it secretly."

She wrote honestly about the incest of her childhood. She wrote about her father's sins. She wrote the insidious dreams that invaded her at night. She thought the act of writing the words, describing the horror, would help pacify the past that just wouldn't leave her alone. It was all too personal for her to expose.

She never read anything to me. She sometimes started to talk about what she wrote that day or the day before, but she'd always stop herself. For the first few sentences it was as if she were talking about another person and then suddenly her eyes would widen, and she'd realize she was talking about herself.

She had the momentary escape until the escape caught itself.

However, she loved to read Nin aloud to me. It appeased her need vicariously. We spent long afternoons in the Golden Gate Park reading to each other, talking, sometimes I'd sketch and she'd write. We'd leave the journal for another day or hastily write some ideas down just before Xeno returned home.

"We have an opposite Henry and June thing going here," she'd say.

"Yeah, two men instead of two women. And we're all straight."

"So we think," she'd say.

"You question it?"

"Don't you feel a connection among the three of us?" she'd ask.

"Yes, I do."

"The two of us?"

I nodded.

"In what way?"

"I don't know, just a connection," I'd say.

"Did you get lonely driving here?"

"Extremely."

"Are you lonely now?"

"Not so much."

"Me neither."

Our flirtatious conversations went further every time. No leaps, but incremental steps, which made it even more exciting. She started wearing lower-cut shirts, bra straps and skin more visible.

My attraction on multiple levels was gaining velocity.

I slept in the living room of the studio. Xeno had turned a big walk-in closet into his bedroom, big enough for a double mattress. He had a milk crate stuffed with books and a lamp on top of it. The closet walls had thumbtacked pictures of Emily Dickinson and Jerry Brown.

"I come to San Francisco, Dixson, and go into the closet," he had howled when I arrived, laughing heartily from the depths of his belly.

So I'd listen to Xeno and Hannah fucking from their closet bedroom. I knew I needed to find my own place and a job fast. I was going to lose control. I wanted her and being a few feet from their moans was making me crazy with jealousy.

Meanwhile, our chemistry was turning more potent and we openly talked about it during our daytime rendezvous.

"Why should we be scared of our feelings?" she'd ask, almost innocently.

"Because it could lead to betrayal, of course," I'd say.

"But the feeling itself is beautiful."

"Yes, it is."

"Why should we run from beauty and love?"

"Is it love?" I asked

"A form of love. It's pure. It's honest. I don't want to be afraid of true connections."

"I feel so strongly for you, but I love Xeno, too. Just differently, of course."

"Is it that different?" She asked with a wry and provocative smile.

"It is most definitely different."

She nodded. "Maybe."

"We're dancing along a scary edge, Hannah."

"I don't know if it can be controlled, but know that I love him, too," she'd say.

"Maybe this is all destiny. Maybe I came west to find you, not for art and Xeno."

"Yeah, true love. I love true love and destiny, my dear Dixson."

We both laughed at ourselves before easing into silent smiles and trying to look away from each other.

I finally found an apartment and a job at a bookstore. The apartment was down the street from Xeno and Hannah, but the bookstore was in Marin County. Some distance from the city would be good for at least part of the day. Some distance from Hannah was vital. I naïvely believed the timing would slow our momentum.

"I am in charge of the art books at Tamalpais Book and Coffee. Head of the art section for $6 an hour. Boy, am I going places, taking the American dream by the fiduciary horns," I told Xeno and Hannah.

Xeno cackled loudly and then responded, "Dixson, my fine artist friend, less money is better for our pursuits. Keeps us real."

We were planning a little party for my last night at the Divisadero apartment. Hannah and I bought some wine and food while Xeno was at work. Of course, we decided to indulge in the wine with a little pre-party in the afternoon.

The conversation led as always to our attraction and the cheap jug of red wine greased the wheels of candid confession.

"What if we make love just one time?" I suggested realizing I was walking off the edge of the plank.

She pondered my idea, sipped some red, and then said, "We just keep it a secret between us. A secret for our friendship, right? Just one time. Our moment to remember the momentum."

"Yes, and maybe, if we do it once, we'll calm this energy between us," I said.

Splash.

"It is too magnetic to halt," Hannah said. "Even Xeno senses it. He says our chemistry is palpable."

"What? He knows?"

"We talk about it. He knows we have a connection and he's not surprised. Kind of even okay with it."

"He's even more foolish than we are. Isn't he wary of more?"

"No, actually. He trusts us. I don't want to hurt him. He knows I love him," Hannah said, tearing up.

"I love him, too. Let's not hurt him."

"It's all about love," she said laughing amidst the tears.

"Maybe some lust mixed in, no?"

"Maybe so," Hannah cooed, replete with coquettishly rolled shoulder and a sideways glance. We were getting good at the game, constant sips of wine at our aid.

"I mean what else is there besides love? Everything else is window dressing."

"I can't think of anything else besides love, Dixson."

"I mean everything we ever do is to get, keep, or recover from love."

She nodded affirmation, smiling, both of us giggling fools in the throes of mind numbing and heart thumping attraction. I gently put my hand on her hand. The first time we actually touched besides friendly hugs. We both took deep breaths.

"It's too much," I said. "Do you feel it?"

"Stupid question," she said.

"It will be our secret. Our one-time secret deviation that no one will ever discover."

"Yes. Our little love secret that is born and dies with us. Something we can treasure when we're lonely."

I took her other hand, pulled her towards me until we kissed. We instantly let every hesitation go, kissing passionately, before I took her shirt off and touched her breasts softly, then aggressively, kissing and caressing. Soon my shirt and pants were off, and her mini-skirt was around her ankles. She pushed me down onto my make-shift bed of couch pillows in the corner of Xeno's studio. A bed fit for a dog, but oh so fitting for me. She took me in her mouth and sensing I was going to come, she stopped.

"One time," she whispered.

In that moment, I had no idea what she meant. I didn't care. All the blood flow was heading south taking any cerebral process with it.

She got on top of me, sliding back and forth, until she eased me inside her, slowly and methodically at first, trying to savor the one time until I couldn't resist completion. Moments after I started, she came, too. As soon as she finished, I brought her down to me, wrapped my arms around her, and held her tightly. We lay there quietly for a while until I got on top of her and we did it again, hard and almost violently.

We lay side by side on our backs breathing heavily, sweat dripping down my brow and temples. I still tasted her, smelled her, senses were hyperactive. We didn't say anything for a while, just held hands while supine and catching our breath.

I was staring up at one of Xeno's found art exhibits, an old, white wall tire attached to the wall with *Aloha* written in chalk in large letters on the top of the tire, between the treads and the white stripe. Inside of the tire there was an ancient, beat up, wooden cuckoo clock. An arrow was sticking into the opening of the clock where the bird would have popped out and a Hawaiian lei hung from the tip of the arrow. Vintage Xeno.

My eyes wandered to the ceiling, where a solar system poster stared down at us. I looked at the planets and observed their varying distances from the sun—Mercury, Venus, and then us. Mars, and Jupiter followed. The sun looked huge in the picture. I remembered a middle school science teacher saying that the sun was four and a half billion years old and that it would last for another five billion years. It would then turn into the White Dwarf.

"Our secret, right? One time," Hannah said, finally breaking the silence and ending my momentary lapse into astronomy.

"Yes, my erotic bird."

She laughed. "Ok, my happiest man alive."

"That's me, right now. The happiest man alive. No money, no hopes, all happiness."

"And no resources," she said, following along.

"No, definitely no resources. Just memories of experiences. The truest of resources."

"And so now we are over the mystery. We have demystified us, right?"

"You think so?"

She sighed, "Fuck, no, I was kidding. It's probably going to be worse!"

"Too damn good for one time."

I turned over on my side, head resting in my palm, and looked into Hannah's eyes as she rolled towards me synchronously.

"We can try," I said earnestly.

"Yes, let's try. Let this memory be a blanket on lonely nights. I know I'll replay us over and over again and—"

"Me, too. All the time!"

"If we stop now. If we keep it up, keep fucking, we're bound to get caught. We'll be sloppy in our distracted state. Then it's all dark. I'll lose you and him. Everyone loses everyone."

"Too much loss."

"Just tuck it preciously away, Dixson, where it belongs."

I fell back supine, staring up again at the oversized sun, thinking how very old it was and how much time remained in the human carnival.

As planned, we celebrated that night with Xeno. We didn't want to betray our friend of the party. But Hannah and I were on a perverse path, tasting deceit and dissolution, even enjoying it despite our bromides. We wanted to break the rules, test the teacher's will and boundaries. We had crossed the line, but it only amplified the desire to do it again and again. I wanted more and I knew I'd want it again and again. Our delusional pact was a fool's promise, and the memory wouldn't soothe, it would burn with urgency. We are a greedy lot. It would be a blanket on fire.

Id was kicking superego ass.

*Don't screw over Xeno.*

*Screw Hannah.*

*Think about the ramifications, the friendship.*

*Think about her on top of you.*

*Think about the deceit.*

*Even better sex..*

We drank wine, chatted about this and that, but it was all a blurry out-of-body experience until near the end of the evening. Xeno had held Hannah's hand firmly all night, clearly conscious of our connection, maybe even that we went further.

He even verbalized it because Xeno believed the road of *expression* leads to Blake's palace of wisdom. It was quite simple, all repression was wrong, all expression right. "Dixson," he once told me years before the San Francisco days, "the Freudian talking cure is real. It's holy. It's my religion. Even the damn fucked up Catholics knew that."

"I know you guys dig each other," he finally expressed. "I told Hannah that a while ago. I knew if she dug me, she would dig you. In fact, you guys are connected more in some ways. Dixson, you had more torture in youth than me. The old man's alcohol, roller coaster parents, divorce, all that strife and stress. I didn't have that. I had that suburban apathy, oh so toxically dispassionate it was, but not the intensity of yours. That's why your paintbrush rages across the canvas, demanding, imploring the demons be released."

"Thanks, Xeno, I guess."

"I'm sometimes jealous of your pain."

"You can have it."

Xeno paused, looked up at the Hawaiian cuckoo clock piece, then said, "Yeah, you know, you're like the Nolte character, the artist, in that Scorsese short film. You know the trilogy with Woody Allen and Coppola. What's it called? Something Stories?"

"*New York Stories*," I said. "Yeah, I thought Scorsese's story was the best."

"Of course, you did," Hannah said enthusiastically. "I actually preferred the Woody Allen one called *Oedipus Wrecks*. Such a great pun. And, well, we're all one big Oedipus Wreck and…" she suddenly stopped midstream, just nodding the unspoken words away.

"Yeah, but the Nolte character, that's Dixson's painting. All raw and manic mad action painting. Pollock would be proud. Hannah's the same way in her journal. Real and raw pain. Art is an open door with room for all of us." He paused, looked at both of us and then sketched an imaginary line in the air between each of us. He repeated the sketch several times so that the shape was clear. "You know, it's a funny thing these triangles. And I was never good at geometry." He laughed hard. We did, too, but it was a stilted laugh.

"I don't know. Can't even say the word I'm thinking of. I want to say every word right now all at once, not just one. You know me." Xeno laughed loudly from the depths of his big belly. "It's all a hootenanny. Love that word. That's the word I want. Yeah, you guys got pain fueling you. Me, I don't have that. I just observe the madness of the spinning earth with a squirt gun like that amusement park game. Just trying to aim the water straight in the clown's mouth and ring the bell above, knock some damn sense into the suburban sheep grazing blindly across life. Missing the drum beat beating right in their ears. Yup! But that's all right. Right honey? You love me, right? Doesn't matter the source of my void. You love all of me, right?"

"Of course, Xeno," Hannah said, hugging him and burying her head in the nape of his big teddy bear neck.

"There, so it's on the table, right?" he asked her directly.

"Yes, sweetie," she said. "All over the table."

"Full house, right, baby?"

"We're a winning hand, my dear."

Then looking at me, holding Hannah tightly, Xeno said, "And you wouldn't do anything to hurt me anyway, my kindred spirit, would you?"

"No, no way." I wanted to crawl onto my doggie bed and hide under the pillows. The libido went limp, super-ego took charge.

Xeno picked up the big, cheap jug of red and filled our glasses, and raised his glass, "To the triumvirate of creativity." And we all clinked glasses, Xeno grinning while we feigned along.

Then he got up and went to the bathroom. We looked at each other, shrugged, slapped down the repressive, pleasure killing superego, and leapt at each other, kissing passionately, angrily, ready to rip off our clothes until we heard a flush.

"What do you say we call it night?" Xeno said on his return. "I got to get up early, and Dixson you got to get your ass out of here tomorrow. Move into your new place and give my sweet lady and me our space back. We have some private carnal adventures awaiting us."

My apartment was in Mill Valley, a posh little town just north of Sausalito and the Golden Gate. I got the apartment out there so I could walk to work. It was just a mile or so away from the cute tree-lined downtown at the base of Mt. Tamalpais, the site of one of the Zen climbs (really more like hilly hikes) in Kerouac's *The Dharma Bums*. I could see the peak of Mt. Tam from my porch and all along my walk to work. I took comfort in knowing Kerouac and Snyder were here nearly 40 years ago seeking...There was even a Zen Center right near the bookstore, just beyond town center, which I presumed was inspired by the novel's location. I would sketch near it, hoping for some Zen transfusion into the art (and my life).

All the Zen and cupcake commute notwithstanding, I took the apartment for distance from Hannah. We'd be one glorious bridge apart, a different county, a swanky suburb rather than the energy of the city. Sure, I'd commute in to work on the journal and hang out with the couple, but I could also find excuses not to go.

We needed distance to resist our gravity.

The apartment was anything but posh, but posh and art don't mix and it was perfect for my needs. It was a studio carved out of a large single family. My little corner unit had a wrap-around porch that was nearly as big as the apartment with enough room for a hammock where I slept many nights, feeling the romance of the moonlight, the dark peak of Tam, and awaking to the morning fog.

The inside was smaller than Xeno's and without giant walk-in-turned-bedroom closets. I bought a bunch of second hand furniture at a hotel liquidation sale. I had a desk in one corner, a mattress on the floor of another, and a bureau against one wall, all with "Holiday Inn" stamps.

I grabbed some milk crates at the local Safeway, and used those for storage, and one for a nightstand, containing the only two books I had brought with me from back East, *A Confederacy of Dunces* and *Bluebeard*.

I squeezed a small "Motel 6" table into the kitchen and my decorating was complete. My one closet was used for all my art supplies.

I really liked the pad except for the tiny bathroom. It was so small that my knees pressed into the wall when I shit. It wasn't long before the dry wall took on the shape of my patellae.

The whole place did have a Gulliver in Lilliput sensation. The ceiling was just about my height so I could feel the hair on my head grazing along. But I couldn't wholly blame the apartment's size for this. I'm six foot five, quite the oxymoron for an Armenian. My Middle Eastern brethren are usually short and squat, thick not long, excelling Olympically in weightlifting and Greco-Roman wrestling. I was always the tallest at Sunday School. It was a family joke that the postman was my father since my old man was barely 5'9".

I'm also a lanky giant, 190 pounds stretched across 77 inches. My other ethnically black sheep quality was not being hirsute. I have barely any chest hair and only need to shave twice a week, at most, so unlike my heavy-bearded, body-haired kin. Some of my uncles have a repulsive full coat of fur on their back. So glad I'm not like that, but I'd like to be somewhere in the middle; a decent 5 o'clock shadow, some chest hair, a little more masculinity, some balance.

But balance was something altogether missing in my life.

I sat at the kitchen table a few days after moving in and wrote a long letter to Hannah. I told her I truly loved her and maybe someday we could be together, but I valued Xeno's friendship so much, too. We got caught up in our little Henry and June thing, but it wasn't us. We weren't perverse enough. We just got consumed in an energy vortex and twirled within it. My moving out would give us some space. We'll do what you said. Hold onto its beauty before it turns ugly and who knows the future? Maybe we'll have our time…

A few days later, when we got together for a journal session, she told me she loved the letter and agreed with everything. It was done. We stopped the madness short. No one gets hurt.

I agreed, but I was hurting bad. Little internal soldiers were taking formation, surrounding the heart and adding reinforcements daily. Trenches were dug wide and deep, numbers proliferating daily. They were far superior to me, outranking my defenses and outflanking my thoughts, preventing me from getting behind enemy lines.

I missed her and wanted her and I was so damn lonely out in Mill Valley thinking about Hannah and Xeno together in the city and me out in this sleepy town.

Alone.

Pathetic.

But when you can't win the war, you learn to exist with it. I bought a used black and white TV and put it on top of the fridge so I could watch Giants or A's games while I ate, which was the loneliest time. Hannah and I spent many meals together, drinking and dancing along the edges of flirtation. Baseball games were surely no panacea, but they filled the prandial void.

When not working, I spent most of my time in Lilliput and turned to my most reliable void filler, especially in those cataclysmic life moments, art. I worked the 2-10 p.m. shift at the bookstore so mornings were on the porch working on the sketches I had done along Route 1, turning many of them into paintings.

I had painted some small canvases right in the moment, but sketches were preparation for the bigger, Pollock-style canvases. And the porch was a perfect art studio. I hung my canvas on the outside of the house and painted in the fresh morning air. I wanted to keep the outside, natural vibe mojo flowing. In fact, I never wanted to paint inside again. My upstairs neighbors thought nothing of my artistic activity. I was in the San Francisco orbit. Here, everyone's aloft.

The mornings were especially ideal. The fog rolled in overhead across the Marin hills and into the mad city. I thought the fog carried with it some mystical molecules of the San Francisco dream. The whole city's history was hunger and want. Gold. Poetry. Drugs. Cults.

The city long screamed to get out of the American strait jacket.

The fog inspired me. It rolled magically and ethereally overhead every morning flowing into each brushstroke. I likened it to Van Gogh and the Arles sunshine.

When the fog really penetrated me, I even perversely hoped an institution loomed in the dark horizon. A place to go. A place to reinstall boundaries and frame this avalanche of freedom. Fill in the crevices of invisibles chasms. Sometimes, it was just too damn much. But that was wishful thinking. I just wasn't mad enough. The fissure was narrow enough to get through the night. It was a gentle madness and my paintings reflected it. They were wishfully mad. Posing in hopes of agony, but expressing anyone's pain. Despite Xeno's analysis, I didn't see the rage on the canvas. Perhaps, I was just too immersed in it to see any of the truth I was trying to express.

The aesthetic Catch-22.

I figured I'd stay as long as it took me to finish the big abstracts. If Xeno and I got the journal going, I'd stay longer. If not, I'd head home, move back in with my grandfather and attempt to start a normal life.

Balance.

Reality.

No more fog.

I could feel the costume shrinking on me.

Meanwhile, I kept my distance from Xeno and Hannah. The longer I stayed away, the more my desperate need for Hannah slowly receded, the soldiers retreating. We weren't real. We were just misplaced, ill-timed distractions. I kept convincing myself it wasn't love, just the alchemy of time, place, and need. The alchemy of loneliness and common demons. What was real was Xeno and me, true friends and kindred spirits.

When he asked me why I was such a stranger these days, I hid behind the art. I kept telling him to get the nuts and bolts part of publication down while I finished my painting. I assured him I was onto something. He hooted and howled with joy over my artistic commitment. He was happy and trusting, while I was dealing with internal waves of disgust and self-loathing. I hated that the urge and energy still lingered and I couldn't outthink and *outpaint* it. Sometimes, when that urge surged and the alchemy found the right potion, I tried to convince myself that we were just in the throes of youth and experience. It wasn't a big deal. Sex is just sex and society has walled us into superficial boundaries preventing physical expression. *Beyond Good and Evil.* Who was I not to dance with Nietzschean ideals in an artist's youth? Hannah and I were just true to the expression of the moment, the expression of experience. It had nothing to do with Xeno. It was bigger than the drama of three.

I romanticized these notions and philosophical sophistries. From time to time, bought into them for a few fleeting here and theres. Absorbing the fog into my blood flow.

But most of the time I just felt like an asshole. Mostly I felt the reality of it.

California is one giant landmass of concocted, cockeyed reality.

The Lost Horizon hotel.


During these lonely couple of weeks work helped. I stayed devoted to the morning-on-the-porch painting routine, getting up early to catch the peak fog and ride its rolling wave until the sun finally turned the sky blue. In Marin this usually happened well before it did in the city, if the blue ever arrived there.

I never ate breakfast. Just filled my empty belly with coffee, which I knew might have long term malefic effects, but I liked painting hungry and caffeinated. When I finished, I'd drink a ton of water to offset the dehydration and quench the uprooted spirits, and then head for lunch at a nearby Mexican restaurant, Sueños Lunares, on Throckmorton Avenue, halfway along the walk to work. I'd invariably eat the standard Mexican plate, rice, pico de gallo, refried beans, carne asada or pollo, and wash it down with one Dos Equis. There was comfort in the creation of habit.

After lunch, I'd go downtown. The bookstore was in the center of Mill Valley. It was half bookstore and half café, which was fortunate. The bookstore alone would have been dull and slow. The café was a shot of adrenalin to the bounded world of words, adding energy and young beautiful women. I spent some of my time in the art section, organizing and researching new books to give the section more breadth. This didn't take long so most of the time I just read about artists, entire biographies on Picasso, Gorky, both De Koonings, and Kahlo. As for women, my self-loathing implored for loneliness. I made no attempts to flirt with any of the lovely women of Marin. They responded similarly. I figured the loneliness was my penance. Perhaps, I just feared more rejection at this moment.

Just simple ego fears.

I usually worked and hid in the art section for the first half of my shift. At six o'clock the manager and other clerks went home. Maggie Gaines worked the rest of the shift with me. We alternated between taking breaks and working the counter until about nine. I'd sit outside in the sprawling terrace, eat free café food, and read the evenings away. For the last hour we were at the counter together before closing up.

Often on the terrace I'd get distracted. There were tables for people to drink coffee and have some light food. Beyond the tables, the patio extended into a social gathering spot for Mill Valley folk; aging hippies chatted politics or played chess, teenagers smoked and flirted, pre-teens had a section for skateboarding, elites discussed business, stocks, or local swanky restaurants. It was a lively, but peaceful scene. I enjoyed the diverse energy, sunshine, and varying voices.

I was all alone, but I was free. I felt good at work. I wanted to take in the freedom without fearing it. Something good would come from that. Something bad would come from running.

Maggie was quintessential Northern California, a sort of female Xeno. Life is altogether too ironic at times. There's got to be some celestial connect the dots at work.

A god in the form of some grand master puppeteer of the universe. Maggie was a poet and her live-in boyfriend was a painter-surfer. She was taking graduate courses in literature, but was not matriculated for a degree even though she had nearly completed one. "I don't want the degree. I just want to study."

She had long, thick black hair, parted simply down the middle, that reminded me of Janis Joplin. And Maggie was the embodiment of the fog. She was Imagine Incarnate. I wanted to tell Xeno I had a member for his mad club. She would contribute to the journal and probably hop on board the dream of his art house, but telling Xeno would have to wait.

For now, Maggie was a good distraction, an older sister I always wanted.

Once a week, I would set up a podium and microphone for a reading in the café. Maggie would set up the author's books at the counter and introduce the writer, which she found to be the worst part of her job. While the writer did their spiel, she would try to convince me to join her distraction.

"Dixson, why don't you bring your paintings Sunday night?" she'd ask.

"They're not ready. Maggie, I'll let you know."

"So what? This isn't a phony, here-to-be-seen reading. It's friends sharing creativity authentically, not competitively."

"I don't know. You need to meet my friend, Xeno."

"You been saying that for a while. Bring him Sunday night."

"Maybe."

"And what don't you know, Dixson?"

"A lot. Everything."

"How long are we going in riddles?" she asked, smiling. Maggie was always upbeat even when she was frustrated during readings and annoyed by my coyness.

"I like riddles," I said.

"So do I."

"You know any?" I asked.

"Just you."

"I'm no riddle. I'm transparent."

"True, not a riddle, just ridiculous," she said, nudging my shoulder affectionately.

"Just like everyone in this floating state."

"I'd rather float than be rigidly stuck in the earth like your east coast. Hey, anyway, I'm serious. It'll do you some good. You've been kind of a mopey Joe lately. You could stand to float a little, so to speak. Loosen that long, lanky body of yours. Put a dent in the Reichian armor."

"I bet you built an Orgone Box."

"I should and put your uptight, east coast ass in there."

I laughed heartily at that. "You know, back east I'm a misdirected, lost artist, but here I fit right in. I'm the norm."

"God bless San Francisco. May it never change. Now do your Rocky Balboa impersonation."

I mimicked opening a window and sticking my head out. "Yo, Paulie, your sister's with me. I'll call yous back later."

That cracked up Maggie every time. She finally said, "So what do you say?"

"Who's coming this week?"

"My boyfriend completed a new painting. He's show-ing that. Phyllis says she's coming, but she usually doesn't show up. She's too good for us with her Columbia MFA, New York agent and novel that might be picked up by the big shots. She thinks she should be reading at the podium, not hunkering down with us salt-of-the-earth artists. Kendra and Nan from the café are going to play some songs. I'll read some poems, of course. I don't know, a few others. What does it matter?"

"Just curious."

"You know the point is to breathe life into art. It doesn't have to be a lonely activity. And it doesn't have to be a business deal like Phyllis' writing. It can be down to earth, even in the kooky, flighty Bay Area. It's about the group anyway, maintaining a new family of friends bound by creativity. Most of us are from fucked up families anyway. That's why we're here, right?

I shrugged. "Probably."

"I mean, why did you come here? Family issues, right?"

"You're oversimplifying it."

"No, you're overcomplicating it. I never met an east coast or anywhere in the States émigré out here who didn't have a messy wake."

"I think I'd be here either way. Maybe not. Whatever."

"Sweetie, truth unravels over time. Can't rush time."

"Maggie, when are you going to get rid of surfer guy so we can be together?"

"The next life, honey. In this one we're siblings."

"Just my luck."

"You're full of shit, anyway. You don't want me. Never mind that stuff. Just come Sunday night. You'll start to get what you want."

"Hmmm, that would be nice."

A few days later, there was a knock on my door around midnight. I was up reading a new Arshile Gorky biography. It was terribly depressing. He was shitting into a bag attached to the side of his abdomen, had rectal cancer, his art was ignored, he was losing his mind and beating his wife. It would end with him hanging himself at home in the foyer, his death greeted by his wife and kids as they walked in the front door one evening. Christ, what damage done, handed down, generation to doomed generation? Why was I reading this? I should have been reading Louis L'Amour or Archie comics. But somehow biographies of doomed artists oddly made me feel better on some level.

I put Gorky down and answered the door.

"Fuck you!" Xeno screamed.

"What?" I stupidly said.

"You're kidding me, right?"

"About what?"

"That you don't know what I'm talking about. You shouldn't be surprised, asshole. You have the audacity to pretend innocence. Come on you fucking asshole. At least be a man, girlfriend fucker."

"No, I mean, I know what you mean. I don't know why I said that."

"Why?"

"I was caught off guard."

"No, no, follow me here, shithead, why did you do it?"

"I don't have a good answer."

"Of course, there is no good answer," Xeno said, throwing his arms up in the air and gyrating hysterically in the doorway. "Then give me a bad one."

I'd actually had this one running through my twisted brain lately. "A brief chemical attraction that got the better of us."

Xeno crunched up his crimson face while I noticed his hands clenched, white knuckled tight.

"You did a lot of horrific damage."

"I know. Let's talk about it," I said. "Let's lay the cards out on—"

"Lay the cards, nice choice of words, bastard! Girlfriend fucking bastard! There's nothing you can say. You know, the first week I wanted to come over with a baseball bat and beat the living shit out of you."

I nodded. "You should have."

"Hannah stopped me. She said she was just as much to blame. She said it was some temporary madness. A moment. Same asshole shit you just said, but she said it's over. Done. She had no real feelings for you then. Has none now. Do you hear that?"

"Yes. It was a mistake. I'm just glad we didn't follow through."

"What?! You followed through pretty fucking good."

"Yeah, but not completely."

"What the hell do you mean? Fucking my girlfriend is not following through? What perverse logic did you come up with to justify that?"

"No, Xeno, no. It's coming out wrong, but I guess the only thing I can take as consolation is that we didn't sneak into hotels and screw for weeks. That I didn't steal her from you. Instead—"

Xeno was shaking his head and gritting his teeth, his jaw muscles twitching. "Well, buddy, thank you, you're a hero. So you let me have my girlfriend after you screwed her. Can you actually hear yourself? Do you have any sense in your insane brain what you've done? What the hell is wrong with you? What happened to you?!"

"That's not what I meant. I mean…Forget it. I know she loves you. I didn't mean anything I said, did, or am saying. I don't know what I mean. I deserve the baseball bat."

"Oh, poor Armenian victim. Woe is you."

"I'm sorry, Xeno."

"Consequences, Dixson."

"I know."

"Every action has a consequence. Next time think before you destroy!"

I nodded. My heart was beating rapidly and my mouth and spirit desiccate.

"We're leaving. We're going to Oregon. This was a sign. A giant, screaming red flag of a sign. We need to get out of this city and get distance from you."

I nodded. At this point, I knew the less I said, the better. It was all coming out wrong.

"You know, and you knew, she has giant emotional issues. Deep childhood shit. You fucking knew that. Incest and painful shit, trouble with boundaries with friends 'cause her family caved in on her as a goddamn kid. Her world crumbled and she's just repeating the same perverse drama of her childhood trauma. You're just a role in a sad play and you played it perfectly. This happened before in her last relationship. It has nothing to do with you. There was no fucking attraction between you two. She has no feelings for you. You got that! You are anybody that would have been in that place. You are nothing. Just the male at the moment in a wretched repetitive play."

"Yeah, I understand. I wish—"

"You just filled a fucking role, a pawn to her psychic pain. You got it! We're going away and she's going back into therapy. I'm going into therapy. I've forgiven her, but not you, Dixson. Never!"

With that, Xeno started walking away.

Still the idiot, I said, "And the journal?"

Xeno was shaking his head and never turned around.

"Never mind," I said.

"Hannah and I will survive. I hope you crash and burn!"

And he was gone.

I stayed in for a while unable to paint, giving myself the baseball bat treatment internally. I took some days off from work. Maggie called a few times to check in and plead with me to come Sunday night, but I never returned her calls. I hated that each time she left a message, I had hoped it was Hannah.

Eventually, I realized that Xeno's attack was a good thing. He snapped me out of a numbness. I needed cataclysm. I had fallen into spiritual hypoplasia. I think I wanted it. Sought it on deep, unseen levels. Their relationship was intact. They were going forward.

I would, too.

In the meantime, I felt an aloneness I had never felt before. An abandonment. Perhaps, I had felt it before when the family had splintered so often. Each period of aloneness in life must carry all the previous pains making the current one exponentially more potent. A storm gathering wind and rain along the way until it strikes with full hurricanic fury. The moment is never truly the moment, but a vicious convergence of many.

But I knew I would survive. It was my modus operandi. Seek disaster and find solution. I believed this disaster would prevent me from falling into another one.

The last drink for the alcoholic.

The last line of coke.

The last break up.

Foolish hubris.

I started taking some yoga classes. I visited an herbal store and got some relaxation remedies; Kava, Valerium, some type of flower oil that you put on your tongue. San Francisco alive. I stopped reading biographies of mad, deeply tortured artists and began reading Buddhism. Tao. Plenty of Eastern self-help books at the store. My heart eventually stopped trying to crash through its ribbed cage and the aloneness went from typhoon to steady winds.

Manageable anxiety and angst. Who could ask for more that? Nirvana in the modern age.

Of course, all the lonely, individual methods could never truly work in the long term. We need others or the walls close in. So I turned to Maggie and she was there for me, adding her hippie Bay area spin to my therapy: she read my palm, did my astrological chart, and even pulled out the I Ching divination, which used yarrow stalks to form random hexagrams that would somehow offer insights into one's past and future.

"Come on, Maggie. Let's draw the line at hexagrams," I said, as she was analyzing the yarrow stalks.

She eventually starting nodding slowly, looked up and said, "Maybe, this was all about your attraction to Xeno."

"That's what the I Ching is telling you?"

"No, I'm going western psychiatry on this part."

"Do tell," I said, rolling my eyes.

"It's obvious. Hannah was just your way of sleeping with Xeno."

"Hmmm, only one problem."

"What?" She asked, with a wry grin.

"Pretty sure I'm not gay."

"I don't think you are either, but part of all of us, straight folks included, is gay."

"Maybe so, but I have come to the conclusion that all of life is gray, one mass of chaos theory, clouds, mysteries, sphinxes, riddles, questions, and stalemate chess games except that I know I am only attracted to women."

"It's even grayer than you think, but one step at a time, Mr. East Coast."

I stayed in California through the summer. In total I lasted about four months. I was getting more peaceful and my aloneness was getting less poignant. It was becoming everyday existential loneliness. I could breathe and sleep at night. I did miss Xeno and Hannah, but I knew all I could do to fix my deviance was stay away.

When I wasn't missing them or thinking of the tragic vortex that I let myself get swallowed by, I saw myself as a dime-a-dozen San Francisco transient. Just another runaway youth sipping some silly western, spiritual mirage. But I still had an east coast work ethic ingrained. I needed something to show for this misadventure. So I returned to what got me through every hard time—painting. I turned all the sketches into completed works, which became a connected collection that I was not unhappy with, perhaps worthy of a small gallery exhibition. At least, I had enough in quantity for an exhibition. I didn't know what the hell to do with them, but I was happy about having them, clichéd youth or not. The mirage has moments of true delusion. We must accumulate some form of currency. Some forum. I liked them on a Maggie Gaines level. Art for art's sake. Creativity as religion. New prayer.

Xeno's level, too.

Their construction helped offset the destruction of a friendship. I gladly would have traded them in for the missteps with Hannah. But I had a feeling something good would come out of the work, someday. The negative energy just exhausted itself and surrendered to a positive flow.

I called the collection *Gone West*, and with it, I was done with San Francisco. I had come west to create my own escape as if I'd never have that possibility again. I said my goodbyes. I would really miss Maggie, but it was time to go. I had a family of one in Providence waiting for me. It was time to return home to the east. My grandfather needed me.

I needed him more.

The day before leaving, I sank into a deep depression, darkness almost visible. The whole escape seemed like such a failure when it was supposed to be some much more. I felt so weak and the only person I wanted to speak to was Hannah. She was the only person that understood the mistake, that understood me. And so I called her, hoping she would pick up.

"Hello," she said.

"I miss your voice," I said. "I miss you."

"We shouldn't be talking."

"Is he there?"

"No, but he'll be back soon."

"I'm so sorry about what we did, but I miss you so much."

"I know, I miss you, too. But we can't, ummm, we can't be."

"I just want to say goodbye in person. I'm leaving tomorrow morning."

"Ohhhh, Dixson, I think that's a mistake. I don't trust us. I don't trust me."

"I'll be at the giant oak tree on the corner of Fell and Masonic tonight at 8. Meet me there. Just a few minutes to say goodbye. Tomorrow I'll be gone."

"Oh, God, where we had our first kiss. Jesus, what are you trying to do?"

"I don't know. It's the first place that came to mind. This wasn't pre-planned."

Hannah sighed. I could hear breathing turn heavy. "If I can, I will. No promises."

I got to the tree a few minutes early and sat on the grass with my back against the mighty oak. I waited and waited and she never came.

I went back to my apartment and finished packing. I put the *Gone West* collection, safely in poster tubes, into my little hatchback along with the few other things worth the haul. Feeling even worse after Hannah's rejection and that I even requested the meeting, I cried myself to sleep. The next morning, I began the journey back east. I didn't paint or sketch at all during the trip. The muse had died and the escape was over.

I was just another California casualty.

I lived in North Providence with my grandfather. I didn't have much of a relationship with my parents after their divorce. I saw them once in a while, but my father had moved to New York years back and had a new family. He kept in touch occasionally, but I always felt like an outsider with his new family and he rarely wanted to meet me without them. My mother lived in New Hampshire in the house I grew up in. I wasn't close to my siblings at all. We talked at holidays and exchanged gifts.

My grandfather was a different story. We were close. I admired him more than anyone in the world. I'd been living with him (and my grandmother until she passed away a few years ago) since I was fifteen when the family finally, officially, thankfully disintegrated. Miscast roles and repressions eventually unraveled and when they did, I told my mother I wanted out.

My grandfather was now in his late eighties. We didn't know his exact age. I reasoned he needed me as much as I needed him, but that wasn't true. He was in great shape, physically and mentally.

I was the mess stumbling along erratic rhythms, seeking large canvases with dark colors.

Kegham Manasian lived through the Armenian Genocide of 1915. His life put my self-absorbed plight in its proper perspective. Patriarchal madness didn't parallel national slaughter. He often told stories of his escape. The stories varied over the years and he seemed to be creative with them—survivor license. He was from a village called Van. The Vanetsis were known for their toughness and unwillingness to go down without an epic fight. He had witnessed his father hold off attacking Turks with kitchen utensils. When word spread that the Turks were going to send a sizable army to exterminate the stubborn Vanetsis, Kegham's father sent him on the run to an orphanage in nearby Russia.

Young Kegham left, but decided to turn back and help his father. He returned during the carnage. As he searched for his father, he was bayoneted by a Turk, injured, but conscious. He crawled under a pile of dead bodies and hid beneath the carcasses. His life instinct somehow allowed him to remain silent as the Turks reviewed the pile of death for any living Armenians. He could hear the sounds of knives puncturing skin and organs and slicing the bones of barely breathing or already dead bodies.

They didn't find Kegham hiding deep beneath death.

He eventually passed out from the horror, stench, and trauma. A gypsy woman, who was looking for any remaining jewelry or valuables, came across a breathing 12-year old boy. She rescued Kegham and took care of him for weeks.

She told him the only way for him to survive was to leave. Even though they stayed in the remote nether regions of Armenia, he would be found. The Turks were ruthless and merciless in the mission to exterminate my ancestors. It was the original Final Solution. She told him that she had heard about a new government in Russia that would save the poor. Perhaps, he could find sanctuary there.

During his journey to Bolshevik Russia, Kegham sneaked onto a farm in the middle of the night. Starving, he was picking and eating grapes as fast as he could. He was caught by the owner of the farm at gun point and put to work to pay off the grapes. He worked so hard that the owner took him in. Kegham got a room to sleep in and meals in exchange for work. He did this for a couple of years waiting for relatives from America to send him money to come to the New World. He knew of an uncle that had escaped to America prior to the Genocide. Eventually, the owner of the farm was able to make contact with this uncle, who wired money to Kegham to pay for the passage. He boarded a ship, sailed to Tiflis, Marseilles and then arrived in America in about 1921. He was a teenager. Dates and ages are all approximate. He didn't even know his birthday.

It wasn't a priority.

My grandfather gave me balance. He had lived through death and still smiled his way through life. He was Buddhist without even knowing what Buddhism was. The best, most authentic kind. The messy, selfish world of my parents was offset by Kegham's simple life. He was married to my grandmother for fifty loyal years. Life resembled what normal might be. They ate meals together. They watched the evening news. She read and sewed and handled the money because my grandfather was illiterate (though bilingual). My grandmother had finished 6th grade and was a voracious reader of mysteries and romance novels. No heavy literary artifice. Just damn good stories. He made the money, she managed it, and they discussed all the decisions. Yeah, they fought, but it didn't have the tension and cataclysm of my parents' fights, which seemed to rattle the earth beneath our house of cards. Each scream might be the last one.

My grandparents' fights were just quarrels that faded away fast and would never separate them.

However, every version has an alternate, especially those versions glorified by those who seek to frame a story to their needs. Admittedly, I needed to see Kegham in a certain light and I refused to see him in any other way. Color my glasses rose, but don't take them off.

My grandfather had two children, my mother and her older brother, Haig. Uncle Haig liked to set the record straight about his father. He didn't visit much and when he did he usually had conversations with me while my grandfather occupied space in the room. I tried to include Kegham in our talks, but Uncle Haig focused on exclusion. It was awkward and it bothered my grandfather, but he didn't talk about it.

During summer breaks from college, when my grandfather wasn't home and Uncle Haig popped in, we would often have conversations about him. We didn't have these conversations when I was in high school. Apparently, he thought I wasn't old enough at that time. During the college years, though, he didn't hold anything back and the pattern was always the same. Uncle Haig would attack. I would defend.

"So how's it going living with my father?" Uncle Haig would say, smoking a Lucky Strike.

"Going well. Peaceful. He lets me do what I want."

"Well, yeah, compared to your parents, but it's funny, he didn't let me do what I want. He used to drag me to the races with him all the time."

"What do you mean all the time? He was working so much," I countered.

"Not at night. I spent my teenage years at the dog track. Can you believe that? He couldn't read the damn sheet, so he had me do it for him. I thought it was fun at the time. Fun comes back to haunt sometimes. He's a lot more selfish than you think."

"I don't see it that way, Uncle Haig."

"Of course, you don't. Do you know the garage door story?"

"Yes, you've told me."

"Your grandmother was complaining to him to fix the garage door. It was jammed and wouldn't open and winter was coming. So what did my dad do? He went to the garage and ripped the garage door off its hinges, and told my mother, 'Now you can park the car in the garage.' We had no garage door the rest of the time we lived on Chauncy Street, unless you count the large piece of wood with broken hinges leaning up against the side of the garage."

Then as reliably as sunrise, Uncle Haig would inject the story of Arthur Shapiro, the blind Jew whom my grandfather played poker with and always won by making sure there was a perfectly placed mirror behind Shapiro. I saw it as survival for an illiterate genocide survivor and also funny like the garage door incident. Uncle Haig didn't see the humor.

"Funny, for you. You know why he had no time to fix the garage or no money to pay someone?"

"Gambling," I drawled, trying to express my boredom with his litigation.

"Dogs and horses were his life. His family was always secondary, if that."

"I know, I know."

"Your grandmother carried the family on her shoulders. He doesn't deserve the pedestal you put him on."

"It's my pedestal, Uncle Haig."

"It's misguided."

"Not for me. Can we talk about something else? You ought to cut him some slack."

"I tried, but I didn't have odds next to my name."

"Do you enjoy the revenge of ignoring him while he's in his eighties? He's been through a bit more in life than you and I have."

"I don't disrespect him."

"You do. You don't even talk to him."

"And you treat your parents well? You reach out to your father?"

"Uncle Haig, ahhhh, never mind. Just never mind. I gotta go."

"I'm just setting the record straight, Dixson. You don't have a father that can't even read or write. An illiterate with all the services in this country. It's a shame. It's embarrassing. You'd think he'd have gone to school instead of the races. What does he do all day besides look at the numbers of the racing pages? What kind of life is that?"

Most of our conversations ended with me biting my tongue and wishing I hadn't.

However, it was true about the racing. It just didn't bother me like it did Uncle Haig. I couldn't understand his bitterness and he couldn't understand my indifference. Human walls. In fact, I enjoyed my grandfather's hobby. I'd read the horse's weights, gender, jockey, and recent record before the night's race. He had some system that would pick a winner and we'd watch the races on cable TV to see how he did. We'd figure out how much he would have won or lost. Amazingly, he seemed to win often at home.

I'd also take him to the track once every week or two. He had a connection at the track that would call him and give him a tip. Whenever we got the call, we'd head to Suffolk Downs. He used to go to the track frequently like Uncle Haig said, but that had changed after my grandmother died. He worried about his money without her managing it anymore. He was more careful now. Sometimes, when I suggested we go to the track without insider tips, he would point to the sky and say, "Freda's watching."

When I got back home, I spent a couple weeks decompressing from the long drive and the experiences of my western days. We watched many Red Sox games and went back to watching and pretend betting on the races. He hadn't gone to the track once during the four months I was gone. The first time we went we didn't have a tip. He pointed skyward and said, "Sorry Freda, it's been a while."

Heavenly invocations aside, time with my grandfather always grounded me. I digested my time out west, the many mistakes and missteps, the drama and damage of it all while being in his routine. He never changed a thing. Instant coffee, cigarettes, two eggs and toast for breakfast, ham sandwich for lunch and dinner at the church with other older Armenians. He had no use for church unless it offered food. Life in his steady, status quo orbit was just what I needed. He was the flip side of California.

It was September and I was too late to start a graduate program in education, but I went to the University of Rhode Island and applied for an education degree with a focus on teaching art. At times I was tempted to go for an MFA, but I stayed true to putting art on the periphery. Art was trouble. There were bad memories associated with creativity. My western tryst of deceit left a bad taste in my mouth about art. My temporary philosophy of regretting what you did rather than didn't do was now the folly of youth. I'd had a momentary dalliance with a Rimbaudian derangement of the senses. Being home with my grandfather would arrange the senses normal. I put the *Gone West* paintings in the basement, back to their true origin where I had painted and sketched myself to escape from the lacerating screams from above. The paintings were home, but now there was tranquility above them and no need for art. That was the plan…

To kill time and get some experience before starting in the Spring Semester, I got an internship through URI as an assistant teacher at an elementary school. Every week I had to go to the university to fill out some paperwork about the internship and while there I'd also check out some course options. Poking around the art department for electives one October afternoon, about four weeks after returning East, I saw an interesting advertisement crammed amidst many ads.

**CEREBELLUM**
**7:30 PM, OCTOBER 30**
**THE NEWEST AMERICAN ART MOVEMENT**
**UNRAVELED**
**NEW ARTISTS STILL NEEDED**
**Contact…**

I thought about it for a while on the train home. I had just buried *Gone West* under sheets in the basement. Dust hadn't even begun collecting, but apparently I couldn't let death become her. It was no easy escape from the escape of art. It whispered and teased, proffered grand horizons and infinite eternities. Extended the tiny orbit of one. In an instant the pendulum restarted its swing.

Life simply seemed insufficient without her.

As soon as I got home, I called.

"Hello," answered a gravelly voice.

"Yes, hi. I'm calling in response to the ad for new artists that was posted at URI. For ahhh—"

"Cerebellum."

"Yes, yes, sir."

"Good, good. Who are you?"

"Dixson Naturian."

"Who's that?"

"Ahhh, me."

"Good, good. Yes, you. I mean who's me or rather who's you? What's behind the name?"

"What do you want to know?"

"Are you an artist?"

"I have some paintings."

"Then you are an artist. Don't hide. Shyness never got anybody anywhere. Tell me more."

"I traveled the California coast this year and painted a series of abstracts along the way from San Diego to San Francisco."

"Abstracts. Hmmmm. In what vein?"

"Gorky, Johns maybe. Colorful drips and—"

"And psychic automatism. Ahhh, well, kind of a throwback style, a bit dead and dated, but I've always loved the first half of the century dream of exorcising the subconscious into art in a grandiose and innocent dream of salvation. Yes, good ole fashion Andre Breton with a paintbrush. Better than that Campbell's soup detour in the 60s. Pop artists just acquiesced. Joined the game. No, no, not Gorky, Pollock, they were fighters. Paintbrush vigilantes. Yes, yes, but, well, all our stuff is quite post-modern, post post-modern, but this could propel the movement with an homage to its once radical origins. We owe a debt to Freud's artistic sons. Yes. Good. Very good."

I had no idea what to say after this mini-lecture so there was an awkward silence until he asked, "What's the name again?"

"Dixson."

"Dixson what?"

"Naturian."

"Armenian?"

"Yes."

"Gorky was too. Yes, you Armenians are tremendous folk. Caucus madmen. You'd bring an ancient, viable will to the evenings. Armenians are survivors. Rubber bands. Like Jews. Never give in to the death instinct, but flirt with it. Juggling thanatos and eros and feeding off the tension. Bards or businessmen, but nothing in between. Good, good. Bring your work to my place."

"When?" I asked.

"Now, of course, we don't have time. Why wait? Waiting is a sin. I hate waiting almost as much as I hate time. Right bloody now," he yelled in a really bad British accent.

"Ok. I will."

He gave me the address and hung up.

I went into the basement and exhumed the paintings. I put them in the back of the car like I had three thousand miles and two months ago. I headed to North Providence where this guy lived realizing I never got his name.

He lived in a rather seedy part of seedy North Providence. His apartment was just across the street from a nondescript building that had *Spa* written in small, red electric lights on the first level. It was a massage joint that ended happily. His apartment was above a pawnshop and a decaying steakhouse that might have been out of business, but it wasn't clear

I rang the buzzer.

"Mr. Naturian?"

"Yes."

I entered through a big metal door painted maroon, but chipped and cracking. It was an old warehouse that looked like a printing press at some point based on some old machines cluttering the corner in a giant room.

"Over here," I heard from the back. I looked up and saw a loft in the rear behind the machines. There was a wooden ladder that led to the loft. "Come on up."

It was a big loft overlooking the aging warehouse. There was a kitchen, a large bed, couches, a TV, a stereo, all the necessities without any separation, a makeshift Manhattan art loft in North Providence. In the far right corner there was a heavy velvet curtain that must have hidden the toilet and shower. The only area of privacy.

"No walls," he said reading my mind from a swivel chair in front of his large, paper-scattered desk.

"I noticed."

"I hate walls. All kinds. The regular ones, of course, but most of all the invisible ones. Still can't rid myself of those, but that's a discourse for another day. I digress, especially during digressions. They beget each other like Genesis. Everyone begets everything. Whole lot of begetting in the old days."

He stood up and walked towards me. He was short and rotund with disheveled, light brown hair. He had on an oversized tweed blazer, covering a wrinkled, white collared shirt, and baggy khakis pulled too high above his ankles by maroon suspenders. It was a mismatched, unhip zoot suit of sorts. He put his hand forth to shake and I gripped his big, fleshy, sweaty paw. My hand disappeared within his, but he had barely any grip. He just effeminately enveloped me like a giant thick cloth draped over my hand.

"My father owned this place. He was a lithographer. My whole family worked here. We had a successful business until lithography went by the wayside. Then my father built this loft and we all moved in so we could sell our house. Soon after, he had a heart attack and my mother died of a cardiac disease. Both at 55."

He made eye contact briefly and then looked away.

"I'm 45. The clock's ticking."

I didn't know what to say so I said, "You'll outlive them."

"No, I like my curse. It's a good curse. Impending death breeds life. I'm going to live the next ten years like a hundred. Lots of living. Lots of plank walking, you know. No fears. No planning ahead. Just great leaps, lunar leaps, not earthly steps."

I nodded, "Good attitude. Carpe diem, right?"

He pounded his chest on the heart side with his fist.

"Like Sammy Sosa. I like when athletes do that. It's big now. They pound their heart to tell themselves their heart got them to gladiator level. I'm not so keen on the pointing skyward to God for every little success. Sosa hit the home run, not God, but hell, God's pretty tempting when you start out dirt poor in the Third World and end up larger than life in the kingdom of America, but that's another story. Lots of stories, but let's focus on ours. Focus," he said with a sudden big twitch, almost a jerk of his head to the left and down, his chin almost touching his shoulder. "We're going to shake the kingdom a little. A few ripples in the moat. Maybe a wave or two that topples the castle. Yeah, waves, tremors, earthquakes." His eyes widened, locking his gaze on mine, and slowly, mad scientist-like, said, "Cerebellum."

"Ahh, huh?" I said, puzzled and incredulous, uncertain whether to laugh or leave.

"The reason you're here. The art movement. The next seminal movement in art that will be studied for years to come, just like your Andre Breton stuff. Cerebellum's post-modern sails need the winds of surrealism. The legacy of Gorky. You know I knew something was missing from the show and then you called. I love the destiny of it. The chance, the randomness. The surrealism."

"Gorky wasn't really a surrealist," I said.

"Everyone's a surrealist," he said dismissively.

"But you haven't even seen my stuff."

"All the better. We leave it to fate. Less thought, more trust."

"I have them in my car. I can just—"

"No, no, no," he loudly insisted. "I don't want to see them. This is instinct. Like a book with no words in it. No, no. I don't mean that. Like a novel manicured and formulaically written like all of them now. The dreaded MFA novel. Then we take the words and throw them up like confetti and wherever they land is the new novel. The real novel. The inner truth exposed. Chaos theory realized. I'd rather read confetti than the nicely constructed lies posing as art today. The written word must be rearranged."

As he babbled on, I was thinking how San Francisco had nothing on whoever this guy was. I returned east, but the west would not let go.

"You know which Surrealist I really liked? Louis Aragon. *La Defénse de l'infini.* What a title! What a book. Hasn't been translated 'cause the modern world couldn't handle it. We have yet to defend infinity and yet that is what we should be compelled to do. Aragon doesn't get much credit, but he was the true surrealist. Madly visionary. I think he succumbed to the bourgeois impulse, though. He lost it and went normal."

"Never heard of him."

"What kind of surrealist are you?"

"I'm not."

"What?" he asked incredulously.

"I never said I was. You did. I like abstract expressionists. My grandmother had some Gorky prints. Got me hooked on that style early on. I liked Johns and Pollock, too, but I'm no expert."

"They're all scions of the surrealists."

"Like us," I said smiling.

"Yes, now you get it. Everyone's a surrealist. Don't care much for Pollock, though. More wannabe eccentric and a mean chap. I'll take De Kooning any day, both husband and wife. You want some coffee? Wine? Beer?"

"Coffee sounds good."

He had a pot already brewed. We sat at an octagon shaped table. He poured black coffee for both of us, not asking if I wanted sugar or milk.

"I want you in the show. You'll have your own room, one of eight, but no walls, just curtains. I hate walls, fences, tall shrubs, partitions, but you already know that. It's the ruination of this damn western world. All of us sniveling inside like turtles under attack. Pervasive sickness. Like the loneliest character in the world. You know the loneliest character in the great world of the lonely imagination?"

I shook my head, but I don't think he noticed. He was looking over me.

"Every character has loneliness as their core. It's why we create, but the loneliest of the lonely has got to be the demented, religious fool in *Midnight Cowboy*. You know, the guy who invites ole Joe Buck into his apartment to turn a trick. Just flat out keeps repeating lonely, lonely, lonely. No minimalism there. Maximum loneliness. That guy or even the red-headed teen that Buck blows in the theatre. It's all one hell of a marvelously lonely film."

I was thinking of getting the hell out of here, then burning my paintings and becoming a math teacher or an accountant. The world of art always seems to lead me to the madly astray, but there was something likable about him that made me stay. He seemed harmlessly mad, almost comically. I did wonder if he was hitting on me with the lonely gay references.

"Ratso and Joe were lonely as hell, too," I said.

"Ahh, you know the film."

"Sure."

"Loneliness spawns art spawns loneliness. How's that for a phrasal palindrome?"

"So, the—"

"The show?"

"Yeah, the show."

"I've been living my whole life for this show. All roads of my life, all the historical forces of my spirit have led me to Cerebellum. We will collect the uncollected energy lingering about today's youth and galvanize it into creativity's full potency. We lead impotent lives, quiet desperation, as Thoreau said. Cerebellum will return potency to the world of art, which has been castrated. Yes, it will burst open the aged and rusted hinges with the half-baked hunger of lustful, youthful youth. We don't want anything polished and formed and refined. We want it raw and fresh like your work."

I was about to say he hadn't seen my work again, but realized the futility. I was standing before the Elmer Fudd of American Art and I very well could be making a mockery of my paintings by putting them in this exhibition, but I knew I would do it. Mockery didn't seem all that disturbing. Maybe there was even something liberation from public embarrassment. Or, just maybe this guy was not the caricature that he seemed to be.

"You know we get tired after a while. It's been one opiate after another. God, egalitarianism, the American Dream, sport, suburbia. Same wolf in sheep's clothing. The car and the black paved driveway is the booby prize. That's Springsteen. *Darkness on the Edge of Town.* No better album title than that. This show will toss some light into the darkness. And this darkness is particularly haunting because we just don't know it's there. Scary, Mr. Naturian. Scary, surly lurking evil. We have opiate fatigue. We need a taste of the truth."

"What truth?" I asked, embarrassed at my need for the concrete and logical.

He threw his hands up in the air and yelled, "That's the unanswerable question, the eternal labyrinth with no pathway out. That is what we—"

I'd had enough. "So where's the show and, hey, I don't know your name?"

"Right now, it's Veris."

"Right now?"

"Yes, I change it often. It's more truthful. Keeps me fresh, alive, and gives rebirth."

"So Veris? Is it still Veris?" I asked, smiling.

"Armenians always have a sense of humor. Good for art, too. The artist should seriously take himself not too seriously."

He gave me a piece of paper with directions.

"See you tomorrow," he said, walking to a desk where he started spinning a Rolodex. I climbed down the ladder and headed out of the lithography museum. As I left, I could still hear the sound of the Rolodex whirling like a roulette wheel. I got to the steel door, opened it, and spotted the thin, neon lights of "Spa" across the street. I thought of returning and asking why he was spinning addresses relentlessly. I thought of going to the spa.

Instead, I went home.


The night of the show I had all my paintings ready to go. I had framed them minimally in black metal. I had cards for each one since there would be an auction at the end of the show, and for a few moments I had delusions of discovery. Delusions of the superficial salvation of fame, artistic triumph, of being hailed heroic, a Renaissance man, groundbreaking. Delusions of fellatio by alive and artsy women.

Oh the sweet high of delusion until the truth gun is cocked, aimed and fired.

The show was on the second floor of a strip mall not far from Veris' home. Below Cerebellum and the next revolution and renaissance in American art, were a pizza place, an adult video store, and a CVS.

It was quiet as I wandered around looking for my curtained-off space. A few artists were setting up their rooms. I came to an empty area with "Gone West" written next to the entrance. There were tripods ready for the paintings. I set up my little exhibition with the works going clockwise from San Diego to San Francisco, each one having the date and location of conception. The last one had the whispering image of the Golden Gate. And that was that. What does an artist do at an exhibition? I guess play artist, whatever that is. Feign importance, perhaps. I decided to walk around and see what the others were doing.

The space next to mine was titled "Linguistics." Hanging from the high ceiling were long strips of paper. They were about the width of toilet paper and hung all the way down to the floor. You had to move the paper out of the way to walk. I looked around for something else, but this was it. This was the exhibit. Each strip had a column of letters from top to bottom. I tried to make out some words, but it seemed like a random collection of letters.

"You might find a word," said a voice.

A form appeared through the paper maze. It was the prototype of the dark gothic looking artist: pale skin, jet black hair, and a long, shapeless, black cotton dress draped over her body revealing no physical shape, no hint of breasts, hips, curves of any kind. An upright rectangle covered in black cotton with tattoos of intertwined black dandelions and red roses circling her neck.

I nodded. "So it's like a word game?"

She smiled, shook her head slowly, and walked away.

The next space was "Tent." There was a tent set up and nothing else. A simple, triangular tent that would sleep two. I looked inside and saw a TV so I crawled in. There was a VCR with the TV and two sleeping bags with the heads of stuffed animals sticking out. One was a deer, the other was a monkey. The TV was showing various images of nature: a stream, a forest, squirrels jumping and frolicking.

I tried one more room. There were chairs with side tables and a newspaper on each table, kind of like a waiting room. Each paper was from a different city and country: *The Washington Post*, *Corriere della Sera*, *Le Monde*, *Al Ahram*, *Saigon Times*, and so on. There was a giant Plexiglas box in the center, maybe ten feet wide and four feet high and the inside was nearly filled with shredded newspaper. I walked out of the room and looked at the title: "Yesterday's News."

That one I liked.

I went back to my spot. Compared to the others, my stuff seemed liked such boring abstracts on traditional tripods and organized so logically by time and place. Everything was quirky, whacky post-modern concept art and here I was old fashioned, mid-century modernist bullshit. I couldn't wait until this was over. I felt foolish, like the only one not wearing a costume at a Halloween party, and the embarrassment wasn't cathartic.

Didn't fit in with the suits or the avant-garde.

Middle ground is turning into quick sand.

A few people came in and looked at the work. They were young hipsters on the pose. After quickly walking by my work without even pretending to look interested, they moved on. I could hear them talking to the Goth woman with toilet paper art. Others came and went, nobody asking any questions. Nobody was going to buy anything. Nobody was interested. I heard more banter from a decent crowd populating all the other spaces.

Then Veris walked into my space and looked at the paintings. "You feel it?" he asked.

"Feel what?"

"Momentum."

"Not here."

"You will. It's building."

I rolled my eyes.

He winked at me. "It's happening. Let it. Don't rain, amigo, on the parade," he said and then left.

I felt like going home and watching a baseball game with my grandfather. I was getting ready to leave and forget the whole stupid California mistake again, burning the paintings as an offering to the muse to leave me the hell alone. As my destructive, self-loathing momentum was gathering steam, a woman entered my room and seemed to be actually looking at the paintings with interest. Finally someone, but not just anyone. She was beautiful. Mediterranean olive skin, silky auburn hair falling along her shoulders, full sensual lips. She was wearing a sleeveless, light blue shirt and white Capri pants, colors darting my mind to an image of clear skies and brilliant clouds. No one part of her monopolized my mind. It was her entire being that captured me.

No, overwhelmed me.

Then she smiled in my direction. Maybe even at me. I tried to smile back, but who knows what my face produced. She turned her attention back to *Gone West*.

Something was different. It wasn't just lust for her, not just a libido gone wild, but something that transcended typical attraction and desire. To me, she had a face that launched a thousand emotions, as if I had known her before. Yes, past life craziness seemed utterly real right now in the chemical anarchy fomenting within. She was the first woman since Hannah to jar me. I had to do something. I had to seize the moment and not shy away cowardly.

I stood by the last painting waiting for her to come to me, both terrified and ecstatic. Was this the purpose of my art? Was she the purpose of going west and painting? Hyperbolized theories of meaning and existence wildly unraveled in my mind.

When she finished looking at the San Francisco painting, she turned to me, and said, "I like them."

I took a deep breath. "Phew, I'm glad."

She laughed. "You surprised?"

I nodded. "A little bit. You're the first."

"You are the painting."

I smiled and relaxed upon her English mistake. She was human and not a descendent from Mount Olympus. I sensed a Spanish or Italian accent. Greek would have been more fitting.

"Wrong English?" she said, cutely.

"I am the painter."

"Sorry, yes, yes, painter. Paintings," she said pointing to the work. "My English makes me fool sometime."

"Your English is beautiful. Language is overrated."

"What?"

"Don't worry about your English. I'm a monolingual fool so you're way ahead of me."

She smiled. I wasn't sure if she understood. I tried again daringly vulnerable. "Your accent is also beautiful. Everything about you is."

"Gracias," she said, turning a bit red.

"De nada."

I wasn't going to let this woman leave without the chance to prove my reaction real or idiotic. I finally experienced the story you hear where people say they meet someone and immediately know they are going to marry that person. I didn't know if she wanted me, but I knew she was instantly right for me. It was utterly ridiculous and made no sense, but it was more real than anything else in that moment.

"So Spain or Latin America maybe?" I asked.

"Spain," she said.

"What part?"

"Barcelona. Can I make you a question?"

"Anything."

"What happened in California? Your paintings have strong, energy, some sad and sweet both. Like life. Can you tell about them? I'm curiosity."

"You are curiosity."

"Another mistake?"

"No. You can't make a mistake with me."

She looked down shyly, but flattered. "You too kind. My English will never improve with you."

I told her I would tell her everything and proposed that we go to a restaurant to talk there. She agreed, "But what about the exhibition? Is not finished."

"It is for me."

Veris was right. Cerebellum would alter momentum, change the flow of history. Revolutionize apathy.

Mine.

I was the happiest man alive. Everything before now seemed a prelude of events to get me right here. Everything after would be all about her and us.

We need a mate to get across the bridge.

As we exited, Veris grabbed my shoulder. We both turned and looked at him. With both hands, he blew us each a kiss. "Look at the power of art." Then he turned back to Cerebellum.

Her name was Sangiella. As we walked to a Chinese restaurant, I could feel she was in the same place as me, or at least in the vicinity. I took her hand and she let me. We were both smiling fools, falling fast and hard. Gravity unshackled.

"Is this really happen?" she asked when we sat down.

"I think it is, but it's never happened to me before. It's loco."

"Mucho loco," she said.

We sat in a maroon vinyl booth surrounded by tacky Chinese paintings, plastic plants, and many red tasseled decorations that I had learned were supposed to bring good luck and money. There were also many beautiful photos of the Great Wall scattered about, eponymously apropos of Veris.

We talked all night, eating dinner and drinking Tsing-Tao beers and scorpion bowls until three in the morning. We laughed and joked and discussed our cultures and all the things we wanted to show each other from our countries. Then we switched to coffee to get us into dawn. We couldn't waste the dawn. We toasted our coffee mugs to Veris and then began to share the pains of our life stories. Alcohol, caffeine, and the moment melted the armor.

I told her everything about my family dramas, California, the paintings, Imagine Incarnate, and Xeno and Hannah, and she listened intently, nary a hint of judgment on my missteps in the triangle. The forgiveness only strangers can give.

Then she told me her story.

Sangiella came to America to change her life, leaving Barcelona to escape her family and her last relationship. She foresaw a cycle of bad repetitive patterns if she stayed and she thought changing continents and a new language would redirect her destiny. Her last boyfriend was a pilot for Iberian Air. He was very handsome, and especially in uniform he was every young Catalan girl's dream. She felt so lucky to be at his side. However, he treated her horribly after the first few months of bliss. He flaunted other women in front of her, which was of course devastating and humiliating, but she didn't leave him.

Their arguments escalated into abuse and he began striking her. Finally, Sangiella's brother sat her down and said she had to do something. He knew she had been lying about black eyes and bruises. If she didn't, he would go to the pilot's home and kill him. At that point, she was suicidal, full of hate and rage at him and even more so at herself. She had lost her identity to this man because she had failed to carve her own identity out before entering the relationship. She had taken on his interests rather than discover her own, allowed him to shape her like clay on a pottery wheel.

She went into therapy and over a few months was finally able to leave him. She spent one year with the therapist, who had changed her life. She recognized her unformed identity, connecting present to the past. She absorbed the impact of the tragedy that had befallen her home.

Her older sister had died in a car crash with her father at the wheel. He had survived, but the family was steeped in trauma and melancholy for her entire childhood. Sangiella had been conceived just months after the death of her eight-year old sister. Her parents never grieved or coped, just leapt into procreation to physically replace the loss and redirect the pain, while sustaining all the emotional damage. Into a womb and world traumatized Sangiella was born.

She felt guilty to be alive. She was a replacement thrust into a world with parents too numb to love again. Too afraid. Too guilty. After she removed herself from the abusive relationship with the pilot, she began to find inner strength. She parented myself because my parents were never able to do it. Her mother even wore a pendant with a photo of her deceased daughter (Santella) hanging on her neck and always visible for everyone to see. She had the perpetual habit of rubbing the photo between her fingers.

Sangiella had to leave. She didn't want to blame her parents. She wanted to understand them and fully process the effect it had upon her. She didn't know anyone in America, and knew almost no English upon her arrival. She had studied some in high school, but was a poor student because of her insecurity and shyness. She wanted to prove herself as a student reborn through therapy, reborn into a new life in a new world. After learning English, she would return home and look for work in tourism because her great passion was travel. She had traveled every year since she was sixteen, European style: four weeks at a time, not the American getaway weekend or week in Orlando or the Caribbean. She had been to almost every European country as well as Thailand, Kenya, India, Cuba, and now the U.S. Her annual four weeks of traveling were the happiest times of every year.

"You're an amazing woman, Sangiella. You've been through so much and you're fighting out of it. I respect you so much."

"No, no, just try to figure me out."

"And America? Do you like it? Are you happy you came?" I asked.

"Happy I came, but don't like too much."

"Why not?"

"I don't like food, people are all such busy and no time for friends. The family I live with never see people. Just work and watch TV at night with the kids. Very bored life. In Barcelona we spend hours each day with friends. We stay late and talk, but we don't have so much money or job there. So con and pro. I miss home. I miss my family. They damaged me, but are my family and we yet have fun moments. I love them. I feel ready to be with them now and forgive. I understand what they are now with the look outside. Make sense?"

"Yes, completely. When do you leave?"

"One month."

There was some silence.

"There is one thing I like about America?"

"Twenty-four hour Chinese restaurants?"

"Yes," she said, smiling wide. "And you."

The castle doors were wide open.

After kissing through the sunrise on Federal Hill, we went back to my grandfather's. We didn't waste the dawn. We had shared pains and truths that take some people years to reveal, if ever in our world of secrets and lies, and we did it in one night.

Our connection felt invincible.

She met my grandfather and immediately fell for him. She knew what he meant for me and this made him more heroic for her, too. We spent every day together, but had had no privacy in my home or hers to make love. The relationship grew without sex, which we thought was a testament to our truth. We kissed and talked and spent time with some of my friends. Eventually, we decided to toss the testament away and leapt in with weekend getaways all over New England, passionately making love and joyously releasing pent up energies. It felt just as right in bed as out of bed.

The elusive dual chemistry.

Her favorite getaway was in Boston where we took the T to Cambridge and walked Harvard University and the Square, which was the closest experience she had to Europe. She was in awe of Harvard. She also loved Provincetown, which reminded her of Sitgis in Spain. The last weekend we went to New York City. Walking around Central Park, we made a vow. I would come to Spain and spend one month just like we had here. She would teach me some Spanish. I would meet her family, friends, live her life like she had lived mine. After that, we would make another vow.

We had no doubts.

We had a dramatic, romantic goodbye at the airport. I would leave in two weeks. My grandfather supported my decision. He told me I was crazy with all this traveling and worried about money, but he liked Sangiella. He nodded at me and simply said, "She's a good girl."

He gave me $500 to help me in Spain.

"One month only, right?" he asked.

"Yes, just one month," I said, not sharing my doubtfulness that I may not return.

Those were the longest two weeks of my life. I tried to read about Barcelona, learn some Spanish, but my head was not in it, perpetually drifting off into our memories, conversations, images of her. We spoke a couple of times a week and those were the only times I felt alive. I understood, finally, the concept of having another half.

During the eternal two weeks, I remembered an old friend, Remy Serenghetti, who had been in a similar position as me. Remy was five years older. I'd met him one summer during college when we both worked waiting tables at a restaurant. He had met a woman from Portugal, another Iberian beauty. When I went back to school for my senior year, they had moved to Lisbon, but I'd heard they recently moved back to the States. They'd married and settled in Providence. I found his number and called him up. He didn't say much when I had asked about his wife, but Remy was the shrouded-in-mystery type. I never truly got to know him, but I had always wanted to, probably because of the enigmatic front. I told him a little about Sangiella and that maybe he could share some of his experiences in an international relationship and living in southern Europe.

"Portugal and Spain can't be that different, right? Plus, it would be good to reconnect," I said.

After a long pause, he invited me to his place.

While I did want to see Remy, I mostly just wanted to talk about Sangiella. Tell someone in my generation about this love-at-first-sight craziness. Hear her name coming from my mouth. The separation was unbearable. My chest ached in glorious, meaningful pain.

I was all anxiety and euphoria and undoubtedly pathetic.

The two-week wait felt like a year. I'd never make it. Perhaps Remy would understand my state of being.

When Remy and I last hung out, he was taking a TESOL training course so he could teach English in Lisbon, but that was just for money. Remy was a writer. He'd written one novel that he was sending out to publishers when I last saw him. He had told me he planned on writing a second novel in Portugal. "I'd write my European, ex-pat novel. Any writer worth their salt must do that. Gotta salute the Lost Generation." At that time, even though he was always aloof, one could tell he was on top of the world. But he never socialized or engaged in the post-work antics of restaurant folk. He did his job and was focused on his art and his woman.

When I knew Remy, he had red hair that was buzzed short. He was muscular thin, and his short hair made his face bonier and more angular. He had bright, azure eyes set deep below a protruding brow that cast a dark shadow over his eyes and nose. Light and shadow. Remy was intense, striking, swirling thought energy. He seemed on the verge of saying a lot, but he rarely did.

I had just gotten off the phone with Sangiella when I headed over to his place. Our conversations always left me in a state of orbit. I never expected love could be so potent. So consuming. I couldn't imagine a life without her, even though all but one month of my life had been that way.

Remy lived in a two-family house. I rang the top bell and heard him yell to come on up. We shook hands. "Come on in, Dixson."

Remy looked the same, if a bit weathered perhaps by the Mediterranean sun. I sat down on the couch. CNBC was on the TV, the stock ticker tape rolling obtrusively below.

"You want some coffee?" he asked.

"Sure."

He disappeared into the kitchen. It was Monday, late morning. In ten days I would be in Barcelona.

His apartment was large and sparsely decorated. Bigger than I expected, minimally furnished, and all hardwood floors, no rugs. There was a greyhound lying in the corner on a puffy dog mattress. His long, skinny snout was aimed at me while his dull eyes gazed apathetically in my direction. I turned my attention to a photo on the wall, a red boat docked in a harbor surrounded by many other colorful boats.

"Costa do sol," Remy said, two espressos in hand, joining me on the couch.

"Portugal?"

"Yeah, near Lisbon. Seaside town Cascais. That's where we got married."

"Where is she?"

"There," he said pointing to the photo.

Remy sipped his espresso, suddenly focused on the TV. Then he wrote something in a notebook on the coffee table.

"I left her," he said

"Your wife?"

"Art," he said earnestly.

"Art?" I asked. "Writing?"

"It's a myth. All skies and seas and suns and silhouettes. That's how I think of it. Trapdoors and trampolines. How's that for alliteration and bullshit poetry?"

"So you stopped writing?"

"I chose real estate, land, something real over imaginary worlds. Took me too long to realize the obvious."

"What happened?"

He got up and gave the greyhound a treat. The dog ate it without much interest and then plopped his face back down, staring at me. I looked away.

"You play the game or the game plays you," Remy said.

I furrowed my brow, started to say something, but Remy took over.

"You know, I've always thought the greatest American of the 20th century was Malcolm X. He fought the game and then he realized he had to play it. Constant evolution. Self-taught behind bars. Not some silver spoon stuck up his rectum, Ivy League phony. Constant evolution rather than permanent revolution. Learn and unlearn, molt and motion."

"Remy, you're on fire, but ahh, what the hell are you talking about?" I looked at the TV and back at him. "You quit writing to buy stocks?"

"Yes, and property."

"Really?"

"Really."

"You've changed."

"I would hope so. Or you get caught in a status-quo quagmire and quagmires are not good places to be. Too often a one-way ticket down the rabbit hole."

"Yeah, I got caught in one."

"You out?"

I nodded. "I like the apartment. Can I ask the rent?

"I charge $800."

"You own it?"

"I got off the trampoline and walked around the trapdoor. You don't have to go through. Just take the easy way."

"Congrats on the house."

"Thanks. I rent out the first floor. Always take the high ground when given the choice. Just think Bunker Hill. Normandy. War and life 101."

"Can't argue that."

"A little luck in the market and I should have another two-family house this year."

"Impressive. Did you hit it big with your novel or something?" I asked.

"No, I told you I left her. No more beards. No more Halloweens."

"Did you ever get it published?"

"Yeah, Marisol got a friend to translate it into Portuguese. Couldn't even get it read in America. So we found a publisher in Lisbon. A small press, but it went to my head. I thought I had my own little, neo-Lost Generation going. About 1,000 copies sold. Then, because of the

European publication, we got some small American publisher to do it, too. He thought we had the next *Tropic of Cancer* and I fell for the delusions of grandeur, an acrobat in the circus in my head. There are a few copies floating around somewhere. The book made enough money for a few meals for Ray, but it wasn't about the money, right, Ray? It's about truth, art for fucking art's sake."

He looked over at the Greyhound and laughed.

"What's the title?" I asked.

He was suddenly jotting down more figures from the TV. "What?"

"Your book. The title?"

"Cascais," he said, looking to the photo on the wall. "Hip fishing town. Last train stop from Lisbon. Swanky nostalgia on Costa Do Sol. We had our salad days of wine and roses."

"You got a copy? I'd like to read it."

Remy didn't answer. He finished his espresso and ran the back of his hand along Ray's jaw. Ray's tail wagged slowly.

"It's standard ex-pat stuff. Love story overseas. Innocent abroad. Lots of stuff about the place. I loved Portugal, Dixson. I want to die there. The coast of Portugal is like no other. Mystical, mad, transcendent. I spent hours sitting on the edge of the cliffs north of Cascais. No people, just the sea. I'd close my eyes and breathe in the briny air and listen to the howling wind and the Atlantic raging into the jagged, rocky coast and then gently settle into foamy, white peace until it would do it all over again. Anger and peace flowing at the edge of the old world."

Remy spoke more tonight than he had ever before, but I got the feeling he wasn't really talking to me.

He continued, "You look out into the sea at dusk along Cabo do Roca and you know why they thought it was the end of the world five hundred years ago. Why they thought there were demons and beasts prowling the horizons. We don't have that external mystery now except for Roswell nonsense. All that's left now is the inside—chemical mind frontiers, neurons have replaced land and space. We're trapped in our own claustrophobia."

"Well, I'd like to read your novel. I remember reading some of your stuff back in our Grill 84 days. Loved it."

"Whatever. Once I buy the second house, I'll have four apartments to rent. I'll head back to Lisbon and have a friend manage the properties. Draw a salary on the rent and be able to work less over there. Have a civilized, normal life. Maybe a family."

"With Marisol?"

"That's the plan. My plan."

"Her plan, too?"

He seemed to ponder that question.

"You know, I've been working like a dog. Work like Ray used to at the track. He ran up in New Hampshire at Rockingham. I've been teaching English classes over at URI full-time and waiting tables full-time over Esposito's downtown."

"Shit, Remy, that's a lot of work."

"Yeah, I got no time except now. Monday daytime. My only free time and I've got to manage my investments. Got my money flowing into stocks and funds. Time to buy now, Dixson. Buy low, sell high. The bulls will be running soon and I'm gonna ride 'em right out of Pamplona and get the hell out of town."

"Back to Cascais?"

"Enough about me. What's your story? Still painting?"

"No, I'm kind of like you. Went west with Xeno. Remember him?"

"Vaguely."

"I painted some stuff and it didn't go anywhere. I was planning to go back to school. Ran into a quagmire."

"Relationship quagmire?"

"More less, but it's over. Met an amazing woman. She's Spanish. We fell instantly. I'm heading there in ten days to spend a month with her. I'm going to ask to her to marry me."

"How long have you known her?"

"One month."

He started to say something and stopped.

"I know, Remy, it's only a month. When you know, you know."

"What do you know, my friend?" He asked, seemingly hostile in tone.

"I know I love her. I know my life changed the moment I saw her. I know what I feel."

"How do you know what you feel?"

"What the hell do you mean? I feel it. I know it."

"You feel, therefore you know?"

"Did something happen to you and Marisol?"

"Time can wreak havoc, Dixson. Whole bunch of therapy has done good. Opened me up. Raw as sushi for a while. Never mind. One month doesn't give you legs for eternity."

"Sure, there'll be bumps and it'll take work. It won't always be this dreamy, but it should start that way, right?"

"When it starts out so dreamy, so perfect, maybe there are things going on inside. Things we run from more so than we are going to. Things that make us go headfirst."

"Remy, I don't know what happened to you and Marisol, but—."

"Stop bringing her up, man. You don't even fucking know her."

"Ok, man, maybe I better go."

Remy got up and was pacing, never looking at me as he monologued. "Things can change. If only everyday could be the wedding day. Had no doubts. I fell in love a hundred times in one day on my wedding day. Every time I looked at her I fell in love again. I was marrying that moment. A thousand times in a moment. You fall in love with an image, a hope. Puts a lot of pressure on the spouse. Kind of like Gatsby old sport and the tuning fork to the sky…the kiss of the dream woman Daisy ended the dream of love…slipped into the cracks of the old, dry earth soul…Time is powerful. Potent. Lethal panacea. Daisy didn't have a chance."

I didn't know what to say. I just wanted to leave.

"Where's your lady from in Spain."

"Barcelona."

"Ahhh, Barthelona, get used to lisping. We made love in La Sagrada Familia. Can you believe that. We were fucking crazy in love. Gaudi would have been proud."

He was silent for a bit and then he began to sing. "Farewell and adieu to you, Spanish ladies. Farewell and adieu to you, ladies of Spain. Best damn movie ever. Not like chasing blue gills and Tommy cats at the pond. It's a big fish. Swallow you whole," Remy said in gravelly, cigarette Quint voice. "You wanna ante up, I'll catch the head, the tail, the whole damn fish. Or you wanna play it cheap and be on welfare all winter…Best character ever. Eating saltines. Peeling apples and eating the insides with a Bowie-like knife, too. Wasn't he?"

"Don't remember that part," I said standing up and heading towards the door.

"The world is bipolar, amigo. We ought to plant some Prozak in mother earth. Get her back into the right spin. Axis must be all out of joint."

"Sure, something is off. Agreed." I wanted to say he was off, but chose avoidance.

"How's her relationship with her parents?"

"Who?"

"Your Spanish lady."

"Not great. She had some shit go down in childhood, but she's working on it."

"And you and your parents?"

"Shitty, but I don't see them much, so it doesn't affect me."

He laughed condescendingly. A smug, insulting laugh.

"Remy, I didn't come for your downer bullshit. All apologies, but—"

"Amigo, Vaya con dios. You are going to need him. You got yourself a subconscious war in the offing. Yellow sun and blue sky time ain't gonna last. The demons will start playing chess with you two. Collisions you won't understand. Moment is never about the moment. Pawns make their move quietly and then it's all bishops and rooks until the queen strikes. A subconscious Stalingrad awaits you two."

"You're like a typhoon on my parade, Remy. Thanks for nothing."

"Ancient rhythms seek music, amigo. Heads up is all."

"Marisol did a number on you."

He nodded. "I would have left me. I don't blame her now."

He went to a closet and grabbed a leash that was hanging on the inside of the door. "You want a take a walk with Ray and me?"

"No, I got to go. I got to get my passport," I lied.

"Vaya con Dios, amigo mio."

"I don't need him. Good luck Remy."

We shook hands.

"Come here, Ray old boy." Ray slowly got up, stretched out his front legs out and then his hind legs, moaning as he limbered up for his walk. He moved really slowly toward Remy and then sat next to him. His tail slightly wagging as Remy showed him the leash.

Remy went one way and I went the other to the nearby bus stop, just as it arrived. I took a seat in the back, looking out the window to see Remy and Ray watching. He waved at me and I returned it as they disappeared from my vision.

In that moment, I decided I would take the $500 my grandfather gave me and buy a diamond. I didn't need to see what the month in Barcelona would bring. I would propose the day I arrived.

No more false escapes.

Just the great and true entrance.

# THE LIVING NOVEL

## Jay Kard

It was time. I knew it.

I wiped the mirror free of steam from my shower and lathered my face. I still used a bar of soap and an old wooden-handled brush to create shaving cream. None of that aerosol produced cream. I took my old west style silver blade and sharpened it on a one of those barber-shop leather straps. My barber right here in Mill Valley, California gave it to me. Then, with nice long precise strokes I sliced the graying whiskers off my face. I liked the sound of the steel severing the stubble. I always tried to finish in the least amount of strokes possible. I strove for shaving efficiency. When I finished, I pulled up the drain stop and let the pool of water disappear into the pipes, leaving whiskers scattered across the white porcelain sink. I have always enjoyed staring at my molted face in the sink. As an adolescent, I prayed for more and more whiskers to dot the sink. The more whiskers, the bigger the man. Testosterone daydreams.

Now, I still do it out of habit, out of peaceful delusion. When I finished, I cupped my hands together and splashed the hottest water I could stand on my face. Then I put the stop back in the hole and filled the sink with boiling hot water that I had already prepared from the kitchen. I took the big cast iron kettle by the wooden handle and poured the bubbling water into the sink. I put a big towel over my head and leaned over the steaming water, letting the vapors blast through my skin and pores. I stayed extra-long in the facial sauna this morning. After the water became tepid, I dried my red face and splashed it with cheap aftershave, enjoying the sting of alcohol.

I took a deep breath.

It was time.

True knowledge, free of the hazy maze of self-doubt. Zen knowledge. Bone and blood flow knowledge. Corporeal awareness, not cerebral chess maneuvering outwitting yourself. I analyzed my skin in the mirror. It looked good for my age—52. I smiled and checked my crow's feet. Disseminating steadily, but not rapidly, maybe an eighth of a centimeter every year. They're like the rings inside a tree that tell you its age. I respect my crow's feet. I inspected my nose, wondering if it was too big as I had wondered since the seventh grade. I never truly knew. Some days I thought it was striking, 50s leading man quality. Other days I felt like Gogol in *Diary of a Madman* and wanted to lop it in half.

My gray hair still had its silver sheen to it. I was happy about my hair. I hadn't lost any and women liked the color. I didn't want to change my hair. Superficial contentment.

I took another deep breath.

Life had been going along fairly well for me, but things had recently changed. Like the Bob Dylan song, *Things have Changed*, from the movie, *The Wonderboys*. I was nearly Dylan's age and adored his music. Loved his namesake, Dylan Thomas, too. *Do Not Go Gentle into that Good Night* is my favorite poem.

I have a lot in common with Michael Douglass' character (Grady Tripp) in *The Wonderboys*. I smoke pot, but not as much as him. I'm an adulterer, but not covertly like him. I'm out in the open. My wife knows it and even strangely endorses it. It's a long story. Grady had an endless manuscript for his second novel that he couldn't finish, even at 2,700 or so pages if I remember correctly. I have a manuscript, too, but I don't want mine to end. There is no end and I like that. Makes me feel eternal. I hate all endings. Nothing should end. If death is really the end, I want my book to end when I do, but hopefully I'll still be writing with divine ink in the cozy white lap of eternity.

Infinite infinity.

I've been putting the living words of my life onto the page for over thirty years. I now have 24 novels, 7,250 pages, and 2,350,000 words. It's really one novel in twenty-four books. My own ego-driven legend, like Kerouac's Dulouz legend (Jack's another favorite of mine). I see the creation of one's own legend as life's highest calling. My enormous 24-volume novel is my life and I could care less if anyone ever reads it. Honestly. My poet friend at the local bookstore balks at my use of the word novel. He says a novel is not something taken down like dictation. Even romans-à-clef have imagined detours.

Yes, my novels are transcribed reality, or should I say, the transcription of my perceived reality since there seem to be so many damn realities. And I do this virtually verbatim. I record events and conversations and they become my novels. I was inspired by Kerouac's novel, *Visions of Cody*, in which he transcribed conversations between Neal and him.

None of this third person, omniscient narrator façade. The citizens of the twenty-first century will see that form as archaic. Turning one's own life into art will be embraced as the only true way to engage realities. Poet friend says a novel involves creativity, manipulation of events, merging fact and fantasy, people real and unreal. I say every moment of every day is manipulation, fact and fantasy, real and unreal. He claims I have an illness, hypergraphia, whereby I'm addicted to writing, an alcoholic of the written word, compulsively obsessed with writing in order to shape an escape from reality; prose as narcotic.

"You've had too much therapy," I tell him.

"You haven't had enough," he parries.

"Writing is my therapy."

"Hypergraphia is not therapy, it's illness. It's a concocted, cockeyed written existence."

"Ahh," I say, waving away his words by swiping them out of the air between us, "you just wish you were as dedicated to your poetry as I am too my novels."

Ultimately, his aspersions at my *raison d'etre* are fine with me because his universe involves verbal fallacy. He writes to please everyone else except himself. Misguided reality. He's written mostly poetry and I really like his poems, but he's also tried a novel, a screenplay, and a play trying to get recognition. He's a feckless artist in pursuit of admiration and not art. He should stick to poetry, but he said he wants to write another novel. "Take another crack at it."

"Crack at what?"

"You know," he says, scoffing at me. "Come on, Jay."

I tell him his problem is the *it* he seeks. "That's your crack."

Poet friend says I'll be his protagonist because I'm virtual fiction already. Of course I'm fiction, just like him. Life is fiction, quicksand, black tar in the desert heat. Constant motion. Change. Reality lasts a second. How could it be otherwise with the earth fully rotating in just twenty-four hours, chasing the sun with the moon clinging on, and everything in hot pursuit of the star Vega. Hell, we all have rotational whiplash and we don't even know it.

And if this weren't enough, our galaxy housing all this mercurial madness is in motion at thousands of miles per second as it expands. Sometimes, I think every action we undertake is to try and just slow it all down.

I've also got a protégé like Grady Tripp did. He had Toby Maguire, and I've got a 23-year-old kid from the East. He believes I'm a true bohemian. In fact, that's what he calls me. He says only a true bohemian "has no concept of the American Dream. Only a true Bohemian lets the Joneses run wild without a hint of jealousy or insecurity."

I told him to read Joseph Mitchell's *Joe Gould's Secret* if he wants to know who I really might be. Of course, that's on the assumption that I know who I am. I do know what I've become. I know what I've done (I'm admittedly obsessed with that). I'm at home with that realization. We must be the sum of our memories. I am all of my writings, but I do not pretend to know who I truly am. That would be arrogant. And worse, a myth.

I've had other protégés, too. They come and go. They come west looking and searching like all exiled, eastern kinsmen of meaning's mystery. His end of America reconnaissance will come undone, unraveled, scattered in a love interest that fails its original, seductive offering. Adam and Eve retells itself over and over again though Adam's fault just as much as Eve's. But I laud protégé's efforts.

André Gide had it right: "Believe those who are seeking the truth; doubt those who find it."

All my writings that I've purged to the page seek truth in a fused reality. Not one has found it and not one ever will. Gleeful missteps on the road to holistic revelry. Poet friend will never even enter the arena of truth until he leaves the arena that entered him. I'm hard on poet friend, but he has one point I give credibility to. He believes my "writing illness" is connected to my being an orphan and then not procreating. I have no before or after and therefore my existential dread is more acute than the average existentialist. My world began with me and will end with me. The birth and death of an ego. Every word I write is the parents and children I've never had.

Maybe, he's onto something.

I put my weary bones on the couch in my writing room. Fifty-three-year-old bones according the Asian method of counting, which only makes sense. You have to count the prenatal nine and call it a year. They might be the most important months of life. Full of absorbed energy creating the deep seas of the subconscious. That's what I humbly presume.

My wife is upstairs watching soap operas as these scattered thoughts flow in my mind. I am tired. Really tired. It should be the happiest of exhaustions because it's from excessive and extensive intercourse. I have been fucking so much, so deeply lately that my body is giving out. I've been fucking like my ne'er-do-well poet friend should be. I've been fucking like my protégé will with some California woman before it all turns inside out and upside down for reasons neither can truly answer. He'll get hooked offstage and off-guard by the mighty dream of connection. Of course, the source of my fatigue is a woman. From Eve to Helen to Cleopatra to Juliet to Joan of Arc to Garbo to Marilyn to the inevitable next. What else is there in life? We are powered by the potent combination of libido and heart. We spend our life trying to keep either side of the seesaw from grounding. It's difficult terrain, but I've been lucky.

I've had many women over the last decade of my marriage. Since my dear wife had a stroke, she has permitted the affairs. Daisy lost her sex drive after the stroke. She told me during dinner one day about ten years ago that I could see other women.

"Jay, my desire died, not yours. I don't want to lose you because of this change or have you live a deceitful life. Here are the rules…"

She made me promise never to leave her and never to fall in love. She said to keep them simple, carnal and short term. Very few people believe me, but it's true. Those that do, called it a naïve plan. I was only moderately surprised. Daisy had always had the bohemian blood. She was always disturbed by the fallacies of conventional marriage. The stroke hadn't changed that.

Poet and protégé are always shocked to hear of my open marriage. Sometimes, I am too. But I've kept my promise never to leave and never to fall in love. The affairs are not constant, just one or two a year. It hasn't been hard to resist falling in love or finding an occasional lover.

Bourgeois women find me fascinating. I'd like to think it's my shiny, silver hair, possibly leading man nose, gentle voice, and calm demeanor, but it's not. They look at me as a circus act. A harmless, side-show freak spicing up their middle-class doldrums. They got money and bills and kids and dull husbands couch-bound at night and televisions and brunches and graduations and dinner parties and video rentals and two-week anxious vacations and car pools and mystery novels and soccer games and the nightly news and weather and lawn mowers and pool cleaners and cleaning ladies and new stereos and soft rock music and and and...the Joneses.

Then they meet me. A dog-shit cleaning, middle-aged man who's written twenty-four unknown novels and refuses to stop his own game of charades.

This current woman though is different. She's outside the circus, or above it on a high wire act, I should say. She's tender, sweet and dangerous. She is brilliant and beautiful. Cataclysmic and seismic. A gorgeous, sensual, intelligent, innately spiritual woman. Not some western poseur. Not some bored housewife. A magical woman of preternatural beauty aptly named Rainbow in Japanese.

Rainbow could be a Geisha girl and let me do things to her that I had never done to any of my many previous lovers. New positions, contraptions, voices, role plays, costumes, places all conspiring orgasms that rattled my middle-aged bones. Rainbow's pussy drove me mad. I never enjoyed engaging a woman orally until Rainbow. I'd always done it just to excite the woman. Dive in solely en route to the next phase, only enjoying it vicariously through their pleasure.

But with Rainbow, I actually got turned on gliding along her velvet Japanese portal. I loved her pleasure. I even came once. I get going just thinking about it.

Rainbow could also be a tough, hard-as-nails, Jewish mother of a woman and set me straight when I would let doubt undercut me or allow the demons to bear their long claws within. Stuck and whining about it. Playing Winey Cronhaeur as we called these moments. She'd take charge and give the carpe diem routine that every partner needs from each other. Next thing you know, we'd be intertwined in bed, Rainbow's long black silk hair cascading all over me, her voice all gentle sensuality.

I loved her more than any other paramour. But Rainbow was dangerous. She was a threat to my cozy, cocoon world, the one affair that threatened my marriage. She could snap the springs of my carefully constructed universe.

That is why I had to leave. She had a hold on me that I hadn't had since I met my Daisy. Everyone else was carnal kicks. Good, meaningless sex and talk and fun and fuel to another day, easing the journey through the night. We each benefited. It added excitement to their life and they had no problem detaching from me because they could never really be with someone like me. I was as safe for them as they were for me and it sustained their house-of-cards marriage.

But Rainbow shattered this pattern. Rainbow truly wanted me. She put my heart and soul back into sex. Rainbow turned sex into making love. I was in love with her.

And I was scared to death.

It was time to leave.

I bought a brand new map of the United States. I'd always loved maps, but this map was different. In appearance it was an ordinary wall map, but on the big side, about six feet in length and three feet high. Big enough to show smaller cities and towns, which was essential for my purposes that superseded dreamy gazing and geographical curiosities.

This map would determine my destiny by going to wherever a dart landed on it.

I knew my celestial connection to Rainbow would pull me away from Daisy and I couldn't leave Daisy. She and my novels are my anchor, my connection to this mad Ferris wheel world. I had to go. We had to go. She wouldn't even question it. We'd pack up and start anew.

I was shaky and sweaty lying on the couch trying to convince myself that escape was the only option. It would be a good surrealist decision to throw the move to the fate of a dart. Aragon and Breton would be proud. I was tired though. I wanted to stop thinking of Rainbow. Stop replaying our deep, soulful conversations. Stop picturing our bodies naked and entwined. I consciously tried to change the direction of my thoughts to my next novel, which I wanted to filter my life into key episodes. An encompassing, Christo-like canvas of my world, rather than the usual specific, tightly-framed period novels. I wanted to spontaneously remember the large events onto audiotape and distill them in a linear retelling of what got me here, to this momentous decision. A scaffold of memories. I drifted into the past, sleepy in body, but alive in mind.

I was adopted by a family in Hoboken, New Jersey and one could argue that my destiny may have been most shaped by my crazy Aunt Hellie, rather than my parents. She was a little Jewish pariah of my adopted family, which was all Catholic before Hellie interloped. My maternal uncle's first wife had had a nervous breakdown and ended up institutionalized. He remarried Hellie, who was in many ways crazier than his first wife. My devout Catholic grandmother couldn't stand to have a Jew in the family. According to grandma, "her people killed our Jesus." This, combined with Hellie's confrontational, brash manners, confirmed her as the outcast of our little clan.

Hellie was an atheist and a communist who never let go of her 60s values. She insisted on changing the world, at least in conversation. Whenever we had parties, she critiqued everyone and everything as bourgeois and phony. She and my uncle traveled everywhere and only wanted to talk about their trips or the politics of egalitarianism.

Aunt Hellie's appearance added to her eccentricity. Her skin was ravaged by the sun and bad genes. If wrinkles measured wisdom, Hellie was a Aristotle. She was about 4'11" (maybe less), about ninety pounds, but she had the Napoleonic complex down.

We called her Aunt Hellion.

Aunt Hellion profoundly impacted my life. Because everyone in my family was virtually the same middle-class mold hatched into life with conversations on jobs, money, sports, all the this and that of no consequence, Hellie was different. She squawked like a septuagenarian Macaw about the mistreatment of blacks, the bullshit middle-class morality, read the Beats, elevated the Soviet Union, and whined with Whitmanesque fervor that the President and the Cabinet should be poets and philosophers. "Leave the legislature to white bread, homogenized gentiles. The frictional amalgam of the two polar opposites would create a real society, not this mockery we endure." However, all the political and social superficial rabble rousing gripes drifted to the background of one sentence she repeatedly uttered at every family gathering.

We'd be having a cookout or Christmas dinner or something and halfway through she'd come to me and stick her little shriveled, baked-apple face into my ear and say, "Jay, every conversation is the same, every time I'm here. Don't you hear it? Déjà vu all over again. It's sick how these people can say the same thing in 1945, 1950, and 1955. Nothing changes, except for maybe the products and brands. Oh, what a life they lead."

Now, I'd just listen and nod because ole Hellie was more or less correct, but what she didn't see was her repetition of their repetition. The irony never dawned on her and I never told her this. The hypocrisy annoyed me, but years later I missed Aunt Hellion. Because I was an orphan, I think we connected since she was more a less an orphan in our family. I think every family should have an Aunt Hellion. She helped disrupt the monotony with her own version of monotony.

I was sitting in a bar on the Lower East side of Manhattan. I'd just finished high school and was pondering attending college, but was truly feckless. It was 1958. I was with my high school girlfriend drinking glasses of house jug wine. It was spring and all was well despite my directionless state. Then my world split open and in the chasm a path appeared.

There was a guy reading a book at the bar drinking five-cent mugs of Narragansett beer and he drank them ferociously under his protruding, heavy brow. The brow of the artist, pained and serious, and wallowing in the gravity of everything and refusing to make that transition into the necessary. Instead of pawning his youth for comfort, he was the kind who'd pine the moment because the moment wasn't what it should have been.

I asked him, "What are you reading?"

"Does it really matter to you?" He snarled.

"Not particularly. Just making conversation."

"*Joe Gould's Secret*," he said dismissively.

"Never heard of him."

"I bet there's probably about five billion or so names you've never heard of," he said derisively.

"Yeah, but there's not five billion titles with names in them."

"Perhaps there are."

"Perhaps," I said, willing to play this game of verbal brinksmanship.

"How do you know he's even real? How do you know it's not fiction?" he countered.

"I don't. Either way I've never heard of him, real or unreal."

"Does it matter?"

"That I've heard of him?"

"No, if he's real or unreal."

"Maybe for him."

"Does it?"

"What's the book about, man?" I asked, sighing in exasperation.

He slid the book my way and took a final swig of his beer and got up to leave.

"Have you finished it?" I asked.

"No."

"Well finish it. I can read it another time. Since you're such pleasant company, we can meet again."

"It's a stupid book. The guy's a fraud. Besides, I hate words. They get in the way. Words are the source of every flagrant lie. Without words, we'd have no lies. With words, we have no truth. Gould should have written that down in his oral history. Put that in your pipe and smoke it. No painter has any use for *Joe Gould's Secret*. It's yours," he said, heading out the door.

My girlfriend, Surya Romanavich, a Russian Jew I'd met at the New York Public Library one afternoon, said, "You know, those abstract painters think they have a monopoly on anger and nihilism, as if the world had only done them wrong."

Turned out this Joe Gould guy was real in the molecular sense. He had graduated Harvard and then dropped everything to settle on a bohemian existence and came up with the idea to pen an oral history by writing down conversations he'd heard on the street, in the subway, at artist parties, anywhere at all. He had claimed to have written 10,000 pages and had them stored away in various Bowery motels, flophouses, second-hand bookstores and other locales where he'd befriended someone. He'd taken up a collection called the Joe Gould Fund and wealthy types involved directly or indirectly contributed to the fund. He was homeless most of his life until a benefactor put him on a stipend to finish the oral history.

Turned out Gould was a fraud, just as the heavy-browed, cheap beer drinking artist had said. He'd written the same couple of chapters over and over again. One was about his father's death and another about an Indian tribe in North Dakota, with whom he'd lived for six months. In sum, the guy was a hoot, an eccentric intellectual clown. He'd sometimes go into a whirling dervish and croon like a seagull, claiming he was fluent in Seagullese. He would do this at parties after too much to drink.

His fraud and failure became my life's calling.

I was eighteen and now I knew exactly what I wanted to do and it had nothing to do with money. I have never wavered a moment, since the day I met the angry abstract expressionist. I'm now fifty-two years old and have been doing just what Joe Gould didn't do. I've been transcribing my oral history. Every time I finish a section, I take the tapes and transcribe them. Then I cover them and bind them at a local printing press and my reward is the book that rests on my shelf. No money, just the defense of infinity. Aunt Hellion would be proud. Money is irrelevant and fame a myth. A sad, pathetic pursuit taking one to the very core of nothingness. This life, my life, has showered me with peace. The books are my currency solving my youthful struggle with voids and eternities. I lost my fear of Hemingway's nada at a young age by knowing pure posterity was in my beautifully lonely hands. When I discovered that my wife and I couldn't have kids due to my sterility, the books became my kids. I knew I would never die and peace has been in my grasp ever since. I lost it only once, slipping into an abyss, but deep down I always knew I'd climb out.

Before I began my oral history, I decided I needed to study. I didn't need an education, which was just the pursuit of a paper for ulterior motives. No, I wanted knowledge. Honest knowledge.

I went to Columbia University and in the fall of 1958 I took my first course, Western Civ. I simply went to the class, got the syllabus, and attended all the lectures, while reading all the books in the New York Public Library.

Nobody ever said anything to me as far as my lack of matriculation. I was considered a bit odd because I wasn't in the Freshman Dorms like new students were required to be, but rather living in an apartment near Times Square. However, I made some friends on campus and went to some parties, had a couple beatnik girlfriends (copies of *Howl*, *On the Road*, and *Junkie* were all over campus), but most of the time I read and studied. The enrollment was a lie, but the education all true.

Because I knew what I wanted, I didn't have to waste time searching classes for inspiration nor did I have to fill those requirements like Math, Economics, and Science. I had my own curriculum: The first two years would be Western History, Religion, Philosophy, Literature and Art. The third year would be the same, except I would study the East. Eastern ideas were just starting to catch on thanks to the Beats so the courses were limited and books were a bit sparse. One year would have to do. My fourth year would be overseas, my study abroad year, learning a language and experiencing a new culture. I'd always romanticized Rome and started studying Italian from the beginning as preparation. In my fourth year I'd master Italian and stow away in some classes over there at La Sapienza. I'd also begin my oral history on my first morning in Roma, thinking it should begin overseas. You've got to leave home to understand home. My Oral

History, in the fourth year of my self-designed education, would be my thesis, one that I would write for the rest of my life.

Nobody asked any questions in the large lecture classes for obvious reasons. When I started taking smaller seminar courses, I always made sure I spoke a lot and exhibited ardent interest, which was easy since it was pure and true. When the professor mentioned I wasn't on any list, I just told him that I was auditing the course in addition to my regular load and couldn't get approval for bureaucratic reasons. I said it would be my honor to just sit in and be a part of the class. The result was always the same. I imagine math and science types would have gotten a little more anal, but the humanities types usually liked my bureaucratic critique and must have felt they were snubbing the system for the benefit of the individual. Sticking it to *The Man*.

They also liked my sycophantic attention. Those in the arts or humanities are too in touch with their lonely cores and adoration worked on them with ease.

My tuition was the cost of NYC Public Library card, but I still needed money to pay rent, eat, and live. I had a bunch of odd jobs at that time: clerked in a cigar store, painted houses in Long Island, worked for the city cleaning Central Park, and walked dogs for rich, upper class types on Park Avenue. Usually I'd work a couple months and then quit when I had a few months' rent paid in advance. Then I'd have more time to plunge into my autodidactic universe. The fact that people pay $100,000 today for an education is insane. It's all right there in the Public Library. Sure the professors helped, but more or less they weren't teaching. They were fulfilling their required presence more than anything, just framing what I needed to do.

When I finished my three years, the energy to explode the oral history out of me was, like the times, atomic. I painted as many houses as I could in Long Island. Whenever I painted one, someone on the block would ask me to do theirs. We bohemians whine about the keeping-up-with-the-Joneses' mentality of materialists, but that's what got me comfortably to Italy. Without the moneyed, how could we live la vie bohème?

I drew the line on that life, unlike Joe Gould, on homelessness. I didn't want much, but I wanted a room and a bathroom. A small kitchen helps, too.

A couple months after Kennedy was sworn into office, I got a passport for one dollar and bought a one-way ticket to Rome for $68. I still can't fathom inflation. Economics will forever mystify me and I think I like it that way. I saved $1,000, a little goldmine to me, and I was off. When I arrived at Leonardo Da Vinci airport, I got on a bus to the center of Rome. One of the first things I saw was a movie theatre with the sign saying, Alberto Sordi in *Un Americano a Roma*. I knew the fates were talking.

The next day I began my oral history.


"I just dropped it all," Walter Graves told me for the thirtieth time or so. We lived in neighboring rooms in a boarding house near Villa Borghese in the center of Rome. "Dropped it all, Jay. Jesus, Jay, I'm swelling up in guilt. Look at me. Don't I look bloated?"

"That's pasta, Walter, not guilt."

"Maybe a little, fine, but I can't sleep at night. I just listen to all the Vespas whipping by and Fiat horns honking, thinking I'm completely insane for having done what I did. I really believe I'm physically swelling from my anxiety, from my guilt."

"You eat a lot of pizza, too. Don't underestimate the caloric effect on your swollen state of mind."

Walter rolled his eyes, tired of my levity over his crisis, which was very real to him. "Jay, leaving my fiancé the day before the wedding is no joke. I humiliated her. I can just imagine her face, the tears. I can't get over it."

"Then go home," I suggested.

"I'm a persona non grata in my family, too."

"Then stay."

"Wrong again, Jay."

"Go to Africa or Asia. Maybe Italy was the wrong choice."

"You always miss the point," Walter said, exasperated that he wasn't getting what he needed from me.

"Sorry, Walter. Listen, it takes time to settle into a dramatic detour like you took."

Walter nodded enthusiastically, excited at a sign of empathy. "It was dramatic, Jay. A dramatic detour, yes, yes."

"Indeed. It took guts. And settling into this detour will take time. *Devi Provare*, Walter."

"Don't speak Italian to me. I haven't learned ten damn words since I came here. I'm too nervous. Nothing sticks. What does that mean?"

"You have to try."

"It's not easy."

"Did someone say it was?"

"Maybe she'll take me back, but it's not right. You know, sometimes, on those rare occasions when I'm not drowning in guilt, I am euphoric, ecstatic with my escape, but after a minute or two, I'm guilty over my euphoria. How dare I feel good after what I did I tell myself."

"Good, Walter, in ninety or so years, all those one-minute moments of euphoria will give you one great day of life in totality."

"You know Jay, you're younger than I am, but you're one sarcastic know-it-all bastard. Real smug, too. You don't get it. When I left Chicago and that life, I saw the sky. For the first time in years, what seemed years, what seemed forever, I noticed the sky without the prompt of a plane or thunder. Just looked up and saw all that blue. Miles and miles of blue. Infinite blue and I realized I'd been sleepwalking all my adult life, head down in depression. All weighed down from my meaningless job, meaningless town, and soon-to-be meaningless marriage."

"What exactly do you mean?"

"You're always breaking my balls. *Rumpo le mie palle.*"

"*Rumpi le mie palle,*" I corrected.

"Huh?"

"You said you break your own balls."

"Did I?"

"Yeah, but it's appropriate. You do. *Poveri i tuoi palle.*"

"Shit, yeah, *Rumpi* is you. I'll never learn Italian. Goddamn verb conjugations kill me. Man, I miss pronouns."

"Walter, your bleakness is starting to get to me."

"Help me out."

"Why don't you try drugs?" I suggested.

"You're no help at all."

"Spontaneously flying to Rome the day before your wedding and dropping everything isn't your scene, but you did it. Hell, you should be proud of yourself, bask in the glee of runaway escape for longer than a minute here and there. Few can do what you did. You realized you couldn't marry this woman before it was too late and you had kids and mortgages, grass to cut, grills, garage doors, hedges, interest rates, linoleum…"

"Ok, ok, I get the damn point. You're right."

"Smoke a little tea with me, Walter," I said, lighting up a joint.

"One step at a time, Jay."

I passed it to Walter, but he shook his head.

"Maybe I should write her a letter telling her my fears and that it was best to do it early, nip it in the bud, rather than down the road, like you said, with kids and a mortgage and all that stuff."

"Good idea. She'll never understand, but it might clear you up a bit. Then start learning the language, get a job, meet one of the many Mediterranean beauties, and really see the sky, leap right into all that blue, Walter ole pal. You did a Henry Miller move. Start appreciating it."

"I did, didn't I? I just want to see the sky every day. Is that asking too much from life?"

"A most down-to-earth request," I said, grinning at Walter and taking a big hit off the sweet joint. When Walter left, I made sure my pocket tape recorder had been running.

I landed a job at Villa Borghese, a public park in the center of Rome. It's surrounded by the mechanized insanity of thousands of tiny cars and motor scooters. Millions of spinning wheels zipping across lumpy, ancient Roman roads. Mixed in were the sounds of humans laughing and fighting, verbal jousts from balconies above and cafés below. Everyone, young and old, complaining about everything. One would walk through this strangely rhythmic score in the theater that is Rome and suddenly land in the sanctuary of Villa Borghese. Noise was everywhere, but I found a quarantine walled in by great trees, softened underfoot by miles of grass. It was as tranquil as could be in the middle of the mighty tragicomedy that is Rome, which at that time was one or two readers of the Communist Manifesto away from going red.

My job? I cleaned up. Not only didn't I mind, but I actually loved my job. I kid you not. I have never understood the American concept of success. It's perhaps a psychic defect of mine. Maybe it was Aunt Hellie's perverse influence or my being an orphan, but working just enough to get by was the goal. My ambition was for time. Time to write, time to enjoy the city, time to meet women. It was late 1950s, the United States of Accumulation was in full conformist throttle, conveyor belt materialism and I couldn't have cared less about things. I took the Beat baton and ran with it across the Atlantic to clean up Rome. I mean, thirty years later I was cleaning up dog shit for a living at a kennel in Marin County, California. A few months before Rome I was cleaning Central Park. At that time I daydreamed ambitious moments of cleaning parks in all the great cities of the world, from New York to Rome and then to Paris to Nairobi, Beijing, Calcutta…I wondered if anybody had literally cleaned the world as I pondered. I think I could sleep peacefully through the night well into the sunset of my life with a million words stolen from my own soul and the unsuspecting voices in my orbit while having cleaned up a little chunk of mother earth.

Now that is the sweet smell of success to me.

I got paid under the table or *Banco Nero* as the Italians say, which was the only way I could be paid, being illegal. Clearly, my boss was skimming from the budget. He must have paid me half the Italian wage and kept the other half for himself. I didn't care because my wage covered my minimal expenses and my job was simple. In fact, of all the various cleaning jobs I've had, this one was the best. I roamed Villa Borghese all day in my green uniform with one white stripe across the thigh and forearm. I worked four hours in the morning and four hours in the late afternoon, with a gorgeous three-hour siesta in between. I was virtually unsupervised. My boss was always in his office working with the books and figures (skimming is hard work). I was free to do what I wanted as long as the litter was under control and garbage cans were emptied every night. *Mio cap*o didn't work much beyond making his end of the black market function efficiently. However, he did do a quick check of the grounds every night at eight o'clock. If the garbage cans were empty and there were no egregious piles of picnic waste, he was satisfied because his *capo* was satisfied.

To relieve my guilt and help clean the world beyond the anemic aegis of my boss, I usually worked the first and last hour of my split shift. The rest of the time, I found a nice place under a tree and read the remaining books on the syllabi from my new Italian professors. Professors who never knew my name. Class sizes were in the hundreds and getting to know students was irrelevant. They were merely there to dispense knowledge to the ignorant. I was getting nearly fluent as a result of living and working in Rome, the rigorous self-study I'd done in New York, going to class and from reading my history, literature and philosophy, all in Italian.

Once a week I'd also clean a small zoo on the Villa Borghese grounds. This was my favorite part. The animals were a mess, shit everywhere. Few cared about them and many mistreated the innocent animals. Zookeepers did the bare minimum. I theorized that after two World Wars on their soil, much of the Italian humane spirit had gone numb. Making sure baboons had a clean cage surely wasn't a priority after the carnage and devastation they experienced, and now an economy that couldn't turn the post-war corner. However, I was the innocent American to whom war was simply discussed or read about in the newspapers. Besides, the animals were also a great relief from Walter's namby-pamby orations.

I was the happiest man I could imagine while being without a woman. I'd lived in two great cities and many more cities awaited my arrival. Permanence seemed a place way down the road, post-wanderlust. I'd be writing my oral history with chapters from everywhere before eventually settling in the States from where the majority of my eternal work would spring. While in Rome, I was particularly on the lookout for Americans. When in cafes, at work, strolling Rome's crooked and crowded streets, I had my mini-tape player tucked in my coat pocket waiting for a conversation. Sometimes, I caught those Americans who could speak Italian and I would translate as well as transcribe. I caught the tourists, ex-pats writing the exiled great American novel, artists discussing the next movement to invade the spiritually naked and hungry, business people scheming for the next great product or import, lovers in love and lovers quarreling, students loosening the seams, and, of course, Walter and me. Rome was simply stop one among many cities where I would prelude American oral history with Americans abroad.

At least, that was the plan until a chance meeting during siesta in a café on Via Veneto. From that point on every city I imagined resided in the eyes of one woman.


"Jay, she's got kids," Walter said nervously after I told him what little I knew of her.

"Walter, I don't care. What's the difference?"

"Jay, she's married."

"Still irrelevant."

"How can a husband and kids be irrelevant?"

"Because she's the one."

"For her husband and kids."

"She can't be the one for her husband and kids otherwise we wouldn't feel this way. One moment of eye contact and I swear I knew it and so did she. Besides, she's already separated from her husband and I'm prepared to be with her kids. This is not conscious. This isn't something you consider. You do it because everything inside you has coalesced into one direction. I don't have a choice. It's not like voting for a president. I'm being carried by our primordial attraction, not by a rational choice of the way she looks or her personality or her background. Logic will not dissuade me. Logic loses here."

"What about your nomadic soul searching ancient cities, cleaning up the world, and all that Joe Gould shit about writing the rhymes and reasons of existence from the voices of the people. Now you'll just be in San Francisco."

"Gould intended to write the oral history of Manhattan. I will switch coasts and write the oral history of San Francisco."

"Really scaling down."

"Much more manageable than trying to cover the globe. I mean, what was I thinking?"

"I don't know, Jay," Walter said, shaking his head slowly, a sad look in his dispirited eyes.

"And San Francisco is the home of the Beats, Howl, progress, change. I'm in. It's not like I'm moving to Oklahoma."

"Jay you're really gone over her."

"We talked for hours and it felt like seconds. Yeah, I'm totally gone."

"I don't want you to go. I'll be lost without you."

"First of all, I'm not leaving yet."

"When?"

"I don't know.

"Let me come with you."

"Walter, you're scaring me. We'll be friends for life, but not Siamese twins."

"Maybe I should go back to my fiancé?"

"You're being desperate. We've talked about it ad nauseum."

"I'm gonna miss you."

"Me too, Walter," I said, putting my arm around him, which he took as an invitation for a big hug. Then he went out onto the balcony that the five second-floor rooms shared and smoked a cigarette. From behind, I watched Walter's plumes of smoke spiral into the Roman afternoon. I joined him for a cigarette and then we took a walk to Fontana di Trevi and like tourists we threw coins into the water, properly facing the opposite way as we tossed.

Walter's spirits buoyed a bit when I told him he could visit me anytime and assured him he had home with Daisy and me in San Francisco if he ever needed one.

"Thanks, Jay, thanks so much," he said, with watery eyes. Mine started to as well, but turned away so he couldn't see.

Daisy and I spent two weeks traveling nearby cities—Florence, Tuscany, and Sienna. The instant attraction deepened as if we'd caught the universe in a starrily aligned moment of amorous generosity. We were like kids building pristine little Lego worlds in the pure and imaginative pre-video game days of childhood.

"Jay, it feels like we're living in a mirage. It's hard to believe," Daisy said.

Except the mirage was real. We made love everywhere—sneaking into bathrooms on the trains, ancient church basements, deep in the catacombs, and of course the cheap hotels and hostels we crashed at. We even got chased out of a museum in Sienna for lewd behavior when we lost ourselves in an empty room that suddenly wasn't empty.

In the hills of Montepulciano, drinking local wine in paper cups and enraptured by the Tuscan vista and each other, I proposed. She said yes on the condition that I wait about six months. She had to complete her divorce and give her kids some time to adjust. When the time was right, she'd send me a letter with the green light to come to Mill Valley, California.

Poor Walter surrendered to the inevitable. He eventually returned to his family and would ask for his fiancé's forgiveness. He told me, "Jay you're better at freedom than me. Freedom beat me. I can't live like this. I have no business here, had no business running away to Italy to be a bohemian fool thinking I could start a new life. The old life never lets you. I'm no Henry Miller."

"Walter, your one is out there and she's not your wife. Otherwise, you wouldn't be here. Freedom takes time to understand. You're just dealing with the culture shock of liberation."

"Nah, I shouldn't have come here in the first place. Jay, I don't have a one. I've fallen in love a hundred times with the beautiful Italian women here. I don't have a one. I have a thousand."

"You're talking about lust, Walter. I see a hundred women a day that I want naked and screaming my name in my bed, too, but that's just biology. I'm talking about spiritual union, universal forces that make our decisions easier. You and your wife don't go together. It's no one's fault. It just doesn't work. I can't explain what I'm feeling with Daisy, but I know you're not feeling it with your wife or these Mediterranean beauties you want to undress. Give the elements time to fuse properly."

"Jay, you'll do well in California, but it's nonsense to me. Maybe I'm not so happy back home, but at least I'm not lost."

Walter finally left a few months before Daisy's green light letter arrived. I wouldn't see Walter again for fifteen years and when I saw him he had finally shed his old life, but not for freedom.

When Daisy went back, I worked on my oral history. I kept my mini-tape recorder in my pocket like an undercover cop covertly gathering evidence. Every night I'd go back to my room and transcribe almost everything I had heard, just cutting out unnecessary detritus. In fantastical fits of onomatopoeia, I'd even try to put a language to the sounds of Rome as Joe Gould did to seagulls and Kerouac did to the sounds of the sea at Big Sur. All my transcribing helped soften the ache of loneliness that penetrated every pore of my young skin while Daisy and I were half apart. We wrote each other every day. I'd sit in Villa Borghese reading her letters, seeing her in my mind as I read: the brown eyes, sensual lips, and long strawberry blond hair that turned me on so. I'd write her back the moment I finished her words.

While recording my oral history, *Book One: Rome*, I finished my university experience. The university of myself. I had finished attending classes in Rome at their great and ancient school, La Sapienza, where four hundred or so Italians and I crammed into two hundred seats, sitting on top of each other in the aisles, standing in the back, taping the usually bored *professore* somnambulantly lecturing amidst a fog of cigarette smoke.

This was the one place I didn't have to hide my mini-recorder.

By the end of these classes, about three months into my exile from Daisy, I decided I was done with my degree. The remaining three months I would finish my thesis, book one of my oral history. At my university, I was my advisor, my dean, my provost, and if I needed to change a requirement or a direction, it was quite simple: all I had to do was ask myself. Ending a bit early didn't bother me. I had done what I had set out to do. It was around the time of this decision in my last class

(German philosophy) that I met the major character of *Book One*, an Italian anarchist named Dario Uguale. While he helped make Heidegger somewhat accessible, we became fast friends.

Dario and I hung out at cafes near La Sapienza, talking for hours, propelled by speed. I often ran out of tape during our talks, which sadly meant that parts of the talks were lost to the universe.

If it wasn't recorded, it didn't really happen.

I was the curator of my reality and my reality was what came from voice to tape to page. The particular reality of Dario Uguale mostly condemned American materialism and bemoaned dysfunctional Italy. As I said, Italy was teetering towards communism after the disaster of WWII, while as a nation it was tenuously held together, fraying fast in its struggle to unify nationally and let go of its city-state regional culture. But Dario hated communism as much as American capitalism. When we met, he had been devouring books by Emma Goldman and Thoreau, but was now "transcending them as well." He knew what he didn't want, but couldn't yet find what he wanted.

When he wasn't criticizing make believe America, he was buying nasal inhalers from the *farmacia* and breaking them apart to inhale the base, which was filled with Benzedrine, a pharmaceutical amphetamine that used to be popular with the Beats before the FDA got hip to it.

"Ohh, Americano, I tell you America is the end of the world, but *grazie Dio* for these sinus *decongestione*. This benzedrine is my *Dio* now."

"Hopefully, the government won't catch on like they did in the States," I said.

"*Il governo non e' stupido, Americano.* They've got a stake in the profits and they figure let's keep the youth drugged out and distracted. They want us in oblivion."

"I don't mind oblivion. Not a bad place. Better than reality."

"Reality will be better in anarchy. There's too much police everywhere. In Italy we have the polizia, the carabinieri, guardia di finanza, and then all the military, American bases everywhere. We're not children, Jay."

"It would be interesting, but I'm not sure I trust humanity without some kind of police."

"A small force then."

"Ok, then I vote for anarchy."

"Now that's a contradiction."

"What?"

"No voting in anarchy. That's anathema. Anyway, I want to move on from anarchy."

"Last time we spoke, Emma Goldman was your new *Dio.*"

"No more *dios,* Americano. We atheists must stop searching for replacements. I got tired of Goldman's arrogance. Damn anarchy to her started sounding like another political party. Now Thoreau's anarchy, I still respect. A more lonely anarchy. Anarchy of the soul without others. He's a great American, *Americano.* His passage on the pyramids is priceless. Everybody goes, how do you say, bananas for the pyramids. People travel thousands of miles to visit the pyramids and Thoreau thought it was insanity. All these fawning people to witness the results of human slavery. His exact words were genius. *So many men could be degraded enough to spend their lives constructing a tomb for some ambitious booby, whom it would have been wiser and manlier to have drowned in the Nile, and then given his body to the dogs."*

"If you follow that credo, you ought to loathe all of Rome."

"And loathe Rome I do. The constructions and sites of Rome are built on human misery. Piazza Del Popolo was an execution ground; Il Colisseo, a symbol of debauchery and the nadir of the human spectacle. It's my brethren, the *popolo* itself that I love. The conversations in the cafés and on the road. Two teenage girls holding hands on their way to school. Boys kicking a soccer ball in a polluted field. That is the true Rome. To hell with Ayn Rand and all that humanity has built because all that humanity built was built on inhumanity."

"And now where?" I asked, curious to hear Dario's follow up to Communism and Anarchism.

"Now, *amico mio*, I've got my new panacea. This is beyond philosophy. Philosophy is a dead end, politics a slow death, and art a tease. This, my friend, is a state of true being, which is the state everyone is searching for—socialist, communist, abstract expressionist, Christian Democrat, capitalist, catholic—whatever your pious, fraudulent road, this is the state of flowing peace all the dysphoric searchers haplessly envision and never see."

It was easy to get pulled into the gravity of Dario's orbit. He was a handsome, dark skinned Italian of Sicilian descent. He had vibrant, mahogany eyes that radiated above tired, dark circles, the consequence of excessive reading, caffeine and Benzedrine. Sleep was an irregular rarity. He didn't want to waste that time. His powerful, piercing eyes bespoke desire and life, set in the appropriately contradictory frame of fatigue. His words and gaze produced an irresistible and mad charisma.

Deceased Joe Gould would have loved Dario. If there were a heaven, Gould would be doing cartwheels in the clouds and crooning seagullese.

Dario's newest fascination was the strangest one I'd heard. He called it Instant Nostalgia and explained it as, "the feeling of nostalgia within the moment of its origin."

"Nostalgia without the wait?" I asked.

"*Essato*, Americano."

"How?"

"You remember, Gianfranco Guerrini?"

"Sure, the neurology student. We had drinks one night with him in Trastevere."

"Right. We're working on this together. I need his scientific expertise. Nostalgia

strikes at the most unpredictable of times and the melancholy of nostalgia frustrates all of us, right? If only we enjoyed the moment in the moment rather than years later. Yet, we can only experience them from afar, with the distance of time gone by. Take, for example, this very moment now. We're talking, kindred spirits enjoying our company, but two years from now, alone, wherever we may be, only then upon reflection, will we realize the essential beauty of what this is now. That is tragic."

"It's better than not experiencing now at all," I said. "I mean I'm enjoying this now. I don't need ten years to know that."

Dario sighed, and threw his hands up in the air. "Si, si, Americano, the glass is always half-full. That's America, *Americano*. That's the spirit of your country. You may be an anti-materialist oddity, but there's still some American in you, *Americano*."

I shrugged. "Guilty."

"But what would be more true would be to capture the feeling of two years from now and experience it today."

"But how?"

"That's where Guerrini comes in. He's taking neurological readings of my brain waves when nostalgia strikes and researching the sensations. He's hoping to find a stimulant, a pill, that can create the same neuron output thereby giving us nostalgia without the pain of separation and time elapsed. Without the loss of the event."

"It would be a miracle."

"What better place for a miracle than glorious Roma?"

"And in the meantime?"

"No idea, *Americano*. I think I'll be in a café talking the rest of my life, creating nostalgia. What else is better than that?"

"*Niente.*"

"If I take a position in life, say a teacher, or whatever, some acceptable role, I therefore declare I accept this life, but I don't. It's an atrocity. It's absurd. So I'll stay in cafés and complain the rest of my life. I'm Italian, true and true. I loathe any group, but my blood is my blood and in my blood I've got a millennia of complaints. We, Italians, are innately cynical and worship what's wrong. You Americans are eternal optimists, but that's cause you're babes in the woods of civilization."

The Benzedrine really fueled Dario's anti-philosophies. We often started light, but invariably, he drifted into the depths of existence and the ideas of new orders, new ways out of the absurdity. He was a true citizen of café life circa Paris in the 20s.

Dario Uguale awakened me to the realization that my oral history was really my desire to capture that nostalgic moment for eternity.

When I arrived in San Francisco, Daisy was waiting for me. We kissed madly at the gate. We got to her house and didn't have the patience to make it to the bedroom. Fortunately, Daisy's two dogs were not jealous and they just watched us rolling around and greeted me after.

For a week we more or less continued rolling around in the various rooms of Daisy's house. Daisy's kids were with her now ex-husband. She had planned our hibernation well by stocking the house with ample food and wine. This was our honeymoon. At the end of the week we went to city hall and made it official followed by a picnic at Baker Beach, staring up at the Golden Gate.

After our honeymoon, I decided to make a change in my life's plan. While Daisy had a house and some money from the divorce, we had her kids to raise and a mortgage to pay. Given my new responsibilities, I tried to get a job that would actually make money rather than get me through each day. And, in fact, I got a good one, but I couldn't keep it. I answered an ad for a sales position in a coffee company. This company wanted to promote Italian-style coffee in America. It was way ahead of its time. They were intrigued by my Italian experience, in particular that I was fluent and that I *had* a business degree from La Sapienza, as my resume indicated.

"We need someone who has lived in Italy and can help us market our product. Americans have no time anymore because of work. So a smaller coffee like espresso with more punch might take off. We want to market the time factor to men and then market the elegance and class of Italy to housewives who long for a better, more interesting life," so said the interviewer in our meeting in the financial district of the city.

Apparently I said the right things because I got the offer, which I took and then quit after a month. Daisy agreed that the madness of marketing coffee as my existence would lead us down a sad road. She said a new dishwasher and a car wasn't worth it. I was making $2,000 a month, which was far more than I would ever make again, but wanted to kill myself sitting in an office all day having these ridiculous meetings and talking about coffee all day. I missed Villa Borghese. I missed the park and cleaning up a piece of the world. I just wasn't fit for normal. Daisy insisted I quit, and we'd figure out ways to get by in jobs that suited me.

A month later I was in Golden Gate Park picking up trash, happy as could be. No one to bother me, outside in a beautiful park, cool San Francisco weather with sheltering fog above, no meetings nor bullshit financial goals. Dario would have been proud and so would Sartre ("Hell is other people").

Like Villa Borghese, Golden Gate Park had a zoo so I could maintain my animal relations while my human relations focused on transcriptions from eavesdropping on the good people of San Francisco. Hell might be other people, but I only dealt with them for material, not real relations. Sometimes I engaged in some real conversations, but my motive was always ulterior.

My oral history was growing and life with Daisy was wonderful. We lived frugally, but happily for many years. Our extended family eventually included a not-yet renowned Sam Billingston, the playwright, who married Daisy's daughter. Their marriage didn't last, but Sam and I became true lifelong friends, spending many days together road-tripping the American West. Our trips, or rather the conversations on the trips, became a volume in the *Living Novel* as I started calling it at Sam's behest.

Sam also wrote a book fusing prose, poetry, and photos from our travels. He gave me a copy, credited me for some of the photos, and I flipped through it, but never read it. I didn't have to. I didn't want to read published, fictionalized reality. Sam and I had lived it and I had the truth down, not some filtered, sculpted version made palatable and dramatic for the public and critics. This was always an issue in our friendship and the conflict and tension led to some of the best conversations in the *Living Novel*. Sam insisted I revise, edit, and publish some of my growing work. The dialectic carried forth from that point.

Sam and Elise divorced and we were given their house as gratitude for the help we had given the young, doomed couple. We were able to sell Daisy's bungalow, make a little profit, and move into the new place just down the street. Elise moved to Hollywood and has struggled through a career of minor parts. Sam has struggled through a career of major plays and parts. Whatever the outside trappings, the spirit shall struggle.

And so we had a perfect home and now with no mortgage to pay thanks to the bungalow proceeds. I still continued cleaning up the park and Daisy worked part-time in an antique store, where she began her own kind of oral history, which was a collection of nostalgic, old stuffed animals. With the *Living Novel* at over 4,000 pages, tragedy struck in 1976.

Suddenly, by some cruel act of the gods, Daisy became a shadow of the person she'd been. She had a stroke and the amount of blood that had been cut off to her brain damaged her mind in the way a lobotomy would. She wasn't totally gone like Mac at the end of *Cuckoo's Nest*, but she would just tune out the world for hours and hours. There were moments of lucidity where we could communicate like before, but those happened rarely and briefly. Her only real link to her previous sentient life was the continued fascination with stuffed animals. She'd spend hours with them, now even talking to them as a child would. It was as if she knew the stroke was coming when she took up the hobby. Adding to the tragedy and apropos for her return to childhood, she no longer would have sex. The first time we tried post-stroke, it traumatized her. I immediately stopped and we never once did it again.

During one of her moments of lucidity, she told me, "Jay, listen to me. I want to tell you something important."

"Go ahead, sweetie."

"You're free to be with other women."

"Huh?"

"We can't, but that doesn't mean you can't."

"Daisy—"

"No, Jay, it's not fair for you. It's not healthy. You still have desire and should be free to act on it. I think it will help us stay together."

Shaking my head and slack-jawed with surprise, I said, "Daisy, I don't know. I am really not—"

"Never mind. Just don't abuse the privilege and never, ever fall in love. Promise me."

"I promise if I ever do it."

"Carnal satisfaction is fine, but your heart is with me."

Shortly after that, lucidity left and Daisy returned to her world of dolls.

I was as shocked as I was relieved. Perhaps my temporary loyalty during the early years of the stroke was good karma. I was honored by Daisy's decision though hesitant to act on it. Did she really mean it? Was that a lucid moment or just cerebral malfunction? Did she really remove the ego from her heart?

To be closer to home in Mill Valley, I took a job at a kennel nearby the house. I would take care of dogs and cats, which for the most part meant cleaning out shit from the cages, but I didn't mind. I loved the animals and the pay was a little better. I could walk to work, too, and no longer had to take the long bus ride back and forth over the Golden Gate.

My job and now Daisy's disability check got us by. We didn't drink fine wines or take big vacations, but we had what we needed. Daisy added to her menagerie from time to time and I forged ahead piling up pages in the *Living Novel*. In some ways, there was no difference between Daisy and my pursuits.

The song of my now sanctioned adultery could be divided into two major verses. The first was a dark depression that rendered me suicidal. The second was falling in love with Rainbow. I never wanted the chorus to change.

The depression hit like a sledge hammer. It was shortly after the carnal high of my open marriage's first few affairs. Perhaps, despite all the bohemian talk of a natural state of sexuality not encumbered by monogamy, my freedom overwhelmed me. Or perhaps it was in my unknown family? My last name is an anagram for Dark. All my life I hadn't really considered the significance of my surname. Perhaps, my name had been Dark and some ancestor played with the letters to try and nominally break the curse. Being an adopted orphan, my name never seemed important. It was just an insignificant tag, label, like one on a shirt. However, maybe it was a case of simple linguistic logic.

The depression slid into my soul, bleak and formless, consuming my days. At work, I'd just sit and cry, like a kid. Sometimes, I would be with some dogs, who tried hard to cheer me up by wagging their tail or nudging their snout into my face. Failing this, they would join my depression in solidarity, lying down all droopy-eyed, heads on the ground, sad eyes staring up at me, forever loyal to all our emotions. Their melancholy made my pain worse. Dogs' eyes are more emotional than ours. They feel as much or more than we do.

Eventually, my boss sent me home to recover. I wasn't any good for animal or human.

The darkness was invisible, which made it all the more numbingly frustrating. There were no images of my past, missteps I'd made, faces of those I hadn't loved or loved too much. There weren't moments of indecision that led to loss. There weren't moments of exaggerated effort that sent me tumbling foolishly ahead when stability was needed.

Something lurked inside, a faceless, crippling monster, omnipotent and omnivorous.

At the time, the *Living Novel* was finally catching up to the present. I'd described Dario Uguale, Italy and

Walter, California, and Sam and me, and was now deep into my sexual freedom. I'd filled several binders, 5,000 typed pages of the voices and conversations around me, the graffiti on the walls, the voices on the street, and my life. I was cultivating Joe Gould's seed and seeing it through to fruition.

When the darkness invaded, I stopped transcribing. I was in a tunnel and the clichéd light at the end didn't exist. I spent weeks in bed, sometimes sleeping sixteen hours a day. Sometimes, the darkness welled up and the tears came down like a long expected rain finally exploding after days of dark, gloomy skies. Words are impotent at trying to describe the sadness that rendered me physically and mentally atrophied. Sadness has its own unknown language.

I got a shrink to come in and talk to me and he kindly wrote that it was for Daisy, so the state picked up the bill. Some days I was too deflated to talk and we just sat in silence.

Eventually on those days I did talk, we came to a conclusion. Since he was of the Freudian school, where the shrink rarely gave an answer, but just paved the road with questions that would lead you to your own answers, I discovered I was terrified of the present; terrified of my newfound freedom granted by Daisy. It was several years and lovers later, but the therapist led me to believe guilt had subconsciously consumed me, pushing me off the cliff and into the sudden, paroxysmal depression. It hadn't hit me when the *Living Novel* was still in the past. But now that the words had caught up to me, the present existed in both life and page.

What I had to do was accept my freedom as legitimate and pure. This was step one. My realization of the fear cast some light on the relentless nights of my recent days. I got out of the house and started slowly living again, going to the café and reading the paper and listening to those around me and recording them. So many of the conversations around had to do with money, possessions, and mortgages. The late 70s had become a very different time, but that was part of the mission: to trace the arc of culture and history from the grassroots of real people.

In therapy, I discovered further guilt over our free house from Sam and Elise and my lack of any significant income in my life. I was guilty over Daisy's government checks, contrite for everything. Naturally, the Freudian led me to childhood and into the underlying guilt and rejection of being an orphan.

Painful realizations seemed to bring me further down after the brief respite of peace. I finally stopped therapy and made a great leap forward from my darkness by a strange and sudden urge that overwhelmed me quite by accident.

Shoplifting.

It started small and comically, just like it would end. I'd stuff a can of tuna in my coat. The next time I'd put some cases of soda in the bottom of my carriage. The cashier wouldn't notice and I just wheeled them out, free of charge. We were now living just on Daisy's monthly disability check of $425 since my kennel pittance was gone. I was only part-time and didn't have the benefit of sick days. Thus, the thieving was both an adrenalin rush of roguish behavior and euphorically practical.

Whenever I was stealing, the darkness dissipated. In fact, I was happy to the point of giddiness in the manic moments after success. It was a thieving utopia. Shortly thereafter, the darkness would begin its steady creep back to dominance like a coaster grinding and churning its way up the first incline before unleashing sudden fury around hairpin turns and corkscrew loops. Fearing the descent after the peak, I started planning bigger thefts.

Oddly, they were all aimed at the Safeway over on Calistoga Road. Suddenly, our house was filled with food, but my obsession with one store made things harder. I was easily recognizable. I got caught twice with my rucksack filled with steaks and dog food for our pair of mutts orphaned at the kennel. After the second time, the manager banned me from the store. The roller coaster was in Coney Island Cyclone gear. I tried stealing from other stores, but it didn't work. It explicably didn't give the same rush. I only wanted to steal from that store and I couldn't satisfy my urge elsewhere.

I went back to Dr. Loom, and, of course, I came to all sorts of quotidian conclusions about childhood needs, adopted and orphan syndromes, and guilt over my extra-marital liaisons, but the talking cure was inept. Besides, Dr. Loom never ventured an analysis. The burden was always on me. Everything was an increasingly annoying interrogative from him when I needed more. I needed declaratives. No, what I really needed was to steal from Safeway. I needed Safeway larceny. I had no interest in the why of my intoxicating, inane urge. I just wanted to follow its lead and the relief it gave. An addict needs their fix and I couldn't wait six roller-coaster months for Dr. Loom's alleged process to figure itself out.

So I said screw Freud and bought a disguise.

I actually went to a costume shop and got a professional set up. I grew a mustache, but bought mouthpieces that changed the shape of my jaw, a few wigs of real human hair, colored contact lenses, and make-up. Once a week I'd go to Safeway in various disguises. Daisy thought I was playing dress up as if Halloween were weekly or this was some game and she started doing the same on those days, which was disturbing. So I stopped letting her see me in disguise and began secretly leaving the house and returning out of disguise.

It all came to a crashing end when I got caught with two prime pieces of steak. The blood had leaked out of my coat and onto my pants at check-out.

"Hey, mister, you ok?" the rent-a-cop said.

"I'm fine, thanks. You?" I said casually, while putting down a couple of cheap items on the conveyor.

"Well, I don't think you are. There's blood on your pants."

"Huh? Oh, well, ahhh, I had a cut there and it must have opened up. It's no big deal."

"There's a lot of blood and it's not in a good area, mister."

"I'm fine. Just a little embarrassing and all. I just need to get home and clean it up. Change the dressing."

"You sound familiar."

"Huh?"

Then the rent-a-cop had his little epiphany, which kind of made me feel good, thinking this is a story he's going to tell for years. The day he caught a thief after years of boredom and flunking out of the Police Academy or something. He pulled off the wig and screamed, "Kard!"

I smiled sheepishly, palms up and shoulders shrugged, while he handcuffed me and called the real police.

Safeway decided to press charges and I got thirty days in the Marin County Reform Center, a minimum security prison. The judge appointed a state therapist to come and visit me. She wasn't a Freudian and didn't hesitate to render judgments and conclusions after a few visits where we actually had conversations.

"Jay, I think a key point is why you were so obsessed at robbing only Safeway and nothing else," Dr. Bensin said. "We can't ignore that neurotic need."

"Agreed."

"You want my state-appointed analysis?"

"Sure."

"Ok, here's my take. You've lived this very bohemian, pariah lifestyle that hasn't really bothered you on the surface the way it would most people. After years and years of just getting by monetarily and staying devoted to your craft of transcribing your world, you had repressed so much angst. The angst of not keeping up with the Joneses as you once called it. Your complete denial of any interest in a middle class life or pursuing the so-called American dream was actually recognized subconsciously and manifested itself into deep depressions. What else could Safeway represent? The name itself is an obvious metaphor for the easy road of the middle class. You'd go there and see all the ease and comfort of people buying cartloads of groceries, while you and Daisy barely got by. With me so far?"

I nodded. "Go on."

"This angst was excavated when your recordings caught up to the present. You must have felt the settled part of your life in this posh little town of Mill Valley. You really didn't belong, aside from the eccentric runaway characters working at Hall's Bookstore, like the ex-cabbie poet. However, they weren't in the Mill Valley community. They were transients like so many in the San Francisco. You, too, but you're here to stay. Years of cleaning parks and dog cages made you bitter, but you've suppressed it for the recollection of the past in honor of some guy named Joe Gold."

"Gould, not gold."

"Sorry, Freudian slip," Dr. Bensin said grinning. I liked her. "When you arrived at the present, it unraveled the buried bitterness. Jay, no man is an island, despite your brilliant efforts."

"Interesting and eloquent. Maybe you're onto something."

"Jay, I'm just scratching the surface here. We haven't even begun to get into the guilt of your affairs or the tragic stroke that has turned your beloved wife into a shadow of her former self."

We did get into them and the only result was I started getting more depressed. All this talk about hidden pain coming to the fore made it worse. Hell, I'd rather have it hidden. Besides, the damn shrink seemed to be culling out neatly placed sorrows tucked away comfortably in neatly arranged subconscious drawers that I didn't want to open. Who says all repression is bad? It's damn human. As much as we want to be Ginsberg stripped naked on stage primally howling vulnerabilities, few can actually do that. Dr. Bensin was disturbing everything. She assured me that while the short run would be hard,

I'd come out of it better off down the road. I disagreed. Hidden truths sometimes hide for a reason.

I stopped confiding so much and cut down my visits. She knew me too damn well. I didn't think that was so healthy and my depression was getting worse. Near the end of my 30-day MCRC stint, I read an article about the long-term effects of amphetamine use. I decided this might be worthy of further inquiry. I'd done a lot of speed with Dario and I continued it for years after to help me transcribe late into the night. Once I was out, I went to see Daisy's state funded neurologist and he filled me in.

"Residual Amphetamine Depression," Dr. Koumans declared once I answered her query on whether I had ever used amphetamines and how much I used. She had an office on 7th Avenue in the city overlooking Clement Street, a busy mix of Asians, mostly Chinese I believed, but the shops and restaurants also catered to Vietnamese, Thai, and Koreans as well. Just outside her window across the street I could see a video store with Chinese characters and subtitled in English: "The Best in Asian Nymph Video."

"Residual what?" I asked.

"Residual Amphetamine Depression. There's a theory that heavy speed use can slowly damage the brain tissue along the synapses. Simultaneously, the chemical activity bounding through the synapses gets altered. The whole process takes many years and even after stopping usage, it can later result in horrific periods of depression. A black hole in the soul opens up and takes you into its void. Just as you described your recent months."

"Do you believe it?" I asked.

"I don't disbelieve it."

"If it's true, what do I do?"

"Well, we can try medication. I'm not a big believer in therapy. I am a scientist, hard science, not that other stuff, so I see most of our problems as biochemical. I'll have to do some neurological tests to determine potential deficiencies or excesses in your chemical activity."

"Let's do it, Doc. I've been down the talking therapy road and back."

While we had to do some tests, he started me out with a scrip for some preliminary pills that might help with this kind of depression. I went to a pharmacy next to the Asian porn video store and got a bottle of the purple and red gel-coated capsules. I walked outside on Clement Street and looked around, watching everyone. I turned on the recorder in my pocket, trying to embrace the present, hopeful that the source of my depression was those Dario Uguale speed days that did extend off and on for many years. Caffeine can't get you to 5,000 pages.

Then I browsed the video store for a while. They had quite a collection, but my focus was on a conversation in Chinese between two quinquagenarians. They were quite animated and seemed to be discussing a particular video that one of them had in their hand and was pointing to every so often. Was he trying to sway his friend to get this video? But then he put the video back and they continued their conversation, loud and proud of whatever they were defending.

I wished I'd understood what those two men were discussing. It was probably nothing, but I so wished I could understand Chinese. What a language! All high-pitched, lilting and multi-tonal, at times piercing and shrill. It was great to be bilingual, but Italian is not a stretch. An

Asian language would be a trip, opening new corridors in my western mind.

I spent the afternoon walking along Clement Street, stopping for tea, then food, then a beer, all the while basking in the linguistic stew of pan Asian languages, and secretly hopeful that Dr. Koumans and those little capsules would slay the dragon of my depression.

A couple or so nights later I was home in my transcription room. Daisy was upstairs with the dogs and dolls. Darkness whispered, but it was at arm's length, just where I wanted it. I didn't want the intensity, but it struck me just then that I didn't really want the depression to completely leave. On some level, I was romancing it. There was a certain aliveness to the deadness, as soon as the intensity was dialed down. It gave life an edge.

The phone interrupted my poetic, if not foolish, notions on my darkness. Suddenly the past became present.

"Jay?"

"Yes."

"It's Walter."

"Walter! Hi! My God, how are you?" I asked, excited to hear an old friend's voice.

"Good, and you?"

"I'm ok. It's been so long. Where are you?"

"California. Marin County."

"Me, too. Are you looking for me?" I asked.

"Not exactly."

"Well, we've got a lot of catching up to do." I said, turning on my recorder, enthused by a variation in my present.

"Yes, but I can't."

"Can't what?"

"Catch up."

"Why not."

"Just can't. But I'd like to introduce you to someone named Gurdjieff."

"Who? Kerchief?"

"I think he can help you."

"Help me with what?"

"Everything," Walter said in a droning monotone. The old plaintive whining tone was gone. Was this really Walter?

"Have you gone religious?" I asked.

"Not really. Maybe."

"Who is he?"

"Meet me at Muir Woods Park tomorrow night at seven."

I arrived at the park a few minutes early wondering just who this guy was going to be. Both the new Walter and the one I'm supposed to meet. I was guessing it was some spiritual guy, some mystical guru. The name didn't sound Indian, which had been all the rage for a spell thanks to the Beatles. Spiritual debris still floated far and wide, especially in 1970s Northern California.

It was a peaceful evening in Muir Woods. The earth was red here beneath the awesome sequoias climbing towards the clouds while the sun dipped just below the horizon. There was a tent with benches beneath it and a podium in the center. About fifty people were walking around drinking from paper cups. Some were staring skyward while others were milling quietly about. One oddball was lying in push-up position with his ear to the earth. It was noticeably silent.

Then I saw Walter.

"Walter! Old friend, how are you?"

He didn't respond. His eyes gestured something indecipherable to me.

"Hey, you can at least say hello."

He gestured no. Not angrily, just no. Then it struck me how loud I sounded in this silent gathering. My words were the only ones in the air amidst the sounds of birds, leaves rustling, the wind, footsteps, running water, plates and other kitchen sounds.

I had my tape recorder, but it appeared that wouldn't be necessary.

"No talking?" I asked Walter, who nodded and gave me a thumbs up.

I spent about a half hour walking around observing others, wondering about their lives. It had the cult vibe, which was soon confirmed when a man in a white, monk-like robe stood by the podium and spoke.

"Can one come into contact with the whole situation rather than force oneself into completion?" he asked.

Silence.

"You won't be here again. Every moment you die and are reborn. How deep and essential you make each rebirth is the approach to the mystery you shamelessly ponder."

Silence.

"Many of you have written that you want to grasp the truth behind words, beseeching me to speak directly, beyond abstract aphorisms, as one of you wrote."

Silence.

"The question is truth and you mock the question by expecting an answer. When we don't know or understand something new, we frame it in words. We surround and therefore stampede the answer under all these weighted words, which aren't even ours, but were given to us by others, always others. It's a cultural labyrinth and the way out of the maze is not by asking or answering, but by allowing."

Silence.

"The comedy of errors that is God has sidetracked us tragically into a millennium of empty tears. It's all been so wrongly manifested by our rush. Our haste. Questions. Every voiceless feeling is the message. Again language has disrupted the processes by which we attain God. It exists within the silent dialectic of messages evolving into questions and again into message and higher question. This is spirituality. Our God is the highest distortion of humanity. Money is the highest defamation of everyday reason. Our feeble attempt at organizing through church is again the innate need to frame the mystery, when the mystery should just be allowed to spread within a wild peace that it deserves. Our relentless sprint has taken a black, Jewish spiritual nomad who might be considered a quack today and made him a white, blue eyed CEO of the corporation that is religion today. We can't go to God. He or she comes to us."

Silence.

"In Persia, a monument reads, *Repair the past, prepare the future*. We don't know how to pray. Pray to a friend. Think of them. Think of your relationship. Inwardly change toward them in the way you feel, not think, you should act towards that person. Elevate yourself in a different, higher way. Eventually, they will unconsciously treat you differently and you will have repaired the past and prepared the future. This is prayer. Never do it with your family. Leave them out of spiritual ascendance. Their weight will hold you down. Our prayers too often center on them. Without involving them, you may one day come to them."

Silence.

"We must release the hierarchy. Truth is on a plane and requires forward steps, not upward leaps. The sky hasn't the answer. We walk and run and take steps every day, but have we ever taken one true forward step to true ego-less spirituality?"

Silence.

The guru walked away. The crowd lingered, quietly of course. I turned towards Walter, but he was gone. Then people went to the tables for a meal in silence. I looked for Walter, but there was no sign of him.

I saw a brochure at a table:

*"A reinterpretation of Gurdjieff though the lens of the ancient stoics, who believed that repression was a glorious, healing path, if the repression was sufficiently understood. This wordless, voiceless ascendancy, mixed with Gurdjieff's religious doctrines of Eastern meditation and calmness, would combat the angst, anxiety, materialism, and ennui of 20th century existence. There is no guru, no leader. We are all leaders and each week at a meeting one member speaks about his/her enlightenments gained during his/her quietude and reading Gurdjieff and P.D. Ouspensky. All money is through donation and strictly limited to maintain an outdoor place to meet and eat. We will never build anything beyond silence and chiseled words*

*spoken by only one each week, the temporary leader. Permanence is another false frame. We offer a book by Gurdjieff for free, which must be read in order to come to a second meeting. Thank you."*

I really wanted to talk to Walter and get some words to frame this whole strange thing, just as I wasn't supposed to. I wanted to have a beer, find out all his news, and wax nostalgic about bygone Roman days. I wanted to hear about the return to his family, which I'd assumed had happened, failed and led him to this ethereal path. Everything just said was against everything I have done in my life. I was obsessed with words and trying to frame my life though the voices around me. Using words to give meaning. Now, I've just heard that more words take one further away from God, from IT, from the intangible and invisible.

As I was thinking, I felt uplifted by a sudden idea, maybe even an epiphany. The *Living Novel* was simply my form of prayer, about which this man had just spoken. In my own way I was praying to friends by giving their thoughts a tangible place. It was prayer to my parents, whom I'd never met. It was a prayer to children I would never have. It was a prayer in my own mad form. My own religion.

As these reckonings multiplied, the deadness dissolved into a redirected darkness that hovered nearby, but far enough away to be controlled. One step ahead of melancholy.

"Jay, wake up!"

Daisy was shaking my shoulder. I opened my eyes. I wasn't sure if I had been daydreaming in a half-sleep or truly dreaming. It all seemed real. I think I thought I was awake. If I had been dreaming, so be it. The dream state might be more real than the waking state. Truth seeps in after midnight.

I got off the couch and went to the bathroom to check my nose and crow's feet. I felt like I had been in some form of sleep for years, like Rip van Winkle. So many events piled upon more events. We don't realize how famous we are in our own living movies.

I looked the same.

"Are you ready?" Daisy asked.

"I'm ready, honey."

"Ok. Who throws?"

"You, my dear."

Daisy stood about six feet from the map.

"It only counts if it lands east of the Rockies, like we agreed," I said.

"Agreed."

I gave Daisy a dart. She aimed at the map, then closed her eyes and threw it.

"You're not going to believe this, honey," I said, after looking at exactly where it landed.

"Home?" she said.

"Damn close. Point Pleasant, New Jersey."

"Time to go home, Jay. Time to go home,"

"Must be a message from the universe," I said.

Daisy gave me a long, lucid stare, slowly forming a wry smile. "Whoever it's from doesn't matter."

Moments later she was carefully packing her menagerie.

# THE SPECTACLE

## Stoker Caudwell

# PART I

Each year in school my classes slid more and more into the avant-garde. My political science classes were taught by unwaveringly ideological Marxists. Lit was European symbolist or American Beat and Art was Dada and Surrealism, but these were not that out there. Some of it might have even been palatable to members of the campus Young Republicans. But my Film class was the clear winner of the unconventional, as it ventured deep into the arcane and esoteric.

It was 1988. The Berlin Wall was still up and so was mine. Everything was escape. The trappings of the excessive left were an umbrella under which I hid.

I didn't want to feel the rain.

During the madness and folly of the higher-ed liberal arts loony bin, Lyra entered my life like a vernal thunderstorm. Her beauty wasn't quick and immediate to the impatient male eye. However, its depth was planted deeply within me. It grew strong and potent with eternal reckonings. She was my classmate in most of the same unraveling, reality-jolting courses. We were swept into the same mind bazaar like psychic lemmings, our hearts following like lost, but obedient sheep. I fell in love with her more and more with each passing, spiritually seductive class. Soon she was all I thought about.

All the time.

I began to make plans of communication. As befits obsession, I developed the a blue print with the precision and fastidiousness of an accomplished thief, who analyzes every possible variable before the mission. However, I was no great thief. I was the timid, bumbling wannabe crook who always backs out at the 11th hour.

That all changed near the end of senior year in that post-WWII Film course taught by a Greek neo-Beatnik, Nick Karcinogenas. Nick wore all the requisite ornaments of the downtrodden seeker. He was thin, had sagging, life's-too-heavy shoulders, complementing a slightly hunched-over posture that seemed to be the onset of kyphosis. He always dressed in black and his salt and pepper bushy hair was an anarchy of waves and curls. He lectured once a week at the Worcester Public Library in connection with the university, but appropriately placed off campus.

Quarantine the madness.

Professor Nick allowed his outcast brethren of the Worcester streets to attend class. They were mostly homeless, harmless local quacks forming an odd diametric cohort with the elitist college kids who sampled sadness and pain like new clothes. Of course, I was on the outside looking in at my superficial classmates. My life wouldn't be mapped out and monetary. It would be open, spontaneous, and surreal. I knew what I was doing by not knowing what I was doing.

Ahh, the glories of YoUtH.

Professor Nick fit right into my plan, or perhaps he fit me right into his plan. His agenda was to breathe life into the dead societies of subterranean, star-crossed cabals. Men and women of the mid-twentieth century European café underworld. Nick trumpeted those hallowed, footnote to history movements like a troubadour. There was the occasional modern art show or dusty, barely read tomes that outlined the transcendent manifestos of blind visionaries. "A secular divinity is what they and all of us seek, consciously or unconsciously," Nick would meekly bellow each week during his lecture that preceded a film allegedly about these movements. The connection between lecture and film was often invisible.

All the better, he probably thought.

I finally met Lyra while Professor Nick was quoting words of Dada offspring movements crawling the postwar weary streets of Europe. A doomed setting I left unconsidered. Lyra's glow had altered my vision and Nick provided the audio of sensory derangement, sowing my madness pure.

"Ahh, yes, they, these two, Dada and Surrealism, are quite known among those in the know, so to speak, but what of those under them, more powerful, more headfirst and reckless in thought, fragmented, ahhh, under their own loftiness of sky-pointed, tainted heaven goals? Yes, the Situationist and Letterist Internationals. They'd claim a week should be six days, rupture the calendar, start all anew, everything always new. Time was a wasted, disturbed concoction of restrictions. But time was only enemy number two. The great counterintuitive thief of the soul was art. Yes, art was the great lie disguised as truth. Art was a beast in sheep's skin. Art tried to transcend time and all our useless assertions of ordered evolution in the most tepid of ways, entrusting the hope of change and transcendence into a frame to be gazed at and forgotten. These two movements wanted to implode the hypocrisy of art, be it paint or word or film or whatever the insulated escalation of feeling might be. Hanging it on a wall to be seen or printed to be read was the lie of art, its consumption into moneyed, upper-crust manipulation."

Professor Nick paused, cleared his cigarette phlegmy throat, "Hmmmm, ahhhh, ahem." His eyes would roll upward as if he were trying to read lecture notes on his forehead, but his head didn't move so it appeared like he was still looking at us, but also not looking at us.

Then his eyes would slowly descend to a straight ahead gaze when he was ready to continue. "And so, art, not money was the real enemy, turning anti-bourgeois sentiment upside down. Art perverted and adulterated its truth into a tepid existence to be consumed by the bourgeois instead of letting it flow in its real, raw form: the impulse to create. The impulse was ripped off and, ahhhh, yes, stolen from the maker, us. The impulse to relive, change, evolve, devolve, turn the whole thing inside out, find the hidden, the elusive road to the true temple of wisdom."

A few in the audience raised their hands with perplexed expressions. Nick ignored them.

"Ahem, ahh, so the Situationists and Letterists International, led by Isidore Isou, Guy Debord, others were a whisper that tried to scream from the primal core only to end up hung up or covered or shown in a dark room to an audience. Concretely, they aimed at artists who sold their works. These were the true liars complacently selling their impulse to those in power rather than revolting against the power. Their complicity put them in the nest of the status quo when the urge of art should be to splinter the status quo. Art became grotesque burlesque belittlement of its true calling to change society. Picasso, Miro, Cassatt, Gorky, Gauguin, all of them frauds, so spoke Situationists and Letterists."

No more hands were raised. Some were antsy in their seats seemingly from frustration, others tuning out in capitulation or apathy. I don't think anyone understood what the hell Professor Nick was talking about, but I thought I did. I thought I got it.

"So these crazy cats produced anti-art art even more anti than Dada trying to concentrate and unify the impulse in its true state of purity. Their works were never sold and only attempted to spread the impulse. They fought and, of course, lost to the spectacle that overran this century into the Michael Jackson world of today. Ironically soon after these movements faded, we get Andy Warhol and Pop Art. If you can't beat the spectacle, join it, chicken soup and all."

Professor Nick took a long swig from a thermos that most assumed was not water though he never smelled of alcohol. He then pointed to the small windows above and behind us cueing this week's film, *The Society of the Spectacle.* As the grainy black and white film rolled into being, I focused more on what I could see of Lyra, who was in the front row. Then the lights dimmed and all I could see was her shadowy profile—shiny auburn hair casually falling to her shoulders and the sharp, perfect nose accentuating an angular face. I vowed to meet her tonight, to get to know her, to learn Lyra. Perhaps, Professor Nick's crazy artists inspired me to finally take a chance.

To follow my impulse.

We always rode the shuttle back to campus after class. It was here I often plotted ways to enter her world, but never acted, overwhelmed by her glow that had become so strong and deified in my seduced mind. We'd then get off the bus at the same stop, she'd go her way and I stood the fool. The meek will inherit the earth, but not Lyra.

Until tonight. Halfway to campus, I summoned the nerve, despite my parched mouth and heart turned into rib cage battering ram. I walked towards the empty seat beside her, stopped to take in some air and press my hand against my chest as if I could manually slow down the thumping mass of anxiety. It felt so loud that I thought she would hear it.

"Hi, ummm, do you mind if I sit here?" I asked.

Lyra smiled warmly, and without hesitation said, "Sure."

I sat down, slightly relieved, but not sure what to say next. All my great and elaborate plans, long conversations that I had even written down and rehearsed, instantly vanished. But Lyra bailed me out by initiating. "It's a little unsettling, isn't it?"

"Yes," I said, thinking she was referring to my obvious neurotic state.

"I mean we're here to critically think, right? That's higher education and if you think about these art movements, and don't dismiss them, their vision isn't necessarily less insane than the spectacle ahead of us."

"Huh?"

"Are you ok?"

"Yeah, I think so."

"You look a little surprised."

"I am."

"Why?" Lyra asked, smiling, but with a puzzled gaze.

"Well, ahh, to be honest, I've been trying to think of a way to talk to you and now that I actually am, I'm a bit overwhelmed," I said, surprised at my confessional transparency.

"What have you been waiting for? I'm just your classmate, silly."

"Courage."

Lyra giggled, maybe even blushed a bit, finally realizing my attraction. This had an instant calming effect on me, as if our seesaw that was so imbalanced had suddenly centered on its fulcrum. I was no longer on the ground looking up at her high in the ethereal air.

"That's cute," she said. "I'm flattered."

"Really?"

"Sure, who wouldn't be? But you know, I'm actually not that surprised if I may be immodest."

"Was I obvious?" I asked.

"Well, I caught you looking a few times in class."

"Just a few? Well, then I did pretty well all things considered."

"That into me? Really? Hard to truly fathom that."

"Yeah, it's just, I don't know. I really am. Guilty."

"Well, I doubt I will live up to the concoction you've created," she said rolling her eyes dramatically. "But I can sure try."

Then she put her hand out with a suddenly serious expression and we shock. "I'm Lyra and you are?"

"Stoker."

"Stoker, nice to meet you."

We laughed and the glow had become less barrier and more magnet.

Lyra told me that she'd thought of talking to me about all this mad subterranean stuff that Nick goes on and on about. There weren't many of us from school in class. In addition to the local homeless, there were some older adults taking this as an adult ed class and most of our few true classmates seemed checked out, just in it for easy credits. "But I did notice you seem to pay attention to the lectures."

"I do. I'm intrigued. This is my favorite class."

"Me, too," she said perkily. "But it is also depressing. I mean I kind of agree with their vision of the future. It's all so nihilistic and empty, but it makes sense."

"Agreed. One big spectacle ahead that I don't really subscribe to."

"Me neither," Lyra agreed. "It's really hitting a nerve. Tapping into some hidden level I didn't know about."

"Yeah, the question is what's the alternative?"

Lyra nodded. "Right, what to do next is the giant looming question. And grad school and a resume are not answers for me."

"All I really want to do is go."

"Where?" Lyra asked, a glimmer of intrigue in her eyes wide.

"Don't know. Doesn't really matter."

"Then, let's just go," she said in a tone lacking any sarcasm.

"Yeah, go until we can't go no more."

"There's always more go."

We both were silent for a bit, looking out the window as the shuttle headed down Main Street, passing by its littered sidewalks and homeless folks buried in dirty blankets or broken down cardboard boxes, just before it arrived at the university in its cleaned up, manicured campus bubble.

Lyra turned to me and broke the silence. "Stoker, I've always veered to the bleak, but that is now strangely energized from Professor Nick. I feel like I'm in a hurry to do everything, follow impulses honestly rather than those societally imposed."

I was nodding, excited at how in sync we were. "Solid ground now feels like quicksand."

"Right, exactly. And if we stand still we'll sink with the rest. So we just gotta go."

"It's almost an obligation if we want to be truly honest."

"Yes, yes, a thousand yeses," she said, smiling and staring deeply into my eyes. "I'm so glad you had courage today. We're gonna go headfirst into truth, my new friend." Then she leaned in and kissed me and we kept kissing until the shuttle driver yelled, "Last stop."

From then on we were inseparable. The times after Film class seemed to be our most intense. We helped each other process the doors of perception that Professor Nick altered, loosening the hinges enough for us to completely remove them. Our talks took on the full-blown bloom of escape, of what to do next, where to go and how to avoid the vacuum of the ominous spectacle secretly mocking ahead.

In my room one night after class, Lyra said, "Stoker, we have to define go. It needs some nuance. Not just philosophically speaking."

"That's the thing. They denounced money, religion, society, and then the last refuge, art. What's left?" I asked her.

"The impulse."

"Right, and love," I added.

Lyra nodded and kissed me. "I think once we step outside the spectacle we'll understand how to properly frame the impulse."

"But that's their whole thing. Not to frame it," I said, noting how she completely ignored the word love.

"We don't have to be them."

"No, and there are other impulses that we can explore."

Lyra smiled, nodding with mischievous eyes. "Naughty ones," she said, unbuttoning her cotton dress, letting it drop to her ankles. Most of our talks ended this way, which was another reason I looked forward to our nihilistic conversations. We made love every night we were together.

I stood up and finished undressing her and then lifted her smooth, petite body, putting her on my desk, sitting where one would write. I pushed all the books and papers onto the floor. She took off my shirt and I got out of my jeans. I turned her body so her legs hung off the side of the desk and then gently pushed her down, caressing her everywhere with my fingertips, lips, and tongue, engaging all the senses. I entered first with my tongue and got her closer and closer, holding her wrists with gentle force, before entering completely and as her head fell off the end of the desk in surrender to pleasure, I came like never before. Each time we made love it was different. Each time it followed a natural path with no awkward moments and no need for anything verbal. I had believed Lyra's glow was our spiritual connection. Literally, the result of our chemistry. We talked about it and she agreed. The talks and sex were beyond what I ever imagined possible. As our love climbed sexually and spiritually, filling every pore with fulfillment, Nick did his best every week to excavate all that had been assumed and consumed.

"So Isadore Isou proclaimed the non-existence of youth was a sickness. It was not an age, nor a billboard of the spectacle, but a feeling and it was being hog-tied like a hapless, helpless calf in a sad, robotic rodeo; chased, overwhelmed, roped and then cheered as an entity of the spectacle. As he said, *Let youth cease to become the consumer of its own élan.* This was all before it became a 60s cliché. Before it became a spectacle within the spectacle as the 60s had been. The great tease decade. Hmmm, now our élan, our vigor to be, is usurped. Just turn on MTV and watch energy unraveled, cremated and stored in cellophane. So they, Isou and his covert cavalry of midnight ideas, begged to start over, remove God from the language, God being semantic weight. New letters, then new words, then new language, new ideas, ahh, ahhem, new cities, then new systems, then, ahhh, the brave new world…new, all new, new, new, new. It was a chant, a plea for new, an eternal mantra imploring eternity. And the connection that Greil Marcus makes in the section of our book for today's class is this desire, this desperation leapfrogged from the café society to some down-and-out kids called the Sex Pistols who tried to disseminate their desperation and all the while being conned by a guy named Malcolm McLaren. Another usurper who sought to market the desperation and possess the élan for a buck. So tonight's film is *The Great Rock 'n' Roll Swindle*."

Lyra and I lay naked in bed. I was still inside her, our bodies were still interlocked. We had fallen briefly asleep immediately after. I gently pushed her off of me and sat up.

I was staring at her room and taking in the material extensions of her personality, waiting for her to wake up. We had been spending all our time together and we always went back to her room after Professor Nick's class and made love. His lectures and films continued to seep inside us. Some elites mocked the words, didn't listen, considered it way out there, illogical babble of a 60s burnout who'd had too many trips inside the kaleidoscope. We both knew it was certainly way out there, but that's what we liked about it. It was logically cosmic. Cosmological. We brought the right internal chemistry to absorb and brew external potions. The loneliness was deeply existential. The earth had become a trampoline. The future a trapdoor. Our physical love the only respite that gave some oxygen to all the nothingness laid before us.

We had spent so much time making love and talking about everything and trying to form senselessness into sense, that I had never really looked at her room in detail. She had several cameras beside her desk befitting her major. On the wall, she had about two dozen or so framed black and white photographs, most of which she had taken. Most of them were from Maine where Lyra was from. Several were beautiful landscapes, typical copies of Ansel Adams. There were several photos of people, seemingly candid shots, in the vein of Diane Arbus, but they were all cut-ups. That is, the photo was three, or sometimes four photos taken to produce one. The various shots were then placed next to each other as a triangle or square to connect the broken images. There was probably a term for this in the photography art world. Cut-ups seemed to work for me. I liked them. They represented the various selves in one self. However, three or four seemed insufficient for everyone's schizophrenia.

On her desk were several texts on photography. There were also several novels stacked up: three from Thomas Wolfe—*Look Homeward Angel*, *The Web and the Rock*, and a giant mother of all novels, *Of Time and the River*, along with novels by Djuna Barnes, Virginia Woolf, and Richard Farina.

There was also a family picture in the corner of her desk. I could see Lyra and what must have been her brother and sister, as well as her parents. It was an old picture. Lyra looked about ten or eleven. I smiled back at her giant, young girl's smile.

The current Lyra started rustling in bed and put her arm around me very tightly as she began waking up to my kisses.

"You know I feel emptied out inside," Lyra whispered.

"Me, too," I said, grinning.

"Not just sexually. I feel simultaneously empty and energized. This strange conflict inside, spiritually undone. How can I describe it? Like a novice on a sailboat, catching the wind sometimes and going and then messing up the rudder and direction and stalling. Going and stalling with no consistency."

"Let's not take Professor Nick too seriously. He's just a strange, retro cat trying to peel off some layers of our vision. Probably just the flipside of a Jim Bakker evangelist or one of the religious con men traveling around with constructed miracles done for the money."

"It's working. And I don't think he's a fraud. You don't either."

"No, I don't, but life is different now that we've met."

"Well, I'm ready to run out into the world and live and simultaneously crawl under a rock and hide. I can't control how I take it. It's taking me."

"I bet if we investigated these Euro Café guys, those Situationists and Letterists, they all came from tortured youths and rather than confront their own agony, they railed at society for distraction."

"Everything is distraction anyway. Besides, who cares about their youth? The path they took doesn't negate the philosophy formed. It doesn't undermine their construction," she said, somewhat perturbed.

"You mean destruction."

"Whatever," she said, now clearly annoyed.

"Let's not fall into the chasm. I don't know. I'm not too broken up about the whole damn spectacle mess as much now since it led to us. I'm crazy about you. That is my overwhelming sensation right now."

"Me, too," she said and rolled over.

I didn't fully believe her.


And on Professor Nick waxed in a new subterranean flight: "Ahh, ahem, so Europe is always decades ahead of us in most things, good or bad. These sub-underground shadow movements crept anonymously, save for some minor, back-page skirmishes trying to throw upheaval at the spectacle and its unwitting followers, such as the assault on Notre Dame. However, the whispers flew across the Atlantic, or across the collective fringe unconscious. Their thoughts were seized because nothing dies, nothing is for not, every thought drifts tangibly despite its invisibility. Nihilism is a lie. The American Beats turned glorified nihilism and existentialism into beatitude. Of course, they were maligned, misinterpreted, consumed and ridiculed by the spectacle, or Moloch, as Ginsberg would *howl* it. They, ahh, ahem, cast stones and yelped at the iniquities and absurdities of post-war conformism, but were also suffused with our uniquely American positive naiveté. Our land, unadulterated with so few wars and so little history of insouciant disruption and distortion, is a tender kitten to Europe's tired, old lion. Kerouac and his fellaheen kinfolk were beatific to Europe's beaten. So this hopeless, destructive, existential, anti-material force crossed the Atlantic and turned optimistic, dreamy, alive, zealous, exuberant existentialism—childlike in hope—innocent enough to merge atheism, Catholicism, and Buddhism. Yes, Kerouac of our nearby Lowell looked at ravaged, drugged and drunk pariahs of modernity and saw divinity and hidden angels swelling with interred spiritualism unable to sidestep the spectacle thereby imploding into mad internal passages and external chaos. They weren't as political as the Situationists and believed in the purity and transcendence of art, so in many ways they were reactionary to Debord. They sought their own Elysian Fields through friendship, sex, love, words, jazz, and most importantly, creativity. To be alive from 1945 to 1950 was a spiritual high when youth could taste experience before film, TV, and pop culture consumed it all into a silly thirty-minute spectacle of disenchanted youth starring Gilligan as the pseudo-Beat, Dobie Gillis."

Nick paused, rubbing his hands together, coughing up years of smoke, and rolling those eyes back into his head with the whites on us.

"Tonight we are going to see the film *Heartbeat*, which was based on Carolyn Cassady's unpublished *Off the Road*. It's a rare woman's perspective of a largely male club. But first let's listen to Kerouac's saxophone soul riffing from *October in the Railroad Earth*. Nick pressed play on an old reel tape recorder. The machine hissed and scratched its way into voice:

> There was little alley in S.F. back of the Southern Pacific Station at third and Townsend in redbrick of drowsy lazy afternoons with everybody at work in their offices in the air you feel the impending rush of their commuter frenzy…truck drivers and even the poor grime-bemarked third street of lost bums even negroes so hopeless and long left East and meanings of responsibility and try that now all they do is stand there spitting in the broken glass sometimes 50 in one afternoon against one wall at 3rd and howard and here's all these Millbrae and San Carlos neat-necktied producers and commuters of American and steel civilization rushing by with SF chronicles and green call bulletins not even enough time to be disdainful, they've got to catch 130, 132, 134, 136 all the way up to 146 till the time of evening supper in homes of the railroad earth when high in the sky the magic stars ride above the following hotshot freight trains – It's all in California, it's all a sea, I swim out of it in afternoons of sun hot meditation in my jeans with head on

handkerchief on brakeman's lantern or on books, I look up at blue sky of perfect lost purity and feel the warp of woop of old america beneath me and have insane conversations with negroes in several story windows above and everything is pouring in, the switching moves of boxcars in that little alley which is so much like the alleys of lowell and hear far off in the sense of coming night that engine calling our mountains. Harrumph!

The scratch and churn of the tape continued while Professor Nick sat on his stool trancelike. Finally, he slowly stood up.

"One shouldn't just hear those words. One should absorb and digest them. Osmotically listen. One should let each word flow into the bloodstream. Poetry should not be heard, but felt. Kerouac was trying to verbalize the instinct that the Situationists and Letterists wanted to capture into daily existence. Kerouac may have considered it possible, but only on a lonely, individual level of salvation."

Professor Nick pointed upstairs to the overhanging projection room where the same, unknown young man ran the projector. He was only seen at the end of class when he and Nick left together. The lights went out and the film began.

Lyra and I continued our odyssey through Professor Nick's orbit. The lectures that disjointed alleged actualities, creating new vacancies once reserved for status quo simplicity. The films darkening the regular and blessing the periphery. In between, we made passionate love and had long, soulful talks about life after graduation.

Spring was coming, it was the middle of March and the end of our four-year term was fast approaching. Parties were more and more prevalent with weekends starting on Wednesdays, but Lyra and I had lost our friends. It was just us and we didn't care. Other relationships seem pretend when a real one is found.

We spent many nights in the Astronomy Lab where Lyra had her work-study job. We'd stay long after closing with the lights out so the campus police wouldn't know. Under an observatory sky-light, inky night and brilliant white stars above, we'd make love, talk, make love again until the inevitable philosophy-in-action crescendo arrived. The unavoidable ignition inherent in the amalgam of Professor Nick, us, and youth long smoldering, finally caught a flame of direction.

It was often after sex, when my thoughts were momentarily cloaked in peace, that Lyra began deep, troubled conversations trying to confront the void, which had become less maddening and worrisome to me since the void brought Lyra and me together. The spectacle had lost its edge. Existential nothingness brought me everything.

Before meeting her, I had confronted nothingness with a kind of art therapy (apologies to the Situationists). I usually wrote every morning with a cup of coffee by my side. It was spontaneous writing about anything that came to mind, an odd, seemingly incoherent blend of fiction and journaling. The Beat school of first thought, best thought. I rarely had blocks or moments of hesitation. There was plenty of childhood that needed expulsion. Families are the great and urgent muse.

In the couple months with Lyra, I rarely wrote. She encouraged me to keep at it after reading some of my spontaneous scribbles, which I had never shown anyone. She wanted to collect and edit them.

With Lyra, with this all-consuming attraction, who needed art.

Despite the aspersions by Guy Debord and his anti-art apostles, art was everything for Lyra. Photography was her main medium, but she also painted and sculpted. She said many times, "When you kill God and embrace existentialism, what's left? Just art."

"And love," I would say.

"My romantic hero," she would say, kissing me and laughing.

In the observatory one night we had the conversation that had been fermenting for months. We were lying supine on the floor, staring up at the night sky, when the linguistic games began.

"Let's go," Lyra nearly shouted. "Just like you said on the shuttle when we first met."

"Where?" I asked.

"Just go."

"Go?"

"Yeah, go," she persisted.

"Where's our go?"

"Anywhere we want it to be, but not here. Here there is no go. Here is a contradiction of go," she said, half-smiling.

"What the hell is so good about go, anyway? Maybe it's overrated. Maybe we should stop. Stop doesn't seem so bad now."

Lyra sighed, "Ugh, you don't have the urge any-more? Are you getting boring on me?" she asked, the disappointment clear in her tone. "Ready for the suburbs already, old young man?"

"Of course not, but the urge and edge have softened a little, but I don't know. I'm probably amenable."

"Don't get soft on me, Stoker. I want more," Lyra said, turning to her side and facing me. She pulled my shoulder so I rolled over and we were face to face, inches apart.

"Hasn't motion been our evolution since the shuttle anyway? We met while going somewhere, while in motion."

"Yes, but just from one end of town to the other."

"Well, let's go from one end of the country to the other. Maybe further."

"This summer? Get the diploma and run west. Cross-country Kerouac descendants? Sure, I'm game for that. Would love it."

Lyra nodded, but there a was devilish squint in her gaze. "Let's go see the country and then the world. It's that simple. We'll slip out sly and unbeknownst in the dead of night alive." Lyra said, eyes now wide. "And before graduation."

"Maybe you've had too much Nick for your own good. Why before? That's ridiculous and unnecessary."

"Maybe so, but all the better. We'll make it original, not Kerouac clichés. It won't be some romp for a few months getting drunk in many cities and passing out in cheap motels like juvenile boys until we get home to mommy and daddy to start the real world of resumes and cover letters. No, I've got a real and true transcendent plan sans platitudes."

"Why don't we just wait until graduation?"

"That's just the cliché we should avoid. It's dishonest and unpoetic. Let's led instincts lead. Let poetry lead."

"So you're a Situationist now?"

"Somewhat. Better than materialists. Poetry in life, at least for a while. Think of all the robotic gray hovering above and ahead of us."

I nodded. "It is romantic. Yes, indeed. Being on the road with you sounds like paradise, but are we truly just gonna go? No other plan?"

"Photography and words. The camera's a truth gun and your words will dress the truth. Here's a chance to experiment. We'll make a novel of words and photos. We'll live it and then create it. We'll get inside ourselves through art and travel and love before it's too late."

"A truth gun, huh?"

She nodded and smiled.

"When?"

"Tomorrow."

I gave her a kiss and we laughed and rolled around as one on the floor.

Lyra gave some specifics to her plan. Lately, she'd become obsessed with railroads from reading a lot of Thomas Wolfe. She read *Look Homeward Angel* for a class and now she was hooked by his amazing passages about the railroad in America. That would be the theme of her photography across the States and the world. We would travel by train as much as possible and she would photograph the trains and stations all along the way and I'd be putting down the words of our journey to complement the photos. At the end we would put it all together into a book.

Meaningful nihilism.

I loved the plan except for one part—leaving tomorrow with the diploma weeks away.

Lyra explained, "It'll give momentum to our muses. Dawn tomorrow, Stoker."

"This is crazy."

"You haven't even heard the crazy part."

I fell back onto the bed, arms extended crucifix style, laughing maniacally, but truthfully I was happy. My protest were meek just out of some innate perfunctory need. I was so gone with Lyra that she could have asked me to do anything and I would have done it. She got on top of me, sitting on my stomach, and kissed me all over. Then she took her top and bra off, grabbed both my wrists and tied them together with her bra. "Let's play a little rough tonight with me in control."

"What about money?" I asked as we packed. It was 3am and we had finished gathering her stuff. Whatever we didn't take, we put in a big garbage bag and would drop it off at the Salvation Army. No possessions but what we could carry. Divest for progress. We were bohemian soldiers seeking visions, not possessions.

"I've got a few thousand saved and a credit card. I don't care what you have. We'll put it together and it'll get us to California. We can max the card out and screw our credit. It's not like we'll be applying for mortgages or anything. Besides, we'll be overseas by the time collection agencies come around."

We would head to Thailand where her sister taught English. We could get certified there as TESOL instructors or we could do it before we leave. The plan was to trot the globe teaching, all the while building our words and photos along railroads everywhere. "There is no end in this journey, just next," Lyra said.

"I only have $300 to my name."

"That's fine," Lyra said, unconcerned.

I took deep a breath. "This is all so crazy, but I'm so up for it. Regret action rather than inaction, right?"

"Our motto."

"Lyra, I love you."

"I love you, too," she said, and jumped into my arms.

There was a three quarter moon and the New England night was clear and cold under low, spring stars. We were in Lyra's '78 Plymouth Reliant K car, which she had inherited from her grandmother. I was driving, watching the university fade in the rear view mirror.

"I think this may be the most boring car ever made," I said.

"Even the names are abysmally dull. K car and Reliant," Lyra agreed.

"Very communist. We're talking practical. Perfect for us. Dropping out of school moments before the diploma is in our hands."

"I know you're a little hung up about that."

"I'm ok. I'll get over it."

"We're getting out all the angst and replacing it with truth in our glorious youth."

"Very half full of you. Anyway, I like the sound of that. Write it down."

We had a notebook in the car handy for thoughts and ideas on the move. Lyra wrote it down.

"There it is. Entry number one," she said, joyfully.

"A big moment."

Lyra lapsed into talking about the spectacle, Situationists, *Nickspeak*. I tuned out the words, stealing looks at her while driving. I followed the sharp angles of her face, perfect skin with just a hint of pink, and the natural waves of her auburn hair. She was a beautiful adventure, but I also wanted more than just adventure. I was drunk with eternity.

I picked up what she was saying midstream, "…a million schools around the world. Everybody wants to learn our language and we automatically qualify by virtue of our native tongue and diploma. Piece of cake."

"What diploma?"

"The one on our resume that no one checks," she said casually. Lyra's free spirited ways were much further down the liberated road than mine. "Anyway, we're a long way from Thailand and our international chapters. First chapter Boston."

"What's there?"

"There's this overpass above railroad tracks near Fenway Park. I think the tracks are out of commission, all rusted iron and rotting ties. We'll begin with decay, death as we burst into life and freedom on the move."

"Look homeward angel, or rather, look wayward angel for us."

Lyra nodded excitedly, loving the reference to her favorite author. "And we should be there at sunrise so we capture both beginning and end."

"You got it all figured out, metaphors and all. How long have you been planning this?"

"I've had this picture in my mind for so long. Every time I drive back to school after a break I pass by it on the Mass Pike. We can take a walk along the tracks and you can put your words down while I take the photos. Simultaneously fused creativity," Lyra exclaimed, slapping my thigh. "So excited to be free!"

"Yes, yes, but what I meant was how long have you been planning this great escape?"

Lyra shrugged. "Seems like forever, but high gear since we met."

I didn't probe further.

The plan was to leave the car at her sister's in Richmond and then it was Amtrak the rest of the way to San Francisco. On the way she wanted to make one stop in White Sulphur Springs, a little town tucked away in the Alleghany Mountains on the West Virginia and Virginia border

"It's not far from my sister's."

"What's there?"

"Alex Clarkson," she said and looked over at me for a pregnant pause as if to check my reaction before retuning her vision to the road. "At least last I heard he lives there."

"Really?" I often wondered what had happened to him. We hung out a bit. He was a year or two ahead of us. I thought he was in grad school, but then he was in some of my undergrad courses. It was always a bit mysterious how he fit into the scheme of things, but his bohemian ways seemed honest, not on the pose. He loved booze, all kinds of drugs, Jimmy Cliff and Karl Marx. We were in a couple of political economy classes together. I remembered he gave this perversely lucid and wildly ambitious presentation on how to restructure the world economy in a neo-Marxist, Rastafarian way. I even remembered his closing line, "Everything equitable and everyone high."

"What's he up to?" I asked.

"Someone told me he was writing a book, or ahh, maybe he was getting his PhD. Pretty sure he's on a farm and living off the land."

"Back-to-lander, huh? Not surprised. That fits his fellaheen mission."

"For me, it'll make for some interesting photos."

"Breaking the train motif?"

Lyra shrugged. "I don't want be tied down."

We made it to Boston. Lyra went off with her camera and I found a quiet spot along the tracks. I took out my black and white speckled notebook and began the spontaneous, Beat-style flow at this moment in this place. It wasn't hard. There was so much going on and I never had trouble externalizing internal visions onto the page. Time stopped and ego diluted in the process of painting daydreams into words.

A Beat marriage of Buddhism and Surrealism.

The process usually lasted half an hour for me. Lyra was done first, but she didn't disturb me. When I finished, I recorded the date and place of the expression. We had decided not to read the words or develop the photos until leaving America. We would never look back at the creativity of one country until we were in another. I rarely read my writing anyway other than looking at the mounting pile of notebooks and feeling an accomplishment of quantity.

Lyra decided we should ditch the car now and jump on the train in Boston. We found a used car dealership and got $600 on the spot. Lyra signed over the title and in minutes we shed the metal. We were in the throes of rapid divestment, materially and every which way. We bought open one-way tickets to California with the car money. We could get off at any stop along the way and get back on for no charge. Sure enough, White Sulphur

Springs was one of the stops. I wondered if Lyra had already known that.

"Right now I couldn't imagine us apart, ever," Lyra said as we settled into our seats, holding hands.

"Just now?"

"I want to think and feel in the moment. Let's not get ahead of ourselves. That's where things go astray."

For the first time since we met I felt some distance between us. I think it had to do with Clarkson. It just seemed odd that we were going to see him out of the blue. And we were away from the sheltering sanctuary of the campus for the first time. It must be that, I told myself. I tried to shift my mind, let it be more open, more Lyra. We were free, alive with experiences, creating memories. She was right. The moment is everything now. Let go of the control that crept along whispering insecurities. I closed my eyes and breathed deeply into my chest, trying to let my mind go blank, go free like it did in the process of writing.

Lyra interrupted my introspection with a gentle kiss on my temple. "Let's make love right now."

"Here?"

"No, silly, in a bathroom."

After we got dressed, we smoked and drank beers in the dining car. We looked out the window at New England fields on the cusp of spring. Lyra took pictures at different shutter speeds and varying aperture settings consciously aiming for the surreal, though that was contradictory to Surrealist principles. The empty fields suddenly became a cemetery and Lyra took pictures of austere, New England graves made of mostly flat grey stones.

"I love cemeteries," Lyra said. "They make me feel peaceful."

She then quickly returned to the world of her lens.

By lunch we had sped briefly across Connecticut and into New York State nearing the great city. She spoke about different photo techniques like overlaying surreal photos into one teasing semi-abstract image and triangular and quadrangular cut-ups like the ones on her dorm wall. She went on about the merging of her photos and my words into a book and how beautiful and pure it would be. Lyra wanted all her photos to be used regardless of their quality. I told her that was silly and logistically impossible. There'd be too many photos. I suggested she go with the Beat first-thought, best-thought ethos, or in this case, first photo, best photo for every image rather than repeated shots pursuing perfection.

Lyra fell asleep with her head resting on my shoulder and her body curled up in fetal position while I watched NYC get closer and closer. She didn't wake up until we gently screeched to a stop in Grand Central Station.

We walked along the tracks there until Lyra found a spot that encompassed views of Manhattan in the background. Lyra said she felt that she was discovering her eye with each shot and no class could ever do what travel was doing now. The thrill came from the fact that we were living the story and had no idea what the next chapter would bring. We walked to the base of the Brooklyn Bridge. Lyra decided to add bridges to the themes.

"Just fits," she said.

We had dinner at an Italian restaurant in Little Italy. We drank a liter of cheap house red wine and ate a simple spaghetti dinner, lots of bread, and salad. We decided to find a hotel to get some real rest before boarding the train again. We checked into a squalid hotel in Chinatown. Under dirty sheets on a lumpy bed in a room of cracked wallpaper and cockroaches scurrying below, we slept deeply.

When I woke up, I saw Lyra wrapped in a white hotel towel. Her wet hair dripped water slowly down her shoulders into rivulets descending between her breasts that rose firmly above the tightly wrapped towel.

"Waking up to a dream," I said.

Lyra approached me and started undoing the towel as I sat up. "Leave the towel on," I told her.

I ran my tongue above the towel, licking the water off her clean skin. She lifted my head and caressed my lips inside and out with her fingers. Then she pushed me down on my back, took off my shorts and mounted me.

She slowly unwrapped the towel and then wound it into rope form, tying my wrists tightly with it. She rode on top of me for a while, drawing me close several times, but pulling away, until she finally took me inside and I quickly came right before her. We fell back to sleep together, still exhausted from all forms of escape.

"Wake up," Lyra said, nudging me out of a deep sleep.

"Will you leave soon?" she asked.

"Huh?"

"Will you leave?"

"Will I leave what?" I mumbled barely conscious.

"No, will you leave me?"

"Why would you ask something so ridiculous?"

"Just answer it."

"No. Hundred percent no," I said sitting up and looking Lyra in the eyes. "Hell, I'm in love with you, Lyra."

"I love you, too," she said, a big smile emerging and fading promptly at its peak. "But it can change so rapidly. You can fall out as fast as you fell in."

"Who says?"

"All of human history."

"Well, to hell with everyone and history."

Lyra sighed. "Ahh, what the hell do we know about love anyway?"

"We're in it. What else is there to know? Just be in it," I said, realizing we were oddly role reversing.

"My turn to be a little tense. Just worried about something coming between us, something stopping our trip and our adventure together."

Later on the train as we passed through Baltimore, Johns Hopkins's campus in view, I returned to my norm, being on the verge of panic, unable to let go of quotidian matters.

"It's your life," she said adamantly after hearing my neurotic venting.

"Yes and no. I don't know if I've got the balls to live in a vacuum."

"We're twenty-two. I don't think we've got to worry about our parents. From what you say, yours are a lot like mine. They're a lot more fucked than we are, stuck in some static doldrums. We've got change, motion, newness. Plenty of time for the slow grind down the road."

"I don't know. What if we run out of money? I don't want to call them begging for help. Hell, they don't even know what's going on. They think I'm in class. What about fucking graduation? Jesus Christ, I haven't thought this through."

"Calm down, Stoker. Let's just pretend they don't exist for a while. Cruel, but healthy. We need true separation to find out exactly who we are. To face our freedom head on."

I was shaking my head. It was hard to argue the mundane with existential philosophy.

"And," Lyra reminded me, "stop being hung up about money. I've got plenty. I mean we. My money is yours. I have no connection to it. Hell, we got enough that we could even stay in Marriott's. Proper bourgeois Beatniks. Or get a sleeper compartment on the train."

And with that Lyra disappeared for an hour while I hung out with my anxiety. When she returned, she grabbed my hand and led me to a sleeper compartment that she'd just purchased.

While lying in our bunk beds, me up top, and her below, both of us reading and drinking red wine, Lyra detoured the relaxation. She climbed up onto my bed, took my book, *Confederacy of Dunces*, and tossed it aside. Then she pulled my shorts down and got me off orally.

After I wanted to do the same to her, but she stopped me.

"No, sweetie, just you tonight. Sleep well."

That I did. A deep, peaceful sleep, anxieties at bay, but resting for another day.

That morning we had a proper breakfast in the dining car, drank lots of coffee, and smiled and kissed each other all the way to West Virginia, deboarding at White Sulphur Springs.

A classmate had given her an address and after asking a few folks along the way, we made our way to Clarkson's.

"You okay today?" Lyra asked as we walked down a country dirt road. All that was missing was a John Denver song.

"I'm good. Relaxed."

Lyra laughed. "Blow job therapy," she said shoving my shoulder. "Men are so simple."

We came to the address and headed up a gravel driveway with an old Dodge pick-up truck parked at an angle.

"I don't see a front door," Lyra said.

"Let's go around back."

We approached a window on the side of the large old farmhouse.

"I hear some voices. One sounds like Alex's, I think," Lyra said quietly as if we were trespassers on the sly.

We bent down and crawled under the window to eavesdrop.

"It's time. I've had it," said the male voice. "Let's just end this bloody thing once and for all. Never wanted it in the first place."

"You're right, I know, but sometimes, it feels so good to escape into it, but moderation hasn't worked. You were right," said the female voice.

"We'll never get to where we imagine to be unless we kill it."

"What the hell's going on?" I whispered to Lyra, eyes wide and palms up.

"I'm pretty sure it's Alex."

"What the hell is *it*?" I mouthed.

"I don't know."

We refocused on the voices.

"We've got to do something," the male said.

"So let the sacrifice begin.'

"Once it's dead, more is possible."

They were giggling now.

Lyra looked at me and mouthed, "What the fuck?"

"Ready?" the male asked.

"Do it," the female said.

We heard a click and cock like that of a shotgun and then the same sound again.

I looked at Lyra and she motioned upward to stand up and stop whatever the hell was about to happen. My heart was racing.

"Stop!" I screamed leaping up into visibility.

I saw Alex and a woman, both armed with shotguns. They turned to me, surprise in their eyes, guns aimed and ready as if they were a firing squad and I the receiver. "Fuck," I yelled, and collapsed to the ground like an elevator having snapped free of its steel wires.

"Stoker?! What the hell," Clarkson said.

"Alex?" Lyra said, starting to stand up, but I grabbed her shoulder and held her down.

"Let's get out of here," I whispered.

"Who's that? Who else is there?" Clarkson asked.

"It's me, Lyra," she said, swatting my hand away and standing up. "What the fuck are you doing?"

Clarkson laughed. "Gonna kill this."

Lyra laughed, too, pulling me up. Clarkson was pointing to a TV that was going to be on the receiving end of bullets from him and the woman standing next to him.

"What gives?" I asked.

"*Televisionicide.* Denise here and I were ready to free ourselves of the box and we got a little dramatic. Just some theatrical fun. Sorry to scare you, but you should've knocked. You know, use the door like most humans."

"Why don't you just donate the TV?" I asked.

"That wouldn't be so ceremonial. Hell, look what the ceremony brought us. Old friends. I never believed

Native Americans could summon rain or what have you with dance and ceremony, but who knows now. I'm less skeptical now."

Denise looked at Clarkson and said. "Maybe you're a shaman, sweetheart."

Clarkson laughed. "Sure, maybe something like that. So come on in you two. Let us give you a proper welcome rather than a terrifying one. The door is around the corner to the right," he said pointing that way. We turned that way, but he shouted, "Wait. Stop!" Clarkson aimed his gun at the TV and fired a shot shattering the screen. Denise followed with another shot.

"Mission accomplished," he said.

We were sitting at a big oak table that had a handmade rather than mass-produced look. The table was in the middle of a giant room that appeared to be the entire house. It looked like a converted barn. There was a loft in one corner that was probably the bedroom because the big main room just had a simple kitchen, the oak table, and a study area with a couch, desk and lots of books piled high horizontally, spines out on the floor. I recognized some of Professor Moss' course books.

We were drinking some white wine and eating hearty turkey sandwiches that Denise had prepared.

"So let me get this straight. You guys quit school on a moonlit whim moments before graduation? Just zoomed out all spontaneously," Clarkson asked after Lyra told the short version of our story.

"Not quite moments," I said.

"More or less," Lyra countered.

"Do you have regrets, Stoker?" Clarkson asked.

"No, no, just clarifying some facts."

"Well, facts unpoetically get in the way of romance and this is certainly more romantic than factual," Clarkson said, behind a wry smile.

Lyra nodded enthusiastically. "Stoker's not quite there yet, but he's en route."

"Facts and facts and facts and more facts. What a boring stack they are," Denise said in a sing-songy way.

"Well, well, the whole escapade is a courageous leap into the unknown. A healthy snub at the groomed, easy life. Unless, of course, it's a little detour prior to getting the dreaded nest egg started." Clarkson said, much to Denise's laughter. Denise was a tall woman, not heavy, but big boned. She had long straight brown hair that went down to the belt line of her bell-bottomed jeans. She reminded me of Mountain Girl, one of the Merry Pranksters riding the "Further" bus and later Jerry Garcia's wife.

"It's no detour." I said. "We're in it for the long haul, Alex."

"I salute you. I'll tell you this, no eternal reward will forgive us now for wasting the dawn, and you've gone headfirst into the dawn without life jackets. Great secular miracles. Anyone trying to un-numb their senses into future truth can stay with me and Denise as long as they want, right sweetheart?"

"We love the dawn," she said.

"Lot of truth in the sunrise," Clarkson said.

There was some silence while he ate and drank. Lyra and I exchanged glances. Her look was inscrutable, one I had never seen before.

"Lyra, why are you so quiet?" Clarkson asked, looking at her with a bemused gaze.

"Ahh, I don't know, bit of a headache. Coming down from our escape. It's been a lot of adrenalin."

"Well, don't come down too much. How can I, we bring you up?"

"Yes, anything Lyra, you name it," Denise said, putting her arm around Clarkson.

Before Lyra could answer, I jumped in. "So how about you? What is all this? Your own farm? A back-to-land thing?"

"Plenty of time for that, but I'd rather find out what's bothering Lyra."

"I just need a couple of aspirin and to lie down. I'll be fine in no time."

"Here," Denise said producing two aspirin from her burlap satchel hanging at her side. "We have an extra bedroom with a big bed. You'll sleep like a baby." She stood up and waved Lyra her way. I could see that the loft was partially bisected by a thin wall that didn't go all the way floor to ceiling.

Lyra gave me a kiss, swallowed the aspirin with a final gulp of wine, and followed Denise upstairs, hand in hand.

"So, tell me, what are you up to?" I asked Clarkson again.

"Farming, my old friend. We are a sustainable farm. This turkey was ours. Killed it a few days ago, fresh and free of government chemicals. Real organic, not just in label. There's nothing better than sinking your fingers into mother earth and nourishing yourself from your own efforts."

I looked behind me out the window to a view of extensive land with farm animals grazing.

"It's all ours," Clarkson continued. "We grow or kill everything we eat. And we don't kill much, eat meat once every week or two. Maybe more in the winter. Keeps you warm. And we have a lot of mushrooms, including the psilocybin kind, which we can sample later if you're into it, which I remember you were. We had a couple fine trips together."

"Indeed we did. I'm impressed. What about the winter?"

"We freeze, bottle and preserve for that. Rice and pasta and things of that sort we go to an organic store in town. It boils down to removing all that is affiliated with exterior sources and living within our own creations and needs. It's not permanent, I don't think, but it is a cathartic detour. Let's call it an experiment, an homage to the 19th century Transcendentalists, Alcott and the other utopian New England movements. The difference is we now know that utopia is a myth, temporary, like a mushroom trip."

"And getting a PhD, too, I hear?"

"I was, but dropped out to actually do something. I'm writing about all of this, weaving together utopian movements, 60s counter culture. Kind of my own personal dissertation."

"Professor Moss would be proud."

"He is. We're still in touch. He's coming down at some point. Might even spend his sabbatical here."

Professor Moss was the resident Marxist professor at our university and it was in his class that I met Clarkson.

"How long are you guys staying? There's so much more to talk about, so much more to do."

"Just a night, I think. We're into movement now." I told him about our artistic project. He was curious, but after I explained it, I wished I hadn't. I felt like I was just doing it to prove Lyra and me. It felt inauthentic and insecure.

Clarkson poured some more wine and our conversation eventually veered back into his macro interests. He was convinced that the nation-system was nearing the end of its phase in history. He envisioned the death of country, patriotism, nationalism, a new world free of borders and passports, as we evolved into a world government that would eventually fail on its way to a return to local communities. He jumped back and forth in time tracing it as far back as Greek city-states and quickly through the age of Empires and the emptiness of religion, up through the French Revolution, the Paris Commune, Taiwanese capitalism at the shores of colossal Chinese communism, the socialized, watered-down capitalism of Europe and into the un-watered-down, almost pure capitalism of Reagan, which put us on the brink of revolution that was only prevented by baby boomer fatigue and greed. He believed the Soviets would fall first, and in the hubris of victory, the West would be next.

He went further, but I tuned out. I was bored. I just wanted to be on a train with Lyra. Our creativity was much more appealing than Clarkson's grandiose theories on the forces of history.

"Sorry, am I getting too heavy? I tend to get carried away."

"It's fine," I lied, downing the rest of my wine. Clarkson refilled it.

"So, aside from world revolution, how do you stay totally self-sufficient on this land? What do you do for money?"

"Whatever we don't need to eat, we sell the excess at a farmer's market over in Morgantown."

"Must be a lot of work."

He shrugged dismissively. After some silence, Clarkson casually asked, "So are you two really in love?"

"Yeah," I said quickly.

"Absolutely?"

"Are you two in love?" I asked him.

"Denise and I?"

"Yeah. Are there others?"

"Not now, but you never know. Ahhh, no, I'm not, but love is very cagey, tough to pinpoint your definition. Anyway, Denise and I aren't too bogged down with monogamy."

Just then there was a knock on the door. I could also hear some mumbling from outside.

Clarkson said, "That's my Marxist friend. You'll get a kick out of him. He's in a different stage. Or, perhaps, on a different stage."

Clarkson let him in. He was short with curly, greasy brown hair receding and thinning. His cheeks were ruby red with the color forming an almost perfect circle on each cheek. He didn't so much walk as stumbled ahead.

"Surplus profit, surplus profit," he wailed. "I tell you I'm going to solve that riddle and then the gates of egalitarianism will swing open so hard it'll knock ten CEOs over like duckpins. Surplus profit will be the big ball down the capitalist alley and those two percenters will be struck down in one glorious strike! Yes, Alex, it's like I always say there are many ways to skin a cat. Ole Uncle Karl'll truly rest in peace once the surplus profit dilemma is finally taken off his tired shoulders. He's tired, he's—"

"Maple, we've got a guest," Clarkson said, interrupting the soliloquy.

Maple seemed to come into focus, registering where he was. "Oh, my manners are gone when I'm thinking out loud. Excuse me, I'm Marcus Edburg, but everyone calls me Maple. Before you ask, that's because I use maple syrup like others use ketchup. Yup, on French fries, on burgers, you name it. I just want to clear that up right away. Yes, my father used to badger me on that for so long. He hated maple syrup and he'd hide it on me. Oh, just the first of a lifetime of things we didn't see eye to eye on, but you can skin a cat many ways. "

"Nice to meet you," I said. I'm not sure I meant it though.

"That's Stoker Caudwell, an old friend of mine from school. He's here with his lover, passing through," Clarkson said.

"Hmmm, passing through, oh, why don't you stick around, join the group?"

"Well, we're traveling. Thanks, though."

"Surplus profit dilemma needs heads. What do you think of the problem?"

"I wouldn't know where to begin. It does ring a bell from Moss' classes," I said turning to Clarkson.

"Surplus profit!" Maple shouted. "Surplus profit is the damn reason Uncle Karl's ghost is trouble. It's why Stalin put an ice pick through Trotsky's skull. It's why Vladimir Ilich's dream failed. It's why Chairman Mao slaughtered his own. It's why Marxism is a mockery in the West. Had the Paris Commune just been given more time to elasticize, stretch into its own being, had, ahhh, oh, skinned the cat another way, things would have, ahhh, never mind. Always a work in progress, let the compass find the right magnetic field. You should have seen those redneck bastards today. They spit on me. Can you believe that!?" Maple's face turned completely red and distended with the sudden blast of anger.

Clarkson patted Maple on the back. "Never mind them, Maple. Fight the good fight."

Maple instantly calmed down as if Clarkson had a guru touch.

"Why don't we have dessert?" Clarkson suggested.

Maple let out a giant sigh, then inhaled deeply and exhaled even louder. He was almost panting like a tired, old dog taking refuge in the shade on a hot, summer day.

Clarkson went into the kitchen area and started preparing something. Denise descended from the loft and helped him.

"So, Mr. Stoker, did I tell you the damn kids spat on me?" Maple began again.

"You mentioned it."

"I'm handing out flyers for a meeting and these kids start calling me pinko and commie and heckling me. I felt like I was back teaching high school in New York when the kids were animals back in the 70s. They threatened to kill me. So this one hippie hater comes real close and just spits in my face. Why? Can you tell me WHY?" Blood poured into Maple's face. Clarkson's touch did not last long.

"You disturb the equilibrium," Clarkson said from the kitchen.

"Listen, Mr. Stoker, if you get any ideas on the surplus profit dilemma, share them."

"You bet. Excuse me for a moment," I said, heading up the loft to check on Lyra and escape Maple.

Lyra was sleeping soundly covered by a thick, soft quilt that had probably been stitched by hand. I sat next to her and gently caressed her cheek with the back of my hand. It was the fusion of peace and excitement that made me know she was the one. There was the tenderness I felt as she lay peacefully, hoping she would feel better soon, but there was also the fire of my sexual attraction. Having these two disparate energies blend with one woman had to be rare. This was the harmony that Clarkson and the genius clown Maple sought, but would never find. I found it.

Lyra woke up and told me she was still feeling weak and tired. Perhaps she had caught a bug. She assured me that plenty of rest would do the trick so we could head out early the next morning. I was sure she would be fine and just needed to refuel after the runaway madness of our escape had come to stillness here in West Virginia. I was happy that we would be alone and going west tomorrow.

I left her alone to rest and recover.

Clarkson did the dishes, while Denise, Maple, and I sat outside. It was an unseasonably warm evening, the first taste of spring. Denise sat in an old rocking chair and was sketching in a big artist's pad. Maple sat on a wooden swing with big, thick twisting ropes ascending to a peeling green metal crossbar. I sat staring at the half moon and the pure black night. I wasn't very interested in talking to either person, but if I had the choice it would have been Denise.

Maple began, "So where you guys heading?"

I could hear the sounds of the dishes clattering beneath running water inside.

"West eventually, but probably south tomorrow."

"Ohh, go to New Orleans for sure. My old man used to take me there every year. Yup, Willy Loman, my old man. He was a shoe salesman and every year we'd go down to New Orleans and it was the greatest time of my life. We'd go into Bourbon Street bars and my father would give me half glasses of his beer and I was the happiest kid in the world. Then that all changed. All of it. Kaboom! You know how? You know why?"

"No."

"My father was a right wing McCarthyite. Worst move we ever made was firing MacArthur and not bombing the Gooks to oblivion, he'd say. He thought Truman was a Commie! That he had been infected by the red plague. So I come home one day from high school and asked him all sorts of questions about Vietnam and why Marxism was so bad if it just wanted equality. It seemed like common sense, I told him. What's so bad about equality? That was it. He went crazy." Maple's eyes widened and blood blasted into every capillary in his face as the memories sought escape.

"Maple, adolescence is tough, man. Your father sounds unreasonable."

"He sounds crazy," Denise calmly added.

"Sounds?" Maple asked, bewildered.

"Ok, sorry, he was crazy."

"Ahh, Christ, what's the difference?" Maple said, suddenly calm. "New Orleans is a great city. You know what, though, why don't you stay here? We need voices. You see Clarkson and I are really different. I believe Uncle Karl was so close if not for the surplus profit dilemma, but Clarkson thinks less of dear Uncle Karl. He's into widely varied dialectics. He's more into social oppression and sexual dysfunction causing economic evils. He thinks about implementing on individual or small group levels. You know, transcendentalism, Fourierism, and all that."

"I know, he told me," I said, looking beyond Maple at the big dipper all brightly lit up.

"We're good complementary extremes, but we need the middle voice. I think that's you."

"Maple," Denise said looking up from her sketch pad. "You can't see what's right in front of you. You just keep harping on your economic uncles and paternal traumas, but just look into this man's eyes."

"What? What are you talking about?" Maple asked, slack-jawed and brow furrowed.

"He's in love. He doesn't give a southern hoot about your Uncle Karl or dialectic jambalaya. His soul is happy, alive in the truest of ways."

"I didn't say he couldn't be in love to join the cabal. He can do both."

"Ugh," Denise sighed and tossed her arms up in the air, almost dropping the sketch pad. "He doesn't need the cabal. And what cabal, anyway? The one among your various selves?"

Maple shot her a dirty look. "I take my medication!"

"To tell you the truth I'm not interested in any groups, real or otherwise. Denise is right. Lyra and I are in love and we're going to travel a little recklessly for a while and then I imagine settling down and being regular. Sorry, Maple, no revolution for me. I have no idea what I'm going to do, but I just know it's going to be with her."

"Are you sure?" Denise asked.

"Yes. Why do you ask?"

"Why did you come here?"

"Clarkson's an old friend of both of ours. And she thought it would make for good photos."

Denise gave me a skeptical, reproachful look.

"What? What is it?" I asked her.

"She hasn't been taking many photos."

"Well, she's not feeling well. What's your point, Denise?"

Denise put the pad on her lap face down. "Look, we can join them or we can let it unnerve us. I've gotten used to it. At first, I reacted traditionally, but I've let go of those bonds. It's just sex and togetherness. Who says it has to be monopolized by only two bodies, two hearts? It's the oldest myth of the human condition."

"What the hell are you talking about?"

"Do you hear any dishes?"

Denise turned her pad over and showed it to me. It was a sketch of Lyra and Clarkson naked and sexual.

I was speechless.

"My version of art therapy," Denise said with a little giggle.

Maple laughed like a snorting pig, then said, "I don't get the need to imprison sex either. We don't own what we should, so we try to own what we shouldn't."

"Your reaction is just the conditioned one. Let it ease into truth," Denise said.

Maple added, "She's right. You can overcome jealously."

"Shut the hell up you Marxist clown!" I finally screamed.

I went inside to disprove the sketch and the cataclysmic image pinballing in my head. My eyes roamed everywhere, but Clarkson was nowhere in sight. I could hear my own breathing all short and gasping like a wounded animal. In between breaths I thought I heard some sounds from upstairs.

I went upstairs hoping not to see Denise's sketch come to life. I came to the top where the thin wood partition divided the loft and walked around it to see Lyra, but instead I saw the sketch.

They pulled apart and both looked at me.

"Stoker, take it easy. We're not in love. Just a physical reunion," Clarkson said as Lyra lay next to him, partially covered by the sheets.

My lips began to mouth words, but I didn't have any oxygen to form them. What little air I had was used for my lungs to function and to prevent me from passing out. So I just stared silently at them in bed together in some state of shock or just a state of distraught.

"We didn't mean for you to find out this way. These things just happen. You know, the human condition," Clarkson said.

"I'm sorry, Stoker," Lyra said. "I have feelings for Clarkson, too. Why should I repress them. Later it will just haunt us in different ways. Getting it out of the way now. This could actually make us better, stronger on our journey."

I stood there shaking my head slowly in disbelief that my lover was in bed with someone else and that they were treating it as a bohemian philosophy lesson.

"Fuck you!" I finally expressed, an attempted scream that came out as a whisper.

"Stoker, she's right. Maybe this isn't the time to discuss it, but tenderness doesn't need to go unexpressed. I feel it for you, too. We can—"

Lyra put her hand in front of Clarkson's face. "Stop, Alex, not now. We're being insensitive. Let him process. We should have talked about it first."

My disbelief slid into frustration at not acting out. I wanted to grab Clarkson, let loose my fists in a barrage, but my body wasn't in control. My arms felt detached.

More words filled the air.

"Stoker," a female voice went on. "Just relax and think about the beauty of sharing physical love without the bonds we're told we must have. You could be with Denise and we don't have to fall victim to hate and jealousy. We can reach a new level. Then we travel with liberation. I love you. We're not over."

"I'll go downstairs. You take my place, Stoker," a male voice.

Clarkson began to get up. I had one instinct in my disconnected body: to run. Finally, I turned and did that.

"Wait honey!" Lyra shouted.

As I ran, I felt my body reconnecting with the strides. The need for escape gathered my senses.

"Don't react this way. It's not even your reaction. It's the reaction you've been told to have," Clarkson lectured.

Maple was in the doorway. "Stoker, just take it easy. We don't have boundaries here. They serve no purpose."

I saw Lyra's wallet on the table. Maple watched my eyes and followed them. I instinctively decided to take it with me in some petty form of revenge. As my hand reached out, Maple's Marxist hand beat me to the money.

"Just hang on, Stoker, don't be hasty. You haven't lost Lyra. You've gained us. Be with us."

"Give it to me," I demanded.

"Just wait." Clarkson yelled from the loft.

"Fuck you!" I yelled back at a normal decibel level.

"Now Stoker," Maple instructed. "You gotta skin the robot cat. We know what's wrong. Let's find out what's right."

"Shut the fuck up, asshole!" I howled, reached back, fist clenched, and hit Maple with a punch squarely on the jaw. As I was winding up and then uncoiling, I remembered Maple frozen and staring at my fist about to crash on his face. He didn't flinch, absorbing the entire punch. His frumpy body dropped to the floor like he'd been shot, the wallet falling free in the process. I grabbed it and headed to the door. Lyra and Clarkson ran after me half-dressed.

I ran and ran until I could no longer hear footsteps or voices behind me.

I made it to the train station and slumped against a wall. My heart battered my ribs and my chest hurt so much. I tried deep breaths, long and slow ones. Maybe I was having a heart attack.

Then the tears came, slowly at first, before upshifting into a full-on weep. A woman then approached and sat down next to me. She put her arm around me and I kind of collapsed into her as if I knew her. She held me and in the comfort of a stranger, I cried it all out.

When the tears finally stopped, I apologized, embarrassed and humiliated.

"Never mind that," she said and just held me tight. "You'll be fine."

She never asked me why I had the breakdown. She just guided me through it in her arms and caressing hands. When I was stable, she kissed me on the cheek and said, "Safe travels and a good life, young man."

I thanked and hugged her and then she vanished.

I was on the side of the tracks for the train heading back north to Boston. I sat and thought about what I should do. My first instinct was to go back and get Lyra, but that was quickly rejected. Heading back to school seemed the logical thing to do. Put this strange and tragic few days of misadventure in the rear view mirror, finish school, get my degree, and figure out my life.

I heard the whistle of the approaching train and got it line to board. When it came, I stood there, unwilling or unable to get on. I watched it leave and then took the underground passage to the other side of the tracks, where the platform for the train heading west was.

In that underground passage it crystalized. I would do a version of what we had planned, just alone. I would get off the train every day, take in a different town or city, and find a proper spot (not near the train) to sit and write the journey across America all the way to San Francisco. I'd have a notebook full of adventures, observations, unknowns, dreamy conversations, verbal cubism, magnetic fields, all surreal truths and Beat spontaneity. Hell, I already had plenty to write about.

I took out Lyra's wallet and counted the money. She had over a thousand dollars. I don't know what led me to take it in the middle of a broken heart crisis. Maybe subconsciously I knew that I wanted to continue the journey even in that catastrophic moment.

I boarded, got a window seat, took out my notebook, and started.

# INTERLUDE

Cars all piled up upon cars. It was this massive junk-yard of dead cars and a sign read, "Entering Dragon Falls–The city with the most junked cars." These piled colors of metal sandwiches with a giant crane magnet towering ominously above, screaming metaphors of youth once on the run and on the road, ready to pick up more dead cars to add to metal mountain and the road was strewn with road kill–squirrels, birds, raccoons, cats, dogs–more so than I had ever noticed before. Then stopping at a tiny nowhere diner eating a BLT, smoking cigarettes and watching the townies talking about sports and a couple of stooped over cooks cooking the dead–and into motel memories of her strong–a mighty migraine emerging rendering supine and madly lonely for her with phone imagining ringing and considering return-ing and dumping the whole absurd idea and confessing some crime to someone…some crime I hadn't done and here it is coach, one more try on the mound. I won't get screw up. No, next time I will be all Zen like I am alone in my own universe so perfectly concocted with a masking tape square on the garage door and a tennis ball whapping the paint off speck by speck–finally it recedes a bit, so off to the lobby. It was small and peaceful if sad and sitting down watching the young girl behind the counter making small talk, but not beyond, just small, small talk between cigarettes then off to a bar nearby full of unsuccessful businessmen in bad insurance salesman suits, piano music, chatter, lots of chatter, voices, perhaps I had a fever and was a bit delirious. Someone asked if I was ok and I felt little beads of sweat on my forehead, yes, yes, just drinking chilled straight Stoli that tastes so great wishing I was a cosmonaut…Back to the room after a quick smile at lobby girl and lying in bed realizing everything was really hilarious, really funny in the monstrous microcosms floating everywhere and the silly exaggerated anthem of love lost for Lyra was all part of the indulgence, but the indulgence could be expurgated like sticking a hose in your colon and hydrically flushing out all the residue until it came clean. Here's a big wave to the new and the little cities in every city I'll see and this girl in the lobby I might see everywhere.

Pouring rain of Nashville at midnight in a little pub and a lonely 23rd birthday celebrating the romance of movement and flow, of cities new every day and dawns and twilights angling original visions all conspiring bright shaded possibility if the mood and moment were freed to run. Couples talking quietly and watching TV and nothing happening, but friendly southern small talk. Looking over at two young lovers not talking, but imagining something, imagining going to go…thoughts of the friends who would try to create creativity as the motivating moment of everyday days, but that falsehood wasn't the springboard of this all. Must be some sort of lost unity severed unknown along the way and whose secret, strange loss rerouted all inclinations higher and more potent than the unrequited love of a constructed angel gone down right before one's eyes…and a café on the fringe of Vanderbilt where students and blue collar types ate big American breakfasts of butter soaked eggs and flapjack meals with their isolated groups. Sounds of cracking eggs plopping on the black griddle and spatulas scraping the surface and bacon sizzling and coffee splashing into mugs…and across Tennessee over its eponymous river into Memphis and a blues club at night soothing the ennui of miles and miles alone…and the darkness, music and cold beer blanketing the foolish fears of pilgrimages done over and over and over again always thinking this one will lead anew, when the true and only real anew would be the taste of a woman, but not a woman besides those lost to the past knitted visibly in memory in sight so conversation begins with a neighboring stool, who begins his story, or was it imagined…

He transferred here from Michigan. Got so tired of friends and family going through the stages, hated the stages, the so-called biological stages, goddamn transgressions, intransigent transgressions, he called them. Boom. He says you finish your school and go out a few years settle in to a job and then marriage and buying a house and a kid and the holidays become a relentless talk of the cyclical plateaus from job, to wife, to property, to kids, to investments in kids' lives, and it all recedes. It just shuts down. So he turned his back on it all, transferred out of his "goddamn" city and came here to Memphis with the same job. Now he sits in a cubicle and plays with people's money, money market mutual fund shit, but the beauty is he only needs a few hours a day, so he can play computer games and listen to music and at night he just comes home and plays video games. Dates and women are rare, but when he has them, he blows it, comes on too strong or too soft. Can't seem to get it just right…just end up back in the virtual world. It's all just transgressions that cast a sticky web over everything…that was the gist of what I think I heard while drinking away and staring at any beauty I could find in some blues supported Memphis honesty and what I honestly needed was the honesty of a woman's body without any entanglements. It's been too long, the next stop's got to have at least the vision of a woman in all her honesty.

Many miles alone into Amarillo and another motel room whispering too much to stay in silence. After a few banal bars without talk beyond platitudes, I found a strip bar with less than five people sitting at tables and a beautiful woman dancing on a protruding stage replete with the stripper's pole. She was thin and Asian with hair short and silk-like, shining under the dusty light surrounding her. I was drinking chilled straight vodkas between beers and drinking fast trying to stem the pathetic loneliness from developing into mad lust, but of course the booze only fomented the desire…A guy at a table next to me slides his chair over starts gushing about how this woman was beyond sexual, in another stratosphere and that he had to have her. He's been coming in every Monday for months just to see her and he wanted to be with her, but he didn't have balls to go beyond money in the G-string… She walked off the center stage and moved to a go-go stage to the right close to us dancing behind the bars all alone while the tiny Monday crowd watched the next act on the main stage. The next woman was larger, full bodied in a cowboy hat and holster with blonde hair, the

Texan type, while the sultry, small Asian seemed unnoticed, except by me and my neighbor. She was wearing a yellow G-string and quietly dancing lost amidst the lust for the American woman. My new drinking and lust stricken buddy kept going on and on about Akeio as he said she was called and I was drinking faster and smoking more trying to quell the mountainous loneliness from the miles and motels alone and from everything for that matter which became maddeningly lucid when confronted with beauty so nakedly near and Gus kept saying how most of the men wanted the big, blonde Texans, but not him. This Asian was an angel, more than beautiful, more than sexual, even mystical. She had an aura, a golden Eastern aura.

"Do something about it, Gus," I told him. "Money works, she's no angel, she's a stripper."

"Yes, yes, I know, but it's more, I've elevated her or she's elevated me about her. The attraction is pure. Paying would corrupt it."

"Please, Gus."

"I know, I know, I'm a fool all caught up in some perverse, irrational, poetic momentum."

Gus was well dressed and had a goatee with messy bohemian brown hair with a couple of earrings in his left ear. Poetic momentum? Yes, the momentum of the unspoken and untried. Well, seize it. Just then a tall man came to our table and joined us. You like her don't you, he said to Gus. $100 and she's yours for the night if you treat her right. Gus got up and left. He said nothing and left fast.

How 'bout you college boy, you wanna get your rocks off like they never been before. I took five twenties out of my wallet and handed them to him under the table. He nodded at Akeio and she left the stage going in back. You got a car he asked me. No, I told him. Ok, he said, here are the keys to my Ford pick-up for another $20. I'll be watching. Wait in the parking lot, she'll be there in five. That will be the best $120 you've ever spent and there are more like her, kid. 20 minutes kid, clock is ticking. An hour later I was alone in my motel room and was even lonelier and strangely I felt like I'd betrayed Gus and I began to miss Lyra more than ever. The alleged antidote served to sharpen and spread the runaway melancholy. More than anyone, though, more than any self-indulgent blues, I thought of Gus wondering why honest poetic sensations were so pathetic.

The sun splintered into dusty rivulets through the tattered curtain of a cheap Amarillo hotel room. I thought of Lyra. I thought of her place in the world. Of Akeio. Then back to Lyra and replayed the cataclysmic night with Lyra…In the morning I was back on board heading to the New Mexican border zealous and more alive now. What if I went to South America? What if I were in a cubicle or in a meeting…Caudwell, we need more analysis of the cost trends of an extra-large drink included in the special as compared to a medium or for that matter the deal with the cinema. What's happening? Did you get the package deal of two tickets with every tenth meal. Movies and meals. Dinner and the movies. They go together. People work all week. They need to go out to eat and then to the movies to escape their doldrums. It's a lock. They win, we win, you win, I win, winners everywhere. Come up with a catchy phrase, lock it up. Ok, Caudwell, remember, you're the best, positivity…What if…no, what will be will be. Che sera, sera…

California alone, new and novel friends, anarchists and artists, anything else is concession. Everything bright and changeable on a capricious notion only fenced in by currency, which despite the lament of the self-indulgent anarchist or artist, remains a needed frame around too many amorphous possibilities. A pursuit gently pursued. Passed through northern New Mexico, thought of O'Keeffe in Taos, red clay earth and various Native Reservations–fenced in societies bound by currency, culture, history, pain, humiliation, pride; dark, deep-souled people with heavy shoulders turned tense and tight. It's in the musculature. That's the gateway. Wandering groups tied harmoniously and justly to sky and earth now chained to poverty, drugs, alcohol...so say the cozy profs in air conditioned nightmare offices...maybe the fences were sanctuary from a money maddened hollow people going back and forth, back and forth, back and forth, why back? Sanctuaries beckoning everywhere like an old college friend's mad thumping inkling for a secret creative society founded on an art journal that would propel and attract youthful winds into temporary eternities...And on through Mosquero, over the Logan river, Ute Creek, through Tucamcari, all this a straight shot on open New Mexican tracks. Finally, heading north through the adobe City of Santa Fe and lunch in the Indian Farmer's market, buying some Indian beads and jewelry on the road and up into Los Alamos and a tour of the first Atomic explosion so poignantly juxtaposed to the native's fences. Here's irony so ironic it'll make you ill. Little biopics of Einstein, Oppenheimer, Fermi, and those who severed the past and began a new era of human history, 1945. Finally, up across the Rio Grande and a steak, black bean and rice dinner in a college town before a memorable New Mexican sunset in front of a little motel in the center of town.

A clean and simple room with all the essentials, a bed, a night table, bible on top, a desk, chair and a window. No TV, clock, or paintings. I sat by the window smoking and peering into the cool April twilight, magnificent orange purple horizon kissing the red, southwestern land. Remembering Isaac MacAuley's call for manipulating facts into untruths thereby unwittingly arriving at truth. One must lie into truth. Bullshit. Truth that is. Unraveling is the essence. The outcome is alleged truth. The outcome is irrelevant and thus truth is an abstraction, da-da-da-da…Catch the now and let it go, not falling prey to the midnight why.

Across the Rockies into Reno. The last stop on the way to SF, where I'd exhale the whole trip into words in the midst of inexorable youth offering the slippery peace of a gnostic. I found a motel across the street from one of the large casinos and took $300 from my stash, Lyra's stash, which I'd use for the night's festivities of gambling and seeing what my final night across America would bring to be vividly remembered in early morning solitude in an unknown apartment. Unknown.

I was walking around the $5 tables looking for a one that seemed to have the right setting when a young, blonde dealer smiled at me. This was the setting. She was very young, maybe 18, with some slight acne and a little pug nose, a shy, seductive smile that made her more attractive than she really was. I sat down and asked for $50 in chips and started playing the minimum hand and after 20 minutes the table was empty. She had a diamond on her ring finger. Soon, I started winning hands that I had actually lost. I smiled every time she cheated in my favor.

"You don't have to do that. Aren't they watching you?"

"I don't care. They don't mess around with the $5 bets. Can we stop talking about it?" She whispered.

"Sure."

"So you're from, sir?" she said in a welcome-to-Reno tone.

"Boston."

"Hmmm."

"And you."

"Right here."

"And you're married," I said looking at her finger.

"Oh this," she said looking at the ring.

"Yeah."

"Oh no, just a deterrent from the creeps."

"Does it work?"

She shrugged and said, "Occasionally. Lot of creeps out there and in here. Are you?"

"Married?"

"No, a creep?"

"I don't think so."

"Nice, honest answer. I'd like to get to know you."

"Likewise."

"Creeps never use that word—likewise. It's a beautiful word. I really like words, especially words like likewise, where two words become one. Isn't that a beautiful thing? Two words becoming one. Two things becoming one. Two becoming one," she said softly laughing through her words.

"Throughout, widespread, hereafter."

"Oh, yes, beautiful, so beautiful. How about this one
– nevertheless?"

"A triple."

She nodded as if she had won. Then she pointed to
another table. "Words are wonderful, but in the wrong
hands, they are abused. You see the dealer over there. You
know what she did to me."

"No."

"Play one more hand and then leave. Can you meet
me at the restaurant on the top floor? You could buy me
a drink, maybe something to eat."

"Sure."

I put up a $10 bet. She widened her eyes and nodded
more. I put up four more $10 chips. She hesitated. I put
up $50 more and she dealt the cards. I had 10 and she
had 7 showing.

"Sir, would you like to double?"

"Yes." I put up another $100 to double.

She dealt me one card. An ace.

She opened. "Dealer has 17. Nice work, sir."

"Thank you."

I had won more than $200 altogether. I left a $10 chip
as a tip thinking if I left more it would be too suspicious.

"Have a good night," she said.

"You, too. Thanks."

We sat in a revolving restaurant high above Reno.
I was drinking Armenian brandy. She was drinking
a screwdriver.

"What nationality are you?" she asked.

"Same as you."

"How do you know?"

"What's the difference?"

"None."

"So we're the same, then."

"You're very sweet. How long will you be in my little sad city?"

"Don't really know, day or two. Who knows?"

"You know what she did to me?"

"Who?"

"The dealer I pointed out to you."

"No, tell me."

"She started working here a couple months ago. She was real shy, quiet, repressed. She told me she took the job to try and change herself. Open up her personality. I helped her relax and let the true self out. We drank and she tried drugs with me for the first time. Just easy stuff like marijuana, a little coke, Quaaludes, but no major stuff. Just enough to let her taste the other side, you know."

"Go on," I said motioning for refills to the waiter.

"So she starts dressing different, gets her hair done, you know drops the nerdy nun image that she had. Starts wearing black and tight things, you now all the clichés like freaking Olivia Newton John in Grease. Goddamn Sandra Dee whoring it up. It was kind of funny. Ridiculous, but guys started looking, of course. The pathetic gender. So she was living with her numb computer programmer boyfriend and wanted out now that she was coming out. She hadn't had real mind blowing sex in her life and he was a real drip, practically asexual. She was full of anxiety about it. Couldn't stand him anymore, so I tell her to move in with me and my brother."

"You really went out on the limb for her."

"You said it. So she's hanging out with me, my brother and my boyfriend a lot. Then I come home from work a few nights ago and—"

"Your boyfriend?"

"Yes, I should have seen it coming, like you just did."

"Easier on the outside looking in with hindsight."

"Well, I was a fool. My boyfriend, I mean ex-boyfriend, had the leather jacket, motorcycle, just what Robin needed, wanted. A little danger. Screw that badass type. I've had it. They're full of shit," she said downing her screwdriver.

"What type isn't?" I asked.

"They're all full of shit, but how do you avoid a type. We can't."

"You're right," I said

"What type are you?" she asked.

"Since meeting you, a very happy type."

"You're just saying that 'cause I let you win a little bit."

"Wouldn't have mattered."

"I hate my own type. I'd like to change it."

"How?"

"With these."

She reached into her purse and pulled out a little plastic container and shook it so I could hear the sounds of pills clattering.

"They're homemade. A little ground peyote, Quaalude, coke, and other stuff I can't remember. My brother made it. He's a drug expert studying pharmacology at Reno City College."

"I don't know. They sound pretty loaded."

"Don't fret my new friend."

"Will it kill?" I asked

She laughed. "This isn't a suicide pact. I've had them. It's only got a touch of sedative so you can mix it with alcohol."

We took the green and purple pill and toasted.

"What the fuck. To your brother," I said.

"To new types."

"To new types," I repeated. Minutes later, I said, "I think the restaurant is spinning a little faster."

"Can you believe Robin?"

"Maybe she did you a favor, getting rid of biker boy."

"You're right. I just can't stand the sight of her face."

"Did I say thanks for letting me win?"

"My pleasure. You're a sweet man."

"You ex-boyfriend's crazy for letting you go."

"You're sweet."

"Should we go somewhere?"

"No, because if someone sees us, I'll get in trouble. A drink is one thing, but the room is another. Maybe, they'll check the video. Maybe, this is dangerous. Maybe, I'm going to get in trouble."

"You're getting paranoid."

"I'm not. I'm just aware of what a fool I've been."

"Take it easy. This concoction is making you edgy."

"If someone's sees me drinking with you and they knew you were at my table and won, they can put two and two together. Christ!"

"Let's leave."

"I've got to leave alone."

"Well, give me your address and I'll come to your place."

"Shit, I'm an idiot."

"Just calm down."

"I need this job. You don't understand. What the hell do you care? You're just traveling through, looking to get laid."

I was about to say her name, but realized I didn't know it or I'd forgotten it.

"I don't even know your name."

"Good. Listen, I want to pretend this didn't happen. I need my job. And I'm not going to lose it to give you a piece of my ass to remember so you can tell your friends about in wherever the hell you're going and whatever the hell you're doing."

"San Francisco to the first question and as for the second question it would require a lot of time to truly answer and I get the feeling time is something you and I don't have."

"You couldn't be more right. I'm gone."

She left and I said nothing watching her go. I accused her of paranoia, but it was really just sudden prescience and she jumped off the game we were playing. I decided to save the money I'd made and just wander Reno, wander the Biggest Little City in the World before hopping on the early morning train for the last leg crossing into California and all its possibilities.

But Reno was depressing after this woman's instant metamorphosis that left me alone again and the drug was starting to freak me out. What the hell did I just take? Got to get out of here is all I kept saying to myself like a mantra through the waves of this ridiculous drug thumping my heart and blood raging in my veins. I went to the train station, slept on a bench, until the whistle woke me up and I was back on the move.

Lingering effects of the homemade Reno drug remained. Everything was soft and melting very slowly. I saw a sign that said Welcome To California. I'd made it. The train stopped in Eureka for an extended mechanical delay. The conductor announced that we'd be here for about an hour. I deboarded and rather than visit the "Historic Truckee downtown," I decided on a short hike up a small hill tucked among many larger ones. All was quiet just after sunrise until I heard some voices in the distance. I came upon two guys, younger than me, maybe still in high school. They had a pick-up truck near them full of equipment. I noticed shovels, pitchforks, large pick axes, and some unfamiliar large machines. I knelt behind some bushes listening to them. The taller one seemed to be in charge. The short rotund one was digging, while the taller was reading a map or something barking out information.

"Jamie, I'm telling you this is the spot."

"That's what you said last night, man. I'm getting tired of you being wrong. Physically tired!"

"Well, there's no guarantee. I'm, we're, undertaking something huge here. You know anybody who's ever done this before? We're pioneers."

"I know Mo, but Christ, I just can't wait for this fucking place to go. We'll be heroes."

I shook my head to try and wake up from the dream or the hallucination I was thrust into by that homemade Reno drug madness. That's the last time I do drugs made by the brother of a jilted dealer in Reno whom I just met. I covered my mouth to conceal the laughter at myself.

I watched Jamie digging and Mo took a pick axe and started hacking the earth in a line seemingly in accordance with the paper he kept checking. The curiosity was getting the best of me and danger didn't seem evident with Jamie and Mo.

"So what exactly are you two doing here? Is there another gold rush going on?"

They stopped their work and Mo spoke, "I don't think it matters to you unless you're going to California."

"Well, that's exactly where I'm heading."

"What for?"

"The same reason anybody really goes anywhere I guess."

"Well, there are lots of reasons to go somewhere."

"Essentially though."

"See, that's a going-to-California answer."

Jamie said, "Yes, you're typical. Just why we're going to make that godforsaken place an island."

"Huh?" I said.

Mo glared at his friend. "Jamie, you know, you got a big fucking mouth!"

"What's the difference if he knows. No one's gonna believe him. First of all, he looks all fucked up and second of all, the story's too insane. Then there's no proof we were ever here."

"We gotta wipe our footprints."

"Yeah, I got the checklist, don't worry. It's on there."

"Just the same, don't tell anyone else, Jamie. This is big shit we're doing."

"Entertain me, guys. How are you going to do this?" I asked.

"Fuck it," Mo said. "Do you see this line here where I'm digging. This is directly above the San Andreas fault line. You know anything about geology?"

"Not a thing other than they cause earthquakes. Plates shifting or something," I said.

"You know the words. The meanings are what we're after. Typical gone west cat. All superficial knowledge. Don't really know anything, you just know to go. We're standing on the most delicate fault line in the world. After last year's earthquake, you know the World Series one, which is all anyone remembers. Stupid baseball game was more important than the results of the natural disaster. The SA fault line opened even more and the earth's crust right here is fragile, quivering actually. The right blast and California goes to sea."

"I might be gone west, but you guys are really gone period."

"This is happening with or without us. We're just accelerating the process. It's geologically inevitable," Jamie said.

"Can I ask why you're creating the island of California?" I said, laughing almost hysterically. "Go 'head and laugh cowboy. Just watch the news though and we'll see who's laughing.

"Ok." I said, trying to keep a straight face. "Tell me why."

"We hate California."

"Really," I said sarcastically.

Mo said, "It'd take all night, but suffice to say Hollywood is the biggest scam of the century. A whole industry of assholes getting rich and making everyone passive in the process. Hollywood has sapped our integrity and energy. Every idea is no longer an idea, but something to put on screen. We want reality back. And the North. They're worse than Southern posers. Those hippie and Beat fools postulating utopia and writing bad poetry. At least, Hollywood is honestly full of shit. Then there's Silicon Valley. More money there than the rest of the world for Christ sake's. It's time to take our lives back from this lost state that is ruining it for everyone else."

Jamie said, "This state has more money than most countries. Now, is that fair?"

"Where do you guys live? Nevada?"

"Look when it's all said and done if you say a word to the FBI, we'll hunt you down. There are others scattered along the fault line doing exactly what we're doing. You'll be followed, so keep your mouth shut."

"Look, this isn't really happening and if it was and I told someone, I'd be put into an asylum, so not to worry."

"We suggest you go home. Where is that?"

"Boston."

"Why would you ever leave? Real people, Boston, a real life, not this phony prophecy of California."

I waved and headed back to the train, wondering if I was really here or would be waking up soon.

Back on the train, hours from San Francisco, I still wondered if Mo and Jamie were real. For that matter, I wondered if any of the last 3000 miles across America had actually happened.

# PART II

I arrived in late 80s San Francisco with no skills, a damaged heart, youth lit up on my sleeve, and convinced that writing would cure all.

I figured I'd fit right into bohemian San Francisco.

I got a cheap little room on Broderick Street across from Kaiser Hospital in the city's Western Addition. It was a transient, week-to-week place called The Gotham, so the initial payment and deposit wasn't bad. And I liked the name. Who doesn't like Batman?

It was one room and a bathroom, furnished with a lumpy twin bed, an old rocking chair, a countertop with some drawers, a rusty sink, and a hot plate with a few dented tinny pots. There was a fire escape that had a view of Kaiser, which became my smoking and reading balcony with a nice view of the emergency room, replete with a steady concert of ambulance sirens whirring below.

After a few days of walking the city, I started to think about a job. Having no diploma and still no skills, I figured I'd get a clerk job in a bookstore, a movie theatre, whatever, but I didn't want to make just six bucks an hour. I was fine with the ascetic squalor of The Gotham and happy about its lack of a commitment beyond a week. Plus it provided a little world of eccentrics and ne'er-do-wells roaming the American fringe, all of whom were of great interest to me and rocket fuel for writing. I mean, who wants to write about accountants and middle managers…

But I needed money for the next step whatever that was.

Scanning the want ads, I saw some bartending positions and realized I was wrong. I did have a skill and bartending should be more interesting than the slow tick of the clerking clock. I had years of unofficial bartending experience. Suddenly, an alcoholic father finally became an asset.

I always bartended for my old man. He was a big martini drinker, dry Stoli on the rocks with two olives. He let me experiment sometimes—shaken, stirred, dirty, perfect. He taught me all of them. We even occasionally ventured into Manhattans and Rob Roys for diversity, but in general, the old man was a vodka drinker. "Those whiskeys and scotches, the brown alcohols, are for real drinkers," he'd say.

His drinking seemed pretty real to me.

Our biggest connections were sports and booze. Better than no connection, I guess. I bartended family gatherings. The women cooked. The men grilled. I made the drinks. My father had made a little bar in the basement and by ten I mastered the corkscrew and shaker.

I'd invent the name of a bar in Boston to feign my experience and tell the potential job that the bar had closed down.

I had more revelations. They seem to come all at once. Epiphanies seem to spawn each other like all the begetting folk in Genesis. After a few months in San Francisco and making a few dollars, I'd teach English overseas just like Lyra and I planned. I'd roll on undeterred, taking this bohemian show around the world, making peace with our tragedy and fulfilling its promise without her. I didn't need her. I didn't truly need anyone. I also considered a fishing venture in Alaska prior to trekking the world in case I was really hard up for money. I'd heard it was hard work, but good quick money.

I had gone 3,000 miles west. Why not keep going west until I got home? A circumnavigating lonely wanderer drinking deep from the well of youth. It was a good idea, Lyra. See the world, create, and settle peacefully into existence knowing the rear view mirror had its days of alternative carpe diem. She could have Clarkson for all I cared. She could have Maple and Denise and the whole sorry aberrant lot. Maybe I was doing everything just to spite her, epiphanies paved in bitterness, but it seemed like healthy anger properly redirected. I'd earned some vitriol. I'd occasionally lapse into angry rants befitting a cuckold, but they were tempered by the memory of the stranger angel at the train station.

It still hurt, but I knew it would wane.

I would tend two bars in San Francisco. The first one lasted one night. The second one a few months. Both ended rather climactically. Everything seems to lead to some form of climax when you're on the run.

The first one was in the seedy part of North Beach. I walked past City Lights bookstore, took a right by Machine Gun Al's Roaring Twenties All Nude Review, passed by some $1 peep show spots, and a few Thai massage parlors.

I had actually gotten the job on the phone. I had called to inquire from The Gotham lobby pay phone. A woman named Tara set up an interview for next week and then called me back in 10 minutes. They'd had an emergency and needed someone tonight. Tara just asked if I'd had experience. I said yes. Then she asked if I minded working with gay staff and clientele. I said no.

"See you at 5:30. 435 Broadway. White shirt, black pants, black bow tie."

I had two hours. I took the bus up to Haight Street, found a secondhand clothing store and got my uniform for $18, including shoes.

A few more buses and transfers and I was in North Beach, wondering where the beach was. I had a half hour to kill so I asked someone.

She never broke stride, laughed, and said, "Welcome to the city, kid."

The bar was on the second floor. I walked up the pink carpeted stairs strewn with purple feathers that floated up with my every step. The place was empty. There was a small service bar with no stools. It was in a lobby type room that led to a huge dining room with big, burgundy-dimpled vinyl booths all around. Some tables filled in the gaps and in the center was a circular couch surrounding a fountain with a statue of cupid with water flowing out its little penis and anus. More purple feathers everywhere.

Pure cheese and kitsch. Film noir meets *La Cage aux Folles*.

I heard voices coming from the top of the stairs behind the bar. I followed the voices to a smoky, windowless office with two desks covered with papers, folders, cheeseburger wrappers, and ashtrays overflowing with yellow cigarette butts. I knocked on the open door.

"Yeah," a man said without turning around.

"Hi, I'm the bartender. I was—"

"Oh, yeah, Tara called you, right?"

"Yes."

"She tell you the deal."

"Not really."

"I'm Billy. What's your name?"

"Stoker."

He swiveled around. "Good name. You from LA?"

"No, Boston."

"You got a LA surfer name."

"Yup, my—"

"You're a long way from home, but we all are in this city, right kid?"

"Sure."

He was smoking and his voice matched his addiction. He looked fiftyish, had brown teeth, and thinning gray hair. His nose detoured a bit to the right, probably from a fist fight he'd lost.

"So Stoker from Boston, what are you waiting for? Show starts at 8:30. Suits show up at 7:30. Big Martini and Manhattan crowd. Some scotches and Old Fashioneds will also come your way. You know how to make those drinks?"

"I do."

"Best chowder I ever had was in Boston."

"It's good."

"Chowdah, I mean," he said, laughing like he was choking on salt water.

I just stood half-smiling.

Coughing his way out of the laugh, he said, "Well, go set up your bar, Boston. They're going to love you here. Ice is in the white freezer at the bar, booze is locked up, keys are hanging on the door where you are. Good looking kid like you all wet behind the ears will make some good tips. You'll do all right, Boston. Make sure the wait staff tips you out 10%."

"Ok, will do."

"Don't worry, you'll have no problems. No, no, easy as pie, kid."

As I started to leave, he said, "Hey, Boston."

I turned around. He had swiveled so that his back was to me now.

"You came west for a reason, right?"

"I guess so."

"Everyone has a reason, but reasons don't matter. Enjoy your first night. Enjoy San Francisco. Ain't nothing like her."

An hour later I had set up the bar. I lined up the alcohols with whites on the right and darks on the left. Filled the containers for olives, cherries, and onions, sliced the lemons and limes, filled the ice, made sure beers were cold while reviewing all the Martini variations. I had no idea what an Old Fashioned was. I'd wing it. During the set-up, a half dozen or so men of varying ages came in and smiled at me before going up the back stairs where Billy was.

Soon those same men were elegant women dressed to the nines hanging around the bar. Drag queens and me. Billy was right—I was as wet as the Pacific behind the ears, but I tried not to show it by striking a cool, blasé pose to the whole queer scene. It wasn't hard because it wasn't really a pose. I had no issues with homosexuality. I just had no experience with it.

"So, sweetheart, where's Jose tonight?" a tall, black queen asked.

"Who's Jose?" I asked.

"The regular bartender," another one replied.

"Well, who cares, I like the fill in," another said. "Where you from handsome?"

"Boston."

"Lot a queens in Beantown. Ought to call it Queen-town. They just aren't as out as we are, yet."

I nodded as if I was in the know.

She continued, "I met my dream man in P-Town. Now that little city is out there more than we are. What a weekend!"

"That's a long relationship for you, Dale!"

"Sweetheart, long or short, they all end up the same," Dale fired back and then asked me, "Are you straight, dear?"

"Yeah."

"Of course you are. Don't worry honey, we don't bite, unless you'd like me to," Dale said winking and grinning.

"Dale, give the kid a break on his first night."

"I'm just playing with him. How long you been in the city?" she asked me.

"Just got here a few days ago."

"Damn, what a welcome! Right to the heart of our fair city in a transvestite club."

We all laughed. "Baptism by fire," I said.

"Attaboy. I bet you've only tended those Irish, manly bars," Dale said.

"Just one, back East."

Turning to another queen, she said, "Look at that nose on our rookie here. It's so nice, big, but straight, full of soul, character, ooh, sweetie, if I had you for a night, I'd welcome you to my fair city."

"Leave him alone. Christ, Dale, you ingratiate yourself when no one's opened the door. You just barge right in, fake tits first."

"Oh, I'm just having fun with him, you don't mind, do you cutie?"

I rolled my eyes.

"What's your name?"

"Stoker."

"Oooh, that hits the spot, stoke me, Stoker." Dale was relentless.

"There you go again," the other queen said. "Listen, Stoker, Dale gives you a hard time, you tell me and I'll take care of her."

"She's fine," I said and I meant it. I found it funny.

My protector asked, "Where'd you get a surfer name like that in Boston?"

"My old man named me after a character in an old film, *The Set-Up*, about a boxer who wouldn't take a dive. Nothing to do with California or surfing."

"Integrity, huh. Very noble," Dale said, "but you won't find any of that here!"

"My name's Melanie. Dale here likes to rattle new bartenders, straight or not. Don't worry, I can tell you're straight as an arrow. Can't hide the core, dear."

"Bullshit, Mel. I've been hiding my core my whole life."

"Dale, you don't have a core."

Dale looked at me. "We're all gay, sweetheart. I'll get you to come out of the closet like a bull in Pamplona."

And she punctuated it with a big hearty masculine, Adam's apple bobbing laugh.

Eventually a crowd formed, one that was very white and corporate. Dale, Mel, and the rest of the drag queens were doing their jobs getting folks drinks. I only had to deal with them rather than directly with the business-men (there were no female customers), which was good. I preferred the queens. Part of their job was also to flirt with the customers, who really enjoyed it.

When 8:30 came, the lights went dim and Billy from upstairs got on stage in a tuxedo and played emcee for the drag singers. First there was Dionne Warwick, then Diana Ross, Judy Garland, and finally Barbra Streisand. Dale came by to keep me company during the music. Dale had big eyes, a very manly jaw, and an Adam's apple like a walnut. She was easily exposed.

"So, Stoker, you never said why you came here?"

"I needed a job."

"No, no, sweetheart, to San Francisco. And give me a shot of Dewars while you're at."

I poured a shot and put it where no one could see it. Dale downed it quickly.

"No reason, really. No good reason, that is. Girlfriend trouble basically. Needed some new geography and San Francisco's the last stop."

"You heteros are all fucked up. You're all doomed."

"Indeed," I said.

"We don't know shit either. It's all a big train wreck."

I laughed and tried to occupy myself with cutting fruit even though it was all cut.

"Sugar, I love that profile. It makes me all loosey and goosey if you know what I mean. Fix me a whiskey sour and I'll leave you alone."

The night went fairly smoothly. I bullshitted my way through some drinks, a few got sent back, but the staff helped me make them right. I got more comfortable with Dale and the banter, even started to enjoy it and give it back to Dale, which just served to turn her on more, of course.

While I was cleaning up, the waitstaff left. The performers were still in the dressing room changing back to their daytime identity. I had about $50 in tips. Not too much, but I would still get my hourly pay, which got me over a hundred for the night. Pretty damn good for an unskilled dropout. Dale tipped me out the most, $20. She also offered non-monetary compensation.

When I finished, I went upstairs to talk to Billy. He spun around on his swivel chair, a plume of smoke floating up behind him. He struck me as a minor league Larry Flynt.

"How'd it go, Boston? I heard you and Dale hit it off," he said, laughing cacophonously.

"Yeah, she was flirty."

Suddenly serious, he asked, "What can I do you for? Trying to wrap it up here so I can have some of the night for my own entertainment." As he said that, I noticed a mirror lying flat on his file cabinet.

"Just wondering when I can work again?"

"Can ya handle it?"

"Sure, I liked it. It went well."

"Look at you. Shedding your east coast skin quickly."

"So can I get a few shifts?"

"Sorry, kid, it was a one-shot deal. Jose will be back soon. But if we need ya, Tara will call. Thanks for the night. Good luck in the city. You got a nice little North Beach baptism tonight."

I nodded and started to leave, but then turned back. "Billy, what about my pay? Tara said it was seven dollars an hour and I worked about 9 hours." It was only a slight exaggeration.

Billy fumbled around with some papers and then found some little piece of crumpled yellow scrap paper and wrote something down. He put the paper off to the side on top of a sea of other papers and folders. It slid precariously to the edge of the desk without him noticing.

With his back to me, he said, "All set. We'll mail it out to ya."

"You don't have my address. I never even filled out an application."

"Ease up, kid. Tara will call you. Don't worry."

I got the feeling I wouldn't get a call from Tara or see a dime from Billy. "I'd prefer to have it now."

"We don't print checks on demand."

"I take cash."

"Kid, time to go home. You're annoying me."

"I'll leave my address on the bar on the way out."

"Sure, now let me to do my work. Go have a drink at Vesuvio with the straight folks."

I headed downstairs, the drag performers were chatting and laughing in the dressing room down the hall. No one was around downstairs. I went behind the bar and decided to take my paycheck right now. I grabbed bottles of Crown Royal, Johnny Walker Black, Stoli, and Courvoisier. That's close to $100. I figured it would help get me through some lonely Gotham nights. I put the bottles in a box as quietly as possible, throwing in some paraphernalia like a wine opener, martini mixer, and a cutting knife and board, and headed for the exit, purple feathers aloft with every step.

Before I got to the stairs, I could hear footsteps behind me. I kept walking, but I was suddenly yanked backward by a handful of my hair. I went down fast and flat on my back. The box of stolen booze snatched from my hands in the process. Above me were the scowling faces of Judy Garland, Diana Ross, and Barbra Streisand, behind me Dionne Warwick was holding my arms down with her knees on my wrists.

"Don't fuck with Billy, straight boy, or we'll fuck you up," one of them said.

Then I saw Streisand pull her clenched fist back and crashed it down on my face, landing flush on my left eye. I tried to break free, but Judy Garland now had a handful of my balls and was squeezing them like a lemon. I felt as if I'd been hit with a brick. I could feel my eye simultaneously closing and ballooning up, but that pain was nothing compared to the agony in my groin. I squealed in testicular pain. Sweat was pouring down my forehead. My vision was gone and all I could see was a kaleidoscope of black and white fuzzy stars and fleeting flecks of jagged diamonds behind my eyelids.

"You ever come in here again, we won't be so nice."

They finally got off of me and I lay there in fetal position, clutching my crushed balls.

It took about a week for my eye to return to near normalcy. During that stretch I had a mighty fine shiner.

Maybe it was West Virginia karma gone west because of Maple. I spent a lot of the shiner time in my Gotham room. I wondered if loneliness could get any lonelier than this. I was running from the world, but I really wanted to run backwards. I couldn't quite fathom the mysterious sensations brewing within. Lyra was the obvious, quick explanation, but I knew there was more simmering in the subconscious.

I hated the subconscious, the invisible and devious puppeteer, the true Big Brother dictating all. I continued my daily spontaneous expressions, but they turned more internal now as if I were in dialogue with some buried self. As if I were a miner trying to get to the source of the strings of the autocrat marionette. I had little hope, but plodded on for lack of a better pursuit, stumbling along the edges of depths. Or, at least, thinking I was. Maybe the void was the last place I should be entering. Maybe my internal trespasses were causing, not preventing, the breakdown momentum I sensed trailing close behind me.

I smoked a lot, bought some cheap wine (instead of the good hard stuff re-stolen from me) to get through the evenings, and walked a lot, mostly in Golden Gate Park, spending hours in the serenity of the Japanese Tea Garden where that miserable momentum seemed to ease. I wrote some long letters to Lyra, pining, let's-get-back-together letters. At the end of that miserable lonesome week, I threw out the letters, but saved the spontaneous prose. The first notebook was nearly filled, 100 pages of who knows what.

One day on the way back from the park, I saw a help wanted sign posted at a pub called The 1907. It was on the corner of Geary and Masonic, the border of the

Richmond and Western Addition Districts. Another strange bartending scenario was headed my way, but this one would be the polar opposite of 435 Broadway.

A middle-aged woman was behind the bar. It was quiet. A few people were at tables eating breakfast. I could hear the griddle sizzling and saw a cook whisking eggs furiously in a large silver bowl.

I sat at the bar and had a cup of black coffee, inquiring about the job. The woman's name was Eileen. She told me they needed a bartender immediately. I seemed to have a magnetic field for emergency bartending gigs. She was the manager and had just fired a bartender this morning, which is why she was tending bar. I told her about my fake job back east, leaving out the one-night gender bender gig. I preferred not to discuss getting my ass kicked by Barbra Streisand and Diana Ross.

Boom! Once again I got the job on the spot. In fact, I was behind the bar ten minutes after walking into the place. People here seemed to trust me instantly, or I was just good at finding desperate folks.

Eileen sat at the bar with some paperwork and a calculator. She told me my timing was great and then explained the new drama that I was walking into.

"We are in the midst of an overhaul. The 1907 has been a local tavern forever. You can guess how long. There is a loyal group of regulars who come in nightly and daily for that matter and we're lucky if they pay for one drink on their way to getting sauced on our dime."

She pointed out the window towards Masonic Street.

"You see that?"

"Sears?" I guessed.

"It's going to be gutted and turned into a mall pretty soon. They're also putting in a Target adjacent to all the small shops. Construction workers will be in here every day for breakfast and lunch and then drinks after their shift. After they've finished the work, we'll have thousands of consumers at our beck and call, but we need to give the place a new look. You know, modernize, get with the times. This isn't 1907 anymore. And the new look starts with bartenders who actually collect money for the drinks they serve," she said, laughing. "A novel idea, huh? Is that too much to ask, Stoker?"

"Seems pretty reasonable to me."

"So far I've caught everyone in the act and fired them. They can't sue because I've had spotters in to nail them, documented evidence. Needless to say, I'm not too popular around here. They say I'm sucking the soul out of the place. Well, I say, we can have a soul and make money at the same time. Besides, it's a bar, not a church. I fill my soul on Sundays."

While she was talking, the waitress put up some drink orders. Mostly regular and Irish coffees.

"You ready?"

"Sure."

I made the drinks while Eileen went into more detail. Apparently, they didn't train anyone in San Francisco. No applications or reference checks. You just go in and work. It fits the laid back California image, countering the uptight beast of the east where you get sent to a 40-hour training workshop to be a video store clerk.

"So there's only one left that gives away the house. The dreaded and infamous Oscar LaGrange. The owners want him out desperately, but there's a catch."

Eileen paused and I felt her staring at me as I finished a drink order. I looked over at her as the waitress took two Irish coffees away.

"He's also an owner. Think about that for a while."

As I did, the chef walked over and delivered a plate of eggs, bacon, toast, and potatoes to Eileen. She thanked him and he scowled back at her as she looked away from him. Then he looked at me with a friendly wink.

"Reilly Port. Pleasure to meet you," he said, shaking my hand.

"Stoker Caudwell."

"Welcome ab-b-b-b-b-b-b-oard," Reilly said, face contorting wildly during the stutter.

"Thanks."

Reilly left and Eileen told me the whole story in detail. This guy, Oscar LaGrange, owned a third of the joint. The other two-thirds were owned by an elderly couple, who rarely came in, while LaGrange worked here, "and practically lives here, pathetic as that is." The other owners wanted him out, but it was hard to fire a co-owner. LaGrange had run the place for years before Eileen was hired. He was also a horrible drunk so he alone drank away a chunk of the profits and gave away the rest and more "to his crony regulars." The 1907 was deep in the red and might not survive long enough to cash in on the construction project. The owners hired Eileen and fired LaGrange as manager, but he still bartended four days a week. Her job was to get LaGrange fired completely. Needless to say, the battle was on.

"So I put in all new rules. No comps. Before you could give out a few free drinks to loyal customers. No more. Every bartender has been caught in the action except

LaGrange. He's bound to screw up. When he does, he's fired. He'll still be an owner, but he won't be allowed in his own bar. We've had a lawyer check into it all. Then the other owners will offer him a nice buyout package and we'll be done with his sorry, sodden ass."

"Sounds like a plan," I said. I didn't care too much about all the drama. I was really only concerned with getting a regular schedule and making some money. I'd follow her rules, make my money, enjoy the city for a few months and then ship off to wherever was next. One step ahead of the momentum. The little soap opera had nothing to do with me. I had my own going on.

"Ok, Eileen, all sounds good. I'm your guy," I said confidently. I kind of liked her and knew I would hate LaGrange.

"Great. Let's get some paperwork done, get you hired on the up and up, and put you on the schedule."

"Excellent."

"One more thing, Stoker. LaGrange will be tough on you. He'll try and break you and get you to give him and his crew drinks on the house. Don't do it. You're on my team."

My first night shift was a Sunday. It was a slow night. LaGrange walked in about an hour into my shift. He put two packs of Camels on the bar, scanned the joint, and then sat down on a stool while eyeing me. He had a salt and pepper mustache, dark, puffy halfmoons under his eyes, and was well on his way to the great drinker's nose. The gin blossoms were on the verge of permanent bloom.

"Scotch and water, twist," he said. No introduction, no hello. Clearly, I was already an enemy by default.

I got him his drink.

"Is this Dewars?"

"No," I said.

"I drink Dewars."

"You didn't ask for it. You just said scotch so that means the well."

He gritted his teeth, muscles in his jaw aquiver. "Do you know who I am?"

"I think so."

"Eileen didn't tell you what I drink?"

"No."

Shaking his head, he repeated, "Do you know who I am?"

"I said I think so."

"I ain't like everyone else. I own this bar. And you know damn well who I am. I'm sure Eileen gave you the scoop, bitch that she is."

I didn't say anything. My feelings for LaGrange were confirmed.

"Do you think I should be paying for my drinks?" he asked.

"It's not my decision. I'm just doing my job."

"Would you pay for the drinks if you were me?"

"I couldn't tell you. I've been told to charge everyone. Even the owners."

"Davis and Helen are in here once a month. Big fucking deal. I'm here every day. I work here. I put my sweat and soul into this place and now this bullshit hot shot from a chain bar wants me to pay for drinks. It's like charging me for a drink in my own home. Just ain't right. Just ain't the way we've been doing things here for the last twenty-five years. Who the fuck does she think she is?"

I didn't say anything, but I could feel a little smile creeping out as a result of his tirade. His anger just seemed a bit funny.

"Stop smirking. kid. Ahhh, what the hell do you know? You're as green as Golden Gate Park. Don't know shit. I'll pay you today, but when you know the ropes, we'll talk. Work out an understanding. For now, here's your fucking $4. Next time use Dewars, punk."

LaGrange put a $20 bill on the bar. I gave him his change. He was quiet for a while. The bar was dead except for him and a few people at the tables.

After a while when it got a little busier, he said, "Hey, kid, you see those guys over there? You see the table of ladies. Let me teach you something about the bar business. What we do here is you pour me a pitcher and a round of Irish coffees and I'll bring it over to them compliments of you and me. Compliments of The 1907. That's how I've been doing business for years. I've been running this place since 1968. Did you know that?"

"No."

"This place is like family for me. People come in to see me, not the bar. You seen my tokes? Hundred dollars a shift during the day. You know how many barkeeps do that in this city? I'll tell you. Less than a handful. I love people. I like to see a smile on their face. That's what bartending is all about."

He coughed loud and deep from the depths of his blackened, Camel-unfiltered lungs, swallowing back what was hacked up, and then washing it down with a big gulp from his scotch and water.

"You buy someone a drink and they smile. I've been here twenty-five years and that's what keeps me going.

The smile on a customer's face. That's my calling. When I put my head down at night and think about the day that just went by, I want to smile. That's the last thing I want to do every night. Isn't that the meaning of life? A smile as your head hits the pillow."

Oscar slurred his way through the mawkish monologue. From what Eileen told me, he started drinking around eleven in the morning every day. A few cups of black coffee for breakfast and then it was time for the first of a nonstop marathon of scotch and assorted shots. During his shifts at the 1907, which were every weekday except Wednesday, he did it here. On his days off, he boozed at other pubs with the bartenders he served free of charge. There was a club throughout the city.

Since it was now eight in the evening, his buzz was in high gear.

"Oscar, I can't comp any drinks. That's the rule."

"No hard feelings, kid. Fuck it. She wants to play hardball and so do you. Well, I say fuck her and fuck you. Bring a pitcher to the softball players and Irish coffees to the ladies. Hell, pour yourself a shot and bring me a shot of peach schnapps. That's what kind of guy I am."

I started making the Irish coffees.

"I'm paying for these drinks so bring me my shot first. Don't make me fucking wait. It's bartending 101. I ordered them and I own this fucking place. Christ! Don't be an asshole."

Without looking at him and biting my tongue on what I wanted to say, I stopped making the Irish coffees and got a frozen shot glass, poured peach schnapps into it, and brought it to Oscar.

"You forgot yourself."

"I'm all set."

"You're not gonna let me drink alone, are you?"

"I don't drink when I work."

He laughed mockingly. "Jesus Christ, you're a hard on. You ain't got a clue how to tend bar. Your tip jar's gonna collect nothing but air."

"I'll take my chances."

I brought the drinks to everyone and they all toasted, thanking Oscar profusely from their table, which he took as a sign to stumbled over and join them. I could hear him telling stories about his days playing minor league baseball in Buffalo. Oscar moved on to the table of women. They bought him a shot. In a half hour everyone left, laughing as they exited. No doubt at the drunken spectacle of LaGrange and his Casanova efforts.

As they left, Duncan James came in after his shift down the street at Trader Vic's. I had already met some of the regulars when I worked that first shift for Eileen. Duncan bought Oscar another shot.

"So they're trying to run me out, Duncan," Oscar mumbled.

"What? Who?"

"Eileen and her little protégé," he said, pointing at me.

"Really?" Duncan said, not so incredulously.

"Yeah, they want me out. Ain't that right?" he asked me.

"I haven't got a clue."

"Fuck you. You know the scoop."

Duncan pressed for details, but Oscar was all over the place. Slurred speech now traveled disjointed notions. His head was bobbing slowly in a circular motion and his eyes were all but closed, yet the alcohol still had a voice.

"Trying to get me, but they tried before. Ahhh, ugh, I'll be back. They haven't learned. I know what's going on. I made $120 the other day. Who does that on a Thursday? No Tuesday. Whatever the fuck day it was. Don't matter. I was telling Mark, AIDS, you know AIDS is fucking San Francisco up the ass. Why don't they just get the ten best scientists? Best in the world, lock 'em in a lab, pay 'em whatever they want and they'll come up with a cure. Eileen is fucking me. My sister's fucking gay. What a mess she made of her life. My old man, damn, breaks his heart. Should have been our bar. Instead, I got to deal with this corporate bitch, Eileen. Yeah. The job. Family. The 1907 is my home. I want to be buried here. Buried under the bar. Smile on my corpse and, and..."

Duncan and I watched Oscar's scattered soliloquy fade as his head slumped to the bar, knocking over his scotch and water, falling on to his packs of cigarettes, which cushioned the impact. The scotch spread into a puddle near his mouth. He was nearly out, but his eyes were slightly open. Then, as if on instinct, his tongue slowly extended and started licking the puddle of scotch.

"Jesus Christ!" Duncan said to me. "He can't stop."

A few moments later he was out cold. Maybe due to the pressure of the bar pressing on his jaw, there seemed to be an odd smile on his face as he lay there, a tired, old, beaten dog of a man.

Sunday nights were always slow and my tips were lean, but I quickly picked up more shifts. And I actually got paid my hourly rate of six bucks an hour this time. I was working four nights a week, one day shift on Oscar's day off, and one early morning shift. I was making pretty decent money and was able to start saving. I started doing research on English teaching jobs and the Alaskan fishing scene. I figured in about two months, I'd have enough to leave San Francisco and begin the around-the-world adventure.

In the meantime, I was getting to know The 1907 regulars more and more. They were the core of the pub. The hard core. There was Sean McGrath, who worked the morning shifts on Saturday and Sunday. He was an unemployed welder. He'd always claim to be hard pressed about finding work during the recent economic downturn, but he picked up odd jobs here and there, often with local pubs he frequented that needed minor handyman work done. Somehow he managed to get by on minimal income.

The cook, Reilly Port, was also a regular. His extreme stutter originated during his days at Colorado State. He said it was part stutter, part Bell's Palsy. Reilly left a forty-grand-a-year-plus-benefits job as executive chef at a swanky hotel downtown to take The 1907 kitchen manager position at half that salary and no benefits. Reilly explained the pay cut as "m-m-m-money c-c-c-can't buy f-f-f-friends or hap-p-p-piness. It was too corporate, too sterile. I like it here. K-k-k-k-k-kitchen is right in the action not hidden all l-l-l-l-lonely in back."

Duncan James was Reilly's best friend. He worked at The 1907 for eight years, but quit the day after his wife died. She was on her way to the hospital to pick up their newborn boy, who had stayed a week later because he was a preemie. Duncan asked Oscar for the afternoon off to get his son, but Oscar said no. As a result, his wife went and was killed in a car accident by an afternoon drunk. Duncan quit the next day in a rampage at LaGrange. He went to work down the street at Trader Vic's and was now the manager of the restaurant. He was doing okay on the surface.

About two years later, he reentered The 1907 on Reilly's suggestion and quickly became a devout regular again, without one word to or from LaGrange about what had happened.

Carter Eddy was one of the younger regulars. He was often with LaGrange, kind of a sidekick. Carter was the only local, having grown up in the East Bay. He dropped out of Napa State after two years and apparently played football there. He talked a lot about it, but it was mostly how he tore up his shoulder in practice. It wasn't clear if he actually ever played a down. He carried a photo of himself in uniform in his wallet, evidence at the ready. About three months ago he quit selling water filtration systems and started bartending here. Like countless others, he went from regular to bartender (or vice-versa). An incestuous vortex it was.

LaGrange, Sean, Duncan, Reilly, and Carter were all perched on the left side of the bar (from my view), the L-shape section, on my Thursday night shift. They were venting their rage at Eileen and a hinting at revolution.

"We've got to stop this. They're killing the heart and soul of my bar," LaGrange said.

"Damn straight. Davis and Helen are making a huge mistake," Sean said. "I gave her a chance, but she promised me a raise to seven dollars an hour soon after I started if I took those brutal weekend morning shifts. She's testing us. I got offered full-time at my old job, but fuck it, I'll stay and spite her."

"Jesus, Sean, you've been trying to find a job for years and now you ain't taking it to screw Eileen over fifty cents an hour?" Duncan said.

"Yeah, it's about principles, Duncan. Integrity, dammit!"

"Foolish and unnecessary integrity," Duncan said, laughing alone. He looked over at me. "It's like I said Stoker, if I could bottle common sense and sell it for ten bucks, I'd be a rich man and help this God-forsaken race of humans, too."

"I don't need you to tell me what common sense is," Sean said, tugging on his thick reddish brown beard. "What I need is for my fellow bartenders to back me up. We all should get that raise. What do you say Stoker and Carter?"

"It's not that important to me," Carter said.

"Ahh, Fluffy, nothing's important to you," LaGrange chided.

"That's not true, Oscar. I'm a new bartender getting experience. I'm gonna stay with this thing, so I'm not gonna let fifty cents screw me. And cut out calling me Fluffy. I'm tired of it."

"I'm just busting you."

"It's getting old."

"Ok, Fluff, take it easy," LaGrange said, shoving Carter on the shoulder.

"Hey, that's my bad shoulder!"

"Oh, yeah, ended your big football career. You never played a down." LaGrange laughed hard at that and high-fived Sean.

"I got hurt. I would have—"

Sean put his palm practically in Carter's face. "Please, Fluffy, enough. What about you, Stoker?" Sean asked.

I was listening closely to the silly banter, but pretended to be watching the Giants game on the TV above their heads. "Huh?"

"You gonna get your raise? You gonna ask for it?"

"No, I just started."

"So what? It's about solidarity for all of us. Why the hell not?"

"I don't quite see this on the Lech Walesa scale."

"Smart ass. Goddamn Bostonians think they're better than everyone."

"It's just fifty cents. Carter is right."

"Young people are selfish these days," LaGrange said to Sean. "Gen Xers are out for themselves, different generation from ours. They are about I and my whereas our generation was all about we and our."

"You got that right," Sean said. "Hey, Stoker, just so typical of you Red Sox fans. Just like what happened to Dwight Evans."

"Sean, not this conversation again." He was obsessed that the Red Sox did Dwight Evans wrong. They showed no loyalty by trading a the long-time veteran.

Reilly jumped in, "Stok-k-k-ker, Sean's right about Evans, the Sox d-d-d-dissed him."

"No, they didn't, man. It was time to move on for him and the Sox. Mutually beneficial."

Sean was shaking his big bearded head. "There's the I-my generation case in point. The guy's got kids with major health problems. He'd been with them for fifteen years and two World Series and they basically dumped him like yesterday's news. Real class act."

"They have Phil Plantier ready to go in right field. You have to go with the better player. You're too sentimental. Gotta go forward."

"I agree with Stoker," Carter said. "It's about winning and Plantier's a phenom ready to go. Time to move on. Changing of the guard."

"You would be a fucking Sox fan, Fluffy," Sean said dismissively. "And you're from the East Bay. What bullshit!"

"Sean, what are you getting so hot about?" Duncan joined in. "It's just freakin' baseball."

"Then stay the hell out of it if you don't care. You don't even work here. Christ, the Red Sox are pathetic anyway. Seventy-two fucking years. What do they know about winning, Fluffy? And I'll tell you why they're cursed. It's not the Bambino. I'll tell you why. They don't take care of their own. Started with the Babe, but it kept going—Reggie Smith, Fred Lynn, Burleson, Fisk, the list goes on. Dump them for money. They want Plantier for a cheap contract and don't want to pay Dewey veteran money. That simple. The Yanks take care of their own and George pays."

Sean grew up in his father's pub in the Bronx not far from Yankee Stadium. Not one of my shifts had gone by without him reminding me of the Curse.

"I'll tell you this, boys, our pub is turning into the Red Sox," LaGrange said.

"Indeed," Sean said, "Eileen is the Red Sox."

"And we've got to get her bullshit corporate ass out of here," LaGrange said. "She'll lose, just like Stoker's team always does."


The morning shift was strange, but peaceful. Most of the regulars weren't in and I enjoyed the break from them. They usually didn't start feeding their addiction until near lunch and the shift was six to noon. The 1907 was only closed for four hours a day and often it wasn't really closed during those four hours. A lot of times the bartender and the regulars stayed after hours, going downstairs to drink and sometimes do coke, usually supplied by Sean. I partook sometimes at first, but with more and more frequency each week. The 1907 had its own gravity.

This particular morning the TV was off. I put some Al Green songs on the jukebox. Reilly was slicing mushrooms and onions in preparation for the day's soup. He was also chanting his morning rant, which was virtually the same I-ruined-my-life mantra every morning we worked together.

"That's right, ole Reilly Port, you just done gone off and quit C-c-c-c-colorado State to end up cutting onions in a dime a dozen pub. Yes sir, g-g-g-g-g-ood move there kiddo, you were a wise young m-m-m-m-m-an. Right now, I could be down in some chic Embarc-c-c-c-c-adero office being a lawyer handling divorces and servicing beautiful women in and out of court. Oh yeah, g-g-g-g-g-great sex and g-g-g-g-g-g-reat money. Instead, I ain't g-g-g-g-g-getting either. I ain't drinkin' today Stoker, you hear me?" He asked this while looking over at me, but continuing to slice with precision millimeters from his fingers.

"Good idea, Reilly," I said pouring myself a cup of coffee. "How 'bout some coffee to take care of you while you're on the wagon?" I asked, playing along with Reilly's game. He'd be drinking within a few hours, maybe sooner.

"I'm not fuck-k-k-k-k-in' around. I'm off the booze. I'm going back to school. Gonna be a lawyer. Get the law degree I should've gotten t-t-t-t-twenty years ago."

"Carpe Diem, Riles. Quit the booze first and then get your degree. A good plan."

"Yeah, but like I told you, booze is tough for me. I got that Native American blood in me and we're genetically alcoholic thanks to the fuckin' Europeans who introduced liquid evil to my peaceful, proper p-p-p-p-p-pot smokin', land-connected folk. I'm a born alcoholic and my soul comes from folk who don't believe in possessions and materialism. T-t-t-t-t-tough to live in this world with that genetic make-up."

Reilly had a great grandfather who was one-eighth Arapaho, according to some family tree company. That made Reilly one sixty-fourth Native American.

"Yeah, law school's the tick-k-k-et. Ain't too many stuttering lawyers out there, though. I'll show 'em."

"How 'bout that coffee?"

"Hell yeah, I can't quit booze and everything at once, goddammit!"

I brought Reilly a cup of black coffee. He was moving on to green peppers.

"Hey, be a buddy and put a little Bailey's in there, Stoker," Reilly said as I put the coffee down near a mountain of perfectly sliced mushrooms.

I looked at Reilly, shaking my head and grinning.

"I'm just kiddin', Stoker buddy. You're too serious, brother. You need to let go of that B-B-B-B-B-Boston edge of yours. Take off the straitjacket and relax with me, my m-m-m-man."

"It's in my blood, like your alcoholic Arapaho past."

"You're right. Genes are tough bastards. No way around them. Gotta k-k-k-k-k-k-keep fighting."

I sat at the bar after I refilled some coffees for the three or four people eating breakfast. Reilly was now into his Bermuda mantra. "Yeah, the ex-wife was hunting

m-m-m-m-me down with a shot gun. Damn crazy
woman took a few shots at me. I was hiding behind some
big Oak tree. She blasted square into the center of the
tree. The d-d-d-d-d-damn bullet almost went all the way
through. It was peeking its pointy edge outside the back
of the tree. Right between my eyes. She reloaded and I
ran as fast as my Arapaho legs c-c-c-c-c-c-c-ould take
me and jumped on a plane to Bermuda."

Every male regular in The 1907 had been wronged by
a woman. And every time it was the woman's fault. Every
time. It had nothing do with them, their alcoholism, their
issues. The alcohol diluted reality and softened the sting
of the ole angel midnight of truth.

My role at The 1907 was as the essentially unofficial scab
on management's side because I refused to give anyone
free drinks. I was following Eileen's rules, which wasn't
that hard because I had issues with the slow suicide of the
drunken nihilists and their white flag life. My contempt
was surely sown in my own cowardly paternal revenge,
misdirected and then redirected at The 1907 regulars,
but perhaps cathartic nonetheless. The less free drinks
I gave, the less time I spent hearing the stories of their
life over and over and over again. They'd often tire of
me and my parochial policy and head down the street to
the Fireside Pub, time which I relished either in silence
observing the pub universe or meeting new people free
of their monopoly.

But there would be no Fireside Pub visit on this night.
The crew was at their stools, Reilly, Duncan, Oscar,
Sean, and Carter. Another long time regular, Albert
Jones, occupied his favorite corner stool. Albert was a

tall, handsome black man, who carried himself with a dignified air. Not haughty or pretentious dignity, just quiet class. He was a regular in frequency only. He rarely conversed with the others. He would stoically read newspapers, usually *The Evening Chronicle* and the *Bay Area Guardian*, and drink two Jamaican coffees. I had never seen him drink more or less than that, which also conspicuously separated him from the others.

He worked as a security manager at some club in SOMA and had also avoided the incestuous magnet that turned regulars into bartenders. While Albert said very little, there would be a polite nod of recognition, and maybe a hello and goodbye, but he and LaGrange never communicated on any level. I also noticed that LaGrange got quieter and less disruptive when Albert was in for his 45-minute-to-one-hour visit. There was history to that.

One night in the late 70s LaGrange was putting his sloppy drunk Don Juan moves on a beautiful blonde waitress. She politely, under pressure, capitulated to a post-shift drink from her boss. While LaGrange was hitting on her, she informed him that she had a boyfriend so "you can quit flirting, please." LaGrange insisted on seeing a photo and when she showed him a photo of Albert Jones, whom to that point had never been to The 1907, LaGrange screamed the verboten racial slur followed by, "Honey, why on earth would you want that touching your beautiful white skin?" Kathy Granger, the waitress, stood up, said, "I don't work for racist pigs," promptly quit and walked out the door.

The following day when Oscar was behind the bar for his afternoon shift, Albert Jones came into The 1907.

"Are you the manager?" he asked LaGrange.

"Yes sir, Oscar LaGrange, what can I do for you?" he said politely.

"I'd prefer we speak in private?"

"Do I know you?"

"No."

"Would you like a drink?"

"No."

"I'm a little confused."

"I'll clarify. I prefer you come away from behind the bar and I tell you this in private at a table. It's quite important."

LaGrange refilled his perpetual Dewars and water with a twist, grabbed his Camels, and walked around the bar. He never went anywhere without his essentials. LaGrange must have been walking on eggshells pondering his fate with this man he'd never met. Albert was six-foot-five, lean, but muscular. He had powerful, steely eyes that could make you feel half your size if he turned an angry glare at you.

When LaGrange reached the table, Albert stood up quickly and grabbed him by the shirt, practically lifting him off the ground. LaGrange dropped his drink and cigarettes. Albert pulled him close to his face and peering down at a shaken LaGrange said, "If I hear you use that word ever again, I will beat you down. And if you so much as look at my girlfriend or any woman disrespectfully again, I will end you." LaGrange nodded like a scolded child, terror in his eyes.

Albert pushed him away and LaGrange fell on his ass amidst scattered ice cubes and cigarettes.

From that point, Albert became a regular as if he were keeping an eye on LaGrange to see if he would cross the line. Part of me wished LaGrange would so that Albert would finish the job.

So these men sat and drank and talked and complained and drank and talked and complained and drank…while Albert read his paper on this particular evening about a month into my San Francisco chapter. Reilly was bemoaning his latest female trouble and Duncan was trying to cheer him up.

"Let it go, brother. It's over. You've done too much. She was good woman, but your self-respect is at stake here."

Reilly sat with his head buried in his folded arms on the bar. His pint of Bud untouched and warm by now.

Duncan continued. "You know, Meredith actually asked me to tell you to stop the flowers, the letters, messages. It's starting to freak her out. Riles, you gotta move on."

Reilly pulled his head up just enough so he could speak. "I c-c-c-c-c-c-an't believe it. I love her and d-d-d-d-d-d-d-d-did nothing but show her that," he said with his face contorting as he stuttered longer and harder than usual.

"Riles, ole pal, you've been moping around for a month. Come on, snap out of it. Get back on the horse, cowboy."

"Ain't no horse left," Reilly said.

Sean jumped in. "I've seen enough man. Goddamn it, cut the fuckin' shit. You only went out with the girl for a few damn weeks and you're acting as though you were married for a decade. Reilly, you're acting like a goddamn idiot. I give you no sympathy 'cause you eat it up like Red Sox fans eating up first place in June," Sean said, winking at me.

As always, Duncan defended Reilly. "Ease up, man. It doesn't matter how long the relationship was. It hurts. Hurt is hurt."

"Sure it does! Hurt has degrees, man. You of all people should know that."

"Believe me, I know," Duncan said, and shot a glance at LaGrange.

Sean continued. "Look, easing up ain't doing him any good. Look at our buddy Rollins. His first wife was a coke addict and his second he found secretly stripping down at North Beach one night at one of those one-dollar peep show joints. Now he's married again and we all know what a great woman he has now. You pick up the pieces, get up and go on. Christ, when Joline left, I didn't bring everyone else down with me. I moved on. I manned up."

"Huh?" Reilly muttered, lifting his head fully up from the bar and staring at Sean.

"I didn't do the nosedive you're doing when I lost my honey. You're being ridiculous. It's like some teen movie. Fucking covering her car with roses. Christ, what an ass."

Reilly sat up straight. His face was bright red. He got off his stool and took his pint of Bud outside to the few plastic tables on the weedy patio and sat down alone with his back to us.

"Why don't you lighten up a bit on him?" Carter said.

"Oh, Fluffy, man he'll eat that shit up as long as you serve. He needs new medicine. Time for tough love."

"Maybe Sean's right," LaGrange said.

"Seems to me, Sean, you were pretty bad when Joline left you. You were pretty down, too, like you ought to be," Carter said. "I don't think you remember it right."

"I didn't do the shit he's doing."

"We're all different. He's doing it his way, and you did it yours. Besides, you weren't treating your lady the way Reilly treated his."

"Fluffy, what the hell are trying to say?"

"You told me yourself you could have done better. Treated her better."

"This ain't about me. Ain't your fucking business, Fluffy!"

"Some nights it is. You talk a lot when I'm on the other side."

"Says who?" Sean was fuming.

"Easy boys. We're family here," LaGrange said. He peeked over at Albert who slowly turned and caught eyes with LaGrange, who instantly looked away.

"Says you. You go on and on about it some nights when I'm working," Carter said. His voice cracked a little and he was almost swallowing his lower lip, but he was holding his ground.

"You don't know shit. You're talking out of your ass. The point is Riles doesn't have to drag everyone else down. I gave him two weeks before I started telling him to toughen up. Christ, his mourning period is almost longer than the damn relationship.

"When was the last time you had a full time job?" Duncan said, getting Carter's back.

"What's your fuckin' point, Duncan?" Sean barked.

"All I'm saying is you haven't worked full-time since you and Joline broke up. It takes time. Just cut him some slack. I mean, I agree he needs some tough love, but you don't have to bash him over the face."

"I'm not working full-time because I can't get work. Believe me, if I could, I'd be out there, but you check out my union. We're getting no offers. They're hiring non-union scabs for half the pay and I'm not working for 15 bucks an hour and crossing union lines."

LaGrange jumped in. "Listen, why don't you stop your bickering and have a goddamn drink. Stoker, give us all a round of Jägers and send one out for ole Riles," LaGrange said, turning to alcohol as an olive branch. "Time for some medicine."

Reilly came inside just then. "I'll have it in here, you fuckers, and I'm buying. Ole Stoker here needs his money 'cause he's a p-p-p-p-ro doing his job and ain't nothing wrong with that. I've been a dick and I'm goddamn glad Sean let me have it. When you're a dick, you n-n-n-n-n-need someone to say, hey, you're being a fuck-k-k-kin' d-d-d-d-d-d-d-d-dick. But I'm back and getting back on that old horse, goddamn it."

"Riles ole pal, you're alright. Attaboy," Sean said, giving Carter the finger.

"Sean, you were right. You can say I told you so," Duncan said.

"No need for that. Stoker, get Duncan a beer on me and tell me one thing."

"What's that?"

"How many championships have the Sox won since I don't know, Amelia Earhart got lost in the Pacific?"

I was shaking my head, but with a little smile. "I come to San Francisco and get stuck working all day with a damn Yankee fan. Just my luck."

"All part of the sweet curse," and Sean let out a big laugh from deep in his belly. Snapping Reilly out of his funk had Sean glowing. He was feeling proud and had moved on from Duncan and Carter's jabs. Hours later the pride would dissolve as LaGrange's olive branch reached its true delusion.

Sean had been up and down the stairs a few times with Duncan and Reilly to do some blow. LaGrange had slid out of his seat and stumbled across the street to his 3rd floor apartment that had been his home for twenty-two years. Albert Jones had had his two Jamaican coffees and left with his girlfriend, newspaper, and his only words of the night, "Night, gentlemen."

It was one in the morning and I was sitting at the bar with the remnants of the platoon. There were no other customers and the waitress had gone home.

"You want some?" Sean asked me.

"Sure, thanks."

"Here's your tip," Sean said, shaking my hand and putting a little pack in my palm. "You guys go down and I'll watch the bar."

We did a couple lines each and headed back up. The bar was still empty. I got behind the bar and started to clean up after refilling everyone's after hour beers on the house.

"Now I know how to loosen you up," Sean said.

"Temporarily," I said.

We all toasted.

"When our glasses hit, Reilly let out a mammoth sneeze, that made Sean jump in his seat spilling some of his beer.

"Jesus Christ, Reilly!"

"What?"

Reilly let out another sneeze, even louder than the first. Duncan was laughing.

"Fucking Reilly, I hate that."

"What?" Reilly asked, palms up in confusion.

"Your goddamn sneeze."

"How can you hate a sneeze?" Reilly asked sincerely.

"Cause it doesn't have to be so sonic. Why you gotta amp it up?"

"I wasn't amping it up. T-t-t-t-that's my sneeze."

"Bullshit! You exaggerate it!"

"Sean, brother, what the fuck are you t-t-t-t-t-t-t-t-alking about?"

"What the hell kind of question is that?"

"It's a question that means you're being the d-d-d-d-d-d-d-d-dick."

"Reilly, I'm just telling you a sneeze doesn't have to be an earthquake."

"Sean, that's my goddamn sneeze. I like it that way. Christ! You can't c-c-c-c-c-c-ontrol everything."

"Boys, calm down," Duncan said.

"His sneezes drive me crazy. It's not about control. It's simple manners. Just tone it the fuck down."

"Sean, we're all having good time. I let out a bodily f-f-f-f-f-f-f-f-unction and you lose it. What the fuck!" Reilly said, frustration mounting. He got up, grabbed a pepper shaker off a table, poured a small pile into his hand as if he were performing on stage in front of us, and began sniffing.

"Don't," Sean warned.

After a few moments, Reilly, with a dramatic prelude, let out a titanic, over-the-top sneeze.

Sean got in Reilly's post-sneeze face. "You prick! You're lucky I don't knock your sorry ass out right now." He feinted a punch at Reilly, who flinched significantly backwards. Sean shook his head in disgust and walked out.

Duncan, Reilly and I spent the next few hours finishing Sean's generous tip and several more pints. The Sneeze was a major topic of conversation and would be for most of the next week. I did find some humor in this inane topic and so many similar ones, but the regulars beat it to a verbal and monotonous death. The 1907 was wearing me down. I was close to making a decision on teaching English or catching fish in the North Pacific. But as much as I was tiring of these guys, I knew I'd miss them on some level when I was gone.

One evening near the end of my 1907 tour of duty, two semi-regulars were engaged in the same conversation they'd had many times. Originality was not part of The 1907 currency, but this particular banter, though repetitive, was more unique and sophisticated than the hardcore regulars' typical frivolity.

Heimi Frynberg, a short, bald quadragenarian, began his usual lament. "Reagan screwed me, us, everyone, but the top five percent. Can you believe a guy helps a mere five percent of the country and gets elected because ninety-five percent of the country gets duped? What an actor!" Heimi let loose a stunted giggle disguised as laughter.

Wilbur Jacque was a tour guide driving those fake trolleys of tourists all over the city. He lived with his mother, had shiny silver hair and was always clean-shaven. His schtick was twofold: trumpeting support for Chögyam Trungpa Rinpoche's Tibetan Buddhism and Wallace Steven's book, *Necessary Angel*, which he always had a few copies on hand in his satchel. He would give them away to all those who expressed an angstrom of interest in return for a "snifter of Courvoisier, if humbly possible, thank you very much."

Wilbur responded to Heimi in usual fashion. "It's not Reagan that blinded us, Monsieur Frynberg. We're all walking around with cataracts. We need to peel off the layers that have dimmed our vision. Once we see, truly see, we wouldn't even need politics, never mind silly religion. Those are just ruses perpetuating blindness. Politics is part of our collective cataract."

"I know, I know, Wilbur, but I have no cataracts. My eyes are fine. And Bush is still reaming us now. I got screwed in the '82 recession and again right this moment as everyone's downsizing and a forty-something Jewish man's the first to go. Kinder, gentler my ass. I got two houses and real estate's dead. Can't sell 'em and the rent doesn't ever cover the mortgage. I'm under water without an oxygen tank. I'm drowning. I don't know why we can't see through them—"

"Cataracts!" Wilber shouted.

Heimi continued undeterred, "Trickle down my ass. The only thing I have trickling down is the damn runs I've got from shattered nerves. The rich people are laughing so hard at how we bought this Republican package lock, stock, and barrel. When I finish pissing, that's my trickle down. He-he-he-he."

The cognac drinking, Eastern philosopher tour bus driver continued, "We aren't seeing through ourselves. Trungpa didn't get drunk, he got intoxicated." Wilbur punctuated the last word by slowly saying each syllable and raising his right hand high for a dramatic emphasis. Once we understand the difference between drunk and intoxicated, we'll begin to see. No more cataracts, no longer nearsighted. We'll be deep sighted, intoxicated with clarity." Wilbur nodded, agreeing with himself.

"If I sell my two houses, I'll lose $50,000. While I rent, I lose $1,000 a month. Thanks Bonzo. Jesus Christ! Bonzo went to Washington. What a country!"

"When we're intoxicated, we climb. We see. We envision. When we're drunk, we flail, sink, and regress with a hangover. We need the intoxication of Rinpoche. Politics is simply our lack of intoxication. Politics is for the drunks."

Heimi continued his ground attack to parry Wilbur's ethereal deliveries. "The Soviets are dead and we still spend thirty something percent on the military. How do you explain that? We could pump that money into the economy and create jobs and I could unload my damn houses and get the albatrosses off my tired, achy back."

The dialogue in the form of monologues was now aimed at me. Each of them responded to me even though I never actually said anything. Wilbur's turn. "Stevens said, '*The truth seems to be that we live in concepts of the imagination before the reason has established them. Reason is simply the methodizer of the imagination.*' That's my mantra that I say every morning when I wake and every night before sleep. '*Reason is simply the methodizer of the imagination.*' Over and over and over and then the necessary angel gives me peace and I live wholly without concepts of mortgages, recessions, houses, etc."

"You live with your mother," Heimi scoffed.

"Irrelevant," Wilbur responded.

Heimi shook his head, laughing derisively. "No, very relevant. I don't know about this Rimposh guy, but—"

"Rinpoche," Wilbur corrected.

"Whatever. I'm voting for Jerry Brown."

"You know," Wilbur said, dismissive of any political talk, "I came back from Boulder without a dime in my pocket, but rich in the words of Rinpoche. Have you read that book, Heimi?"

"Huh? What book?"

"*The Necessary Angel.*"

"I only need an angel if she's willing to buy my property."

"*Reason is the methodizer of the imagination.*"

"You know, Wilbur, I never know what the hell you're talking about."

Once a night I usually took a cigarette break outside, walking just across the street to the overpass above Geary Boulevard. I needed a few peaceful moments from the maudlin men's club. The 1907 was not well frequented by women, especially at the bar. It was as if women picked up on the scent of the regulars and knew better. Their sixth sense working very effectively, or more concretely, their eyes simply seeing more than enough to stay clear.

The 1907 provided fine writing fodder for sure, filling many notebook pages during lonely hours in my Gotham room, but the daily immersion grew increasingly cloying and started conjuring up too much paternal past. The smoke break was momentarily liberating. From the Geary overpass, looking north you could see the vermillion tips of the glorious Golden Gate and the rolling hills of Marin just beyond it. Morning shifts were a treat watching the billowing, high speed roll of the fog gliding in from the north, draping this part of the city in a sensual and haunting mystery. Sometimes I'd wish the fog would roll right up Geary, into The 1907 and whisk the drunken talking heads away, bathing them in heavenly vapors and transmogrifying their beaten souls into reincarnation. My illusory moment would end when I'd gaze into the bar and see all the faces in the mirror: Duncan, Sean, LaGrange, Reilly, Carter, even Heimi and Wilbur (but not Albert), all the sad old men. Each set of eyes in the mirror. Each head with its mouth moving or pointed vacantly at the television. It was an all-in-one reflected panorama that was a great and melancholic snapshot of existence gone awry. Youth had slipped through their fingertips with no preparation for the loneliness that lay paralyzingly ahead. Nothing left to do, but mourn yourself on a stool, night after funereal night.

It was after midnight. Just a few regulars and LaGrange hanging on later than usual. He'd been out boating in the bay with some friends and looked tanned, even a bit healthy. The fresh air and sun did him some good, temporarily cleansing away his barroom and Camel unfiltered complexion. Albert Jones had gone home. His seat was taken up by an occasional regular, Jean Filbert, who was from France and rubbed Sean McGrath the wrong way.

"Maginot line, Jean, explain that one to me." Sean loved ridiculing Jean on this bit of WWII history. Sean was a history buff and actually had an incredible breadth to his vast 20th century knowledge.

"Sean, explain Vietnam," Jean countered in a heavy French accent.

"Two different things. We learned our lesson. That was growing pains. The Maginot line was sheer stupidity. Sure, let's build this huge, intricate wall with sophisticated transportation systems underneath and spend years and a fortune on it, just so Hitler could walk around it. I mean, Stoker, the Nazis walk up to the wall, think to themselves, hmmm, what should we do, go through it or around it. Pretty fucking easy deduction. So they literally walked around the wall since it ended at the Belgian border and not the Atlantic, marched through Belgium and took down France in four weeks. Can you believe that? France folded like a timid poker player."

Jean sighed. "Yeah, fine, it was stupid. I know. How many times are you going to tell me? Stoker, can I have a Pernod, please? But growing pains? Yeah, my derriere."

"You guys did the same damn thing in Vietnam. Don't throw stones in glass houses, Frenchman."

"Bullshit, Sean. We did it before you, got out realizing we couldn't win after Dien Bien Phu and warned you, but mighty invincible America wouldn't lose like France. Yeah, right. It wasn't growing pains. It was runaway American ego."

I poured Jean a double Pernod. He was going to need it.

"The Germans did it to you in WWI and you let them do the same thing. Déjà vu shall we say," Sean said in a heavy mocking French accent. "You built a wall and they walked around it. What a joke!"

"Why do you care? Can we talk about something else?" Jean implored Sean.

"Historical curiosity. I'm a student of history," Sean said, downing the remaining half pint of his Bud in one gulp.

"Sean, why do you always nail people on one thing and never let it go? The Maginot line, the Red Sox with Stoker," Carter said.

"Jesus, Fluffy, I'm just busting people's balls, making conversation. You're too touchy feely and that's why we call you Fluffy. Go do some yoga."

Jean downed his Pernod quickly and left.

"Au revoir," Sean yelled. Jean flashed the middle finger as he exited without turning around.

"You see, you drove him out of here," Carter said.

"I never liked him. I saw him steal someone's money off the bar."

"Whose?"

"That's not important. He's a fucker. French or whatever, he's a fucker. I don't trust him. I grew up in my dad's bar and the one thing you don't do is take someone's money off the bar. You can insult him, say whatever you want to a point, but touch a guy's money and you've crossed the line. We all leave our money out, go the bathroom, use the phone, and come back trusting each other that the money's there when we get back, but not with Jean. He's a Euro-trash thief. Period."

LaGrange interrupted. "No place in here for those types. It's about trust here."

"Here, here," Sean said, and picked up his empty pint to toast and then scowled at me. "Stoker, empty goddamn beer. Come on, man, do your fucking job. You charge us for every penny so my beer should never be empty."

"Bartending 101, Stoker," LaGrange said.

"You just finished," I said and grabbed his glass to refill it.

"Never mind that," LaGrange said. "Listen to me. Speaking of thieves, I've got to tell you guys something that's been on my mind for a long time. Out in the sun today on the water with my friends and a few beers, it all came together. I know how to take down Eileen and get her ass fired and make up for all the comped drinks we've been robbed of. Like from this guy." LaGrange pointed at me.

"Just doing my job."

"Whatever, you're not the problem. You're just a symptom, a pain in the ass for sure, but not the root of this evil. It's that tyrant of a woman who's the problem. I want her out and I know how to do it."

"Let's hear it, Oscar," Sean said.

"We rob the place," LaGrange said, grinning ear to ear.

"What place?"

"This one."

"It's your place, Oscar." Carter said. "You gonna rip yourself off? Brilliant!"

"Hey, first of all, keep it down, Fluffy. Secondly, it ain't my place. They took that away and turned it into a corporate bullshit pub. They're ripping me off. I can't have a drink on the house in my own goddamn establishment. Fuck that."

"So, have you thought it out? What's the plan?" Sean said calmly.

"Us. I want us to do it. You, Reilly, Duncan, Fluffy and even Stoker. I know you're a by-the- book, tight ass and all, but—"

"For the hundredth time, I'm not taking a side. Just doing my job."

"That is taking a side."

"Anyway, whatever. I'll be overseas soon enough. I'm just passing through."

"I know, I know. Off to Thailand," LaGrange said.

"Taiwan," I corrected. "Maybe. Maybe Alaska first. Don't know yet."

"Whatever. I've seen you come and go in my city over and over again since I came here in '68. San Francisco takes you in and spits you out. Sometimes it's quick, sometimes it takes a while. But you never last. What did you come here for anyway? I bet you can't answer that or you're too embarrassed to."

"What the hell do my plans have to with this?"

"As expected. I oughta write a book about trespassers looking so hard for that something they can't define and thinking they'll find it in San Francisco. Soon they realize we ain't Shangri-La."

"Ok, Oscar, you got it all figured out. You're such a sage," I said, sarcasm masking that he was on to something.

"He makes sense," Sean said. "Really does."

"What you're really looking for is right here, right among us. Brotherhood, camaraderie. Selected family, not the one you're forced into. One you choose." A day of sunshine had Oscar firmly knee deep in his own alcoholic pathos. "The point is we're together by choice. We stick together while Eileen's trying to rip us apart. She wants my ass on the street. Well, we pull off a robbery and she gets fired, and as gravy, we get those drinks we should be getting now."

Sean said, "Again, how?"

"It's as easy as pie. Listen. Ahhh, wait, Stoker, are you in? I was just breaking your balls. Don't take it personal. And the rest of you? I'm not telling the plan without knowing you're in."

Sean said, "I think I speak for everybody by saying we're not in until we hear the damn plan."

"Fine. Fuck it. After closing Sunday night, because that'll include the whole weekend drop, we take the cash from the safe, which is typically around four grand. We take it and make a run to Tahoe. We set aside two grand so that if we lose, we still get a few weeks of comped drinks. If we win, if we get on a heater with some big bets, get to ten or twenty large then we get a nice cut. We split the winnings. Comps for months."

"Wait a minute, I got a—"

LaGrange put his hand up practically in Fluffy's face and said, "Just hear me out. The Sunday night bartender is in the clear because we'll be witnesses saying the drop was made. We've got ex-bartenders all over town who have keys to this place and know the stupid safe combo: 19-0-7. What kind of combo is that? I've been telling Davis and Helen for years to change the door locks and safe combination. I told Eileen, too. She'll get blamed for it and fired."

Sean was nodding approvingly. "Not bad."

"They'll give up trying to outmaneuver ole wily Oscar LaGrange and let me come back as manager. The Eileen experiment fails quickly. And, Reilly, you're the player at the table."

"Why m-m-m-me?

"Because you got luck on your side. You're a new man just getting over that woman. When I got over my divorce, I hit it big in Vegas."

Nobody said anything for a few moments.

Then Duncan said, "Well, I'm out. I got a job to protect and two kids overseas to feed. Best of luck, though." He left me a five-dollar tip and was gone.

I was surprisingly impressed by LaGrange's plan and liked the idea of a quick few grand if we got lucky. Seemed like a properly improper way to end my San Francisco days.

Sean took the plunge first. "I'm in."

Reilly was next.

LaGrange looked at me. "You're the Sunday bartender. We need you, Stoker."

I hesitated.

"I'll give you a grand no matter what for being the one on duty at the time of the crime."

"Well, fuck it then, I'm in."

"Attaboy Boston," Sean said. "Money talks, baby."

Everyone looked at Carter.

"Solidarity," Carter said, smiling.

"Excellent. We got our fab five. How 'bout some drinks Stoker, on the house for a fucking change?" Oscar said.

"What the hell," I said.

"Well, look at that," Sean said.

"Yeah, ole Stok-k-k-ker is l-l-l-l-l-l-l-l—"

"LOOSENING UP for fuck's sake!" Sean yelled.

"Thank you," Reilly said, laughing with everyone else.

I refilled everyone's beer, LaGrange's scotch and water, and poured a round of Jägers, too.

We raised our shots as LaGrange said, "To Operation Tahoe."


Carter, LaGrange, and Reilly plotted out the details and I went downstairs to count out my draw. Sean joined me, pocket filled with ammunition, of course.

Sean sat at the table diagonal to me, carefully opening a small, neatly folded piece of paper. I had told myself to lay off the coke in the weeks before leaving the city to clean up before the next stop. Get healthy and clear headed in transition. Sean left the open packet of clean white rocks staring at me as I tried to count the drawer. Saying no to blow with it staring at you was like saying no to a woman, whom you deeply desire, eagerly beckoning you to bed.

Sean grabbed a mirror from the supply room in back of this cave-like room that had a little door high on the street side wall. That was where the bootleggers smuggled in the booze during prohibition and this cave was where folks secretly drank while the upstairs posed as a law abiding restaurant. 70 or so years later the cave was still the sanctuary for illegal activity.

The mirror had a picture of the Golden Gate Bridge with Anchor Steam written across it. Sean poured the rocks carefully in the middle of the mirror, practically dead center of the bridge between the two giant stanchions. He took a razor blade from his wallet, pulled it from its cardboard sheath, and cut the coke from little clumps into a fine, smooth powder. Sean was focused, almost surgical in the process. He liked his lines to be clean, equal in size and distance from each other. He even traced his lines along the vertical suspension cables of the great bridge. His apartment and life, for that matter, were a dark, cluttered mess, but his lines were meticulous.

He took a brand new twenty-dollar bill from the drawer that I had just finished counting, rolled it up, and held it out to me. I did two lines.

Sean did the same, more quickly and efficiently than me. I always had a little residual on the mirror, but he never did. His nasal passages and sinuses must have been singed of any blockages or obstacles. The cilia must have been burned deep through their tiny follicles. The white poison had eliminated everything in its path, like a mighty river eroding its own banks.

"So what do you think of the plan?" Sean asked, downing his beer. He usually drank his pints of Bud in two large gulps.

"I think it'll work. I'm a little worried about being a suspect, but there'll be no proof. Worst they can do is fire us and I'm leaving anyway, but you guys—"

"I don't need this job. I'm leaving too. Hell, I just did it as a favor to Oscar. Who the hell wants to work the thankless Saturday and Sunday morning shifts."

"Why do you do them then?"

"I just said why."

"But he doesn't care anymore now that Eileen is in charge."

"You don't get it, Stoker. Things aren't so simple. Ain't so black and white as you see them."

Sean licked his finger and cleaned my leftover coke dust off the mirror, spreading it all over his gums and tongue. Then he cut up more lines and took another blast. He had another pint of Bud waiting for him since he had brought two full ones down.

"You know, Stoker, I never ask you or anybody for money for this stuff."

"I know. I appreciate it."

"Things, us, are so much bigger, man. Much, much bigger, man. You people from Boston," he said laughing and slapping my back.

"Yeah, what can I say," I said, not knowing what he was talking about.

"You know I'm only breaking your balls when I go off about the Sox."

"I know. You're just jealous. You wish you could root for a team that never wins. There's something noble and heroic in that."

"More masochistic than noble. Just like this stuff." He pointed to the mirror. After a pause, Sean asked, "So what the hell's in Taiwan, anyway?"

"Well, it's far away, for one thing."

"And for a second thing?"

"I just want to travel before it's too late. Satisfy my wanderlust energy so it doesn't haunt me down the road."

Sean was nodding. "Yeah, that's good. I hope you pull it off. I hope you do it, see the world, a lot of it, and hopefully when you're done, you're not right back where you started."

"Hope so."

"Does it have anything to do with a woman?"

"Yeah, kind of."

Sean nodded as if he knew that was the case before I answered. "You know, it just doesn't get easier, Stoker. No matter how much you unleash in the twenties. I don't know. It's worth a shot. Get it out in the twenties, so we won't be like the parents. Running from that, too, right?"

I nodded.

"Maybe I oughta run, too. Maybe, I didn't get enough out. I saw some ads for courier work in Australia. I got to go to a place with English. Can't deal with not knowing what the hell is going on."

"I don't want to know what's going on. Hell, I don't know what the hell is going on right here in the States. Knowing the language hasn't clued me in on anything."

Sean laughed. "Nobody fuckin' does anyway. We're all just pretending and going along. Riding the conveyor belt. I don't know. Get some career going though, pal. Don't end up behind the bar forever. It's a miserable, god forsaken life."

"Like a LaGrange."

"Yeah, but he doesn't know any better. Too late for him. We all got our own cocoons. That's his. So be it, but get something. I should've taught history."

"You'd be a great history teacher."

Sean bowed to the mirror and snapped up two more. He handed me the bill and I did my share.

"You can fall off the train for only so long before they just don't let you back on board," Sean said. He took out another packet and began cutting. When he was done, he looked me in the eyes and said, "You really don't know. How could you. Haven't earned it yet. You're like a top spinning around with no clue as to who pulled the string. I know who pulled the string now, but I can't get her back and I'm still spinning like a fool. Ahhh, anyway, it's all changed. Back in my day, messin' up was an art form. It was our duty. Jesus, there was more than one damn road and inventing, falling off, taking detours, was what you were supposed to do. Now it's all such a straight line like these," Sean said, pointing at the finely cut foursome.

Sean was racing through his monologue, sweat beading up on his forehead, and his nose was running.

"Jesus, I worked too much. That's what she said. And now? I can't work a full shift outside the bar. I get calls from the union for new construction sites, but no, I just can't do it. Don't tell no one. That's between us. Christ I can't do it. The energy's gone. Now, an eight-hour day is like an eternity. Ahh, the hell with it, who needs the train anyway."

When we went upstairs everyone was quietly and attentively watching TV. Other than the movement of drinks moving from bar to mouth, there was total stillness. I looked up and saw a female lion hunting a turtle. The lioness was growing frustrated with the turtle, who had quickly retracted all his appendages and lastly put his head inside his shell. She pawed at the empty holes and even tried to force her head inside the hole that housed his head. She quickly pulled out shrieking as the turtle had bit her fiercely in the face. There were drops of blood coming from her nose and mouth. The lioness changed strategies in her rage and began gnawing at the turtle's shell. The turtle put his head out occasionally to peer at what was happening, but quickly went back inside when the lioness made a move towards its head. The guys were cheering for the turtle.

"Get the bastard," one of them yelled.

After many tries, the lioness was able to sink her teeth into the shell at its peak point.

Reilly shouted, "She'll never get through. The little guy's s-s-s-s-s-afe inside."

Eventually, one of the lioness' great incisor teeth broke through the shell. Big pieces of the shell were ripped off while the turtle's head madly and wildly circled the outside world trying to bite the enemy, but the lioness smartly had gone to the rear. When the turtle tried to extend his feet to move, she clawed at them, drawing blood. The final scenes were of the lioness and now a lion eating the turtle's totally exposed soft body on a plate of his bottom shell, while his upper shell lay scattered around him in broken pieces.

"Fuck!" Carter said.

"Shit, that sucks. I thought the shell was imp-p-p-p-enetrable,"

LaGrange was shaking his head, a distraught look on his face and sadness in his bloodshot eyes.

Another round of drinks later, and it was back to the plan.

"Next Sunday," LaGrange said.

"I'll drive," Carter said, "but I don't have a car. I'll stay sober though."

"You can drive my car," Sean said.

Everyone would come in at their typical times and leave before last call. I'd make the drop in the safe as usual and hopefully there would be some folks after hours to see me make it. The safe was on the main floor near the kitchen. I would offer free drinks to anyone there near closing to seduce them into being unwitting witnesses. Reilly said that Duncan would come in and be a witness just in case no one was there. "He'll do that for us."

Then with a weekend's worth of cash, I would walk to Sean's apartment a few blocks down Geary and we'd all meet there at 2:30am.

Sunday came and everything went smoothly. Heimi and Wilbur were there doing their conversational dance. They saw me make the drop as did Duncan who was there as promised. I had $5,100 in cash. When I arrived at Sean's, he and Reilly were coked up. LaGrange had just woken up, and was groggy and still drunk. Carter was drinking coke, but not doing coke. We got to Tahoe at 4:30 in the morning. LaGrange slept the whole ride, I dozed off, and Reilly and Sean yapped for a while until their high faded. They soon had that dark, miserable shadow on their faces, the other side of the high.

"I need some fucking coffee," Reilly said.

"Let's get breakfast," Carter said. And we did. A big egg, toast, sausage, bacon, OJ, full on, full throttle indulgent American breakfast. Even LaGrange had a couple of eggs and toast.

We had solidified the gambling plan on the way. We left two grand back at Sean's apartment so we wouldn't lose it and had the guaranteed free drink tab (though I'd take my cut in cash). That left three grand. We weren't in for a long stretch of gambling. Reilly would play thousand-dollar hands, see if he could get on a quick heater, and ride no higher than twenty grand. If we hit that or zero, we'd be done.

After breakfast, the coke shadow was gone and Reilly was perking up with a full belly, new and natural adrenalin, and a boatload of caffeine. He must've drunk eight cups of coffee. He was also constantly rubbing his hands together.

"What are you doing?" Sean asked.

"Warm hands bring good luck," Reilly repeated several times, stutter free.

We went into the casino around six, early morning sun just starting to spread some light in Tahoe while inside the casino was the usual parade of lights and sounds, though quieter than typical. It was early Monday morning after all.

Most of the tables were empty and Reilly picked one with a very attractive female dealer. He sat down in the center seat. It was just him and her and all of us fanning out behind him.

Reilly gave her all the cash.

"Changing three thousand," she yelled towards the pit boss, who came over with a curious look, but didn't say anything.

"Just three chips, young l-l-l-lady," Reilly told her.

"Good luck," she said, laying three gold chips in front of Reilly. He took two and left one in the circle.

Reilly had twelve on the first hand and the dealer had a seven showing. Everyone was saying hit, but he ignored the advice and waved his hand to stay. She opened an eight and then drew a King and busted.

"Never b-b-b-b-b-b-ust. Gotta give yourself a chance to win and the d-d-d-d-d-d-d-d-ealer a chance to lose."

McGrath said, "It's Rile's game. Everyone shut up and let him do his thing. Just one chief here." We all nodded. Reilly seemed to be in a zone.

LaGrange said, "Dude has horseshoes wrapped in four leaf clovers up his stuttering ass."

"Jesus, Oscar, shut the hell up. You'll wreck his juju," Sean scolded.

"Yeah, yeah, you're right," LaGrange conceded.

"Right in the circle, sweetie," Reilly said pointing to the chip he had just won.

Reilly got a pair of eights on the next hand and the dealer had a five showing. He split them, put up the two grand he had left and drew a Queen and a King. The dealer drew a two on fifteen.

"Nice!" I shouted.

"We're up five grand already," Carter

"Shhh," Sean said. "Don't count the money. You'll curse it. Just shut up!"

"Yes, quiet p-p-p-p-p-lease, boys" Reilly said calmly.

Reilly let it all ride on the next hand. All eight thousand. We were huddled together behind him freaking out, but staying quiet.

He had fourteen with the dealer showing a two.

"Fucking fourteen," LaGrange whispered. Sean elbowed him in the stomach.

"Stay, my lady," Reilly said.

She turned her card over. A ten of clubs. Reilly nodded his head slowly as if he was confirming what he expected. LaGrange had his fist partly in his mouth, biting down hard on it. Then the four of us interlocked arms in a moment of pure unity.

As she pulled the fateful card from the shoe, Reilly said, "Let's see royalty, p-p-p-p-please."

And she obliged with a Jack.

"Jack be nimble, Jack be quick," Reilly shouted.

"Holy shit!" McGrath yelled amidst a slew of high fives. The few people in the casino came over to see what all the drama was about.

"Never bust, keep the trust," Reilly said.

We were all hugging Reilly and each other from behind. Reilly got up, asked the dealer to change one thousand-dollar chip to hundreds. He gave her one as a tip and turned to us. "How'd I do boys?"

"Reilly, you crazy son of a bitch!" LaGrange screamed. We were jumping up and down around Reilly like he'd just scored the winning touchdown.

It was a celebratory ride back. Sean drove and after the initial euphoria, Carter finally got some sleep. He hadn't slept a wink all night. We were all exhausted from the all-nighter and by the time we drove out of Tahoe National Forest, the adrenalin was gone, but the joy remained. We made it to Folsom, just east of Sacramento.

"Is this Johnny Cash's Folsom?" I asked.

"Look over there," Sean said, pointing to a sign that said, "Folsom State Prison Next Exit."

We pulled over at the exit after the prison and drove down to Folsom Lake. It was a crisp, blue sky morning. There was a little beachfront with no one around where we all crashed for a restful couple of hours. We stopped in old town Sacramento for lunch and were back in the city by mid-afternoon.

I planned on waiting a couple of weeks to give my notice so it wouldn't look too suspicious so soon after the theft, but I didn't need to. I started giving comps to the guys and Elaine had a spotter in that nailed me. She fired me the next day.

"I was counting on you, Stoker," she said, shaking her head in disapproval.

"Sorry."

"And the theft? You sure you know nothing about it."

"Not at thing. Made my drop and went home."

Eileen nodded, but I didn't think she believed me. She eventually got put on probation for not changing the safe combination as LaGrange had predicted. He assured us that her days were numbered. "You can't outdo and old dog like me with a new corporate puppy," he said.

I gave my one week's notice at the Gotham. I had a little over three grand from the theft and another $1,500 in the bank. I forewent Alaska since that was mostly about building a stash. I'd heard from a customer at The 1907 that it was hard work, 18-hour days, but good money. I still romanticized it in a Jack London kind of way, but was more eager to be overseas taking in new countries and cultures.

There weren't many bohemian types that came into
The 1907, but I did meet a woman who had just returned
from teaching English in Japan. She gave me a contact in
Tokyo and told me it was easy to get a job.

"You got a BA?" she asked. "That's all you need, and
your mother tongue."

"Yeah, just graduated," I lied, thinking of Lyra.

"You'll be all set."

And so I was off to Tokyo to continue the journey.
Didn't know where I was headed after that, maybe Taiwan as originally planned, but India, China, and Vietnam
seemed like good prospects, too. Then over to Africa,
Europe, South America, and home.

But home had changed. There was something magical
about my short stay in San Francisco. I'd miss the trans-
vestites, especially Dale, all The 1907ers, particularly the
now thick-as-thieves crew forever bound by our Tahoe
adventure. Hell, even LaGrange, and Billie on some level.
I realized nostalgia was getting the best of me, but it
was deeper than that. Maybe because it was the place
of my first taste of true freedom or where I persevered
after losing Lyra. Whatever the analysis was, defining it
didn't really matter. The city was special all on its own.
San Francisco now felt like home and the east coast was
just where I was born.

I didn't know what I'd do with all the pages that I'd write
along my way around the world, but the pursuit of a mountain of words written on the move was the only goal I had.

And I wouldn't read a word of it until I was back home
in San Francisco.


THE END

www.ingramcontent.com/pod-product-compliance
Lightning Source LLC
Chambersburg PA
CBHW021057110726
47900CB00007B/1918